CARTEL PUBLICATIONS
PRESENTS

MW00698243

...EYS
...AST
...ASE
& I RIDES WITH
EYONE ALL THE
WAY"

-T. Styles
President & CEO
of Cartel
Publications

A NOVEL

HELL RAZOR
Honeys

EYONE Williams

BEST SELLING AUTHOR OF FASTLANE

PUBLISHER'S NOTE:
This book is a work of fiction. Names, characters, businesses, organizations, places, events and incidents are the product of the author's imagination or are used fictionally. Any resemblance of actual persons, living or dead, events, or locales is entirely coincidental.

Library of Congress Control Number: 2008930410
ISBN: 0-9794931-7-X
ISBN 13: 978-0-9794931-7-1

Cover Design: Davida Baldwin www.oddballdsgn.com
Editor: Renita M. Walker www.myspace.com/hdbeditorialservices
Graphics: Davida Baldwin

www.thecartelpublications.com

First Edition

Printed in the United States of America

Acknowledgements

All parise be to Allah for all that comes my way.

Much love to T. Styles and my true comrade Jason Poole; yall saw my hunger and put me in the pocket. Good looking, now watch my work!

Much love to my loved ones and true comrades. You all know who you are. Thanks for your support!

Thanks to everyone that digs my writing, I love all the love I'm getting.

Write me:
Eyone Williams #06076-007
FCI Gilmer
P.O. Box 6000
Glenville, WV 26351

Eyonewilliams06076007@voiceforinmates.com
www.myspace.com/eyone30

Dedication Page

I dedicate this book to the First and Kennedy Honeys and the 100 Honeys.

My memories of growing up around them and going to school with them in the early 90's inspired this street story. They were some serious females, no bullshit!

I also have to tip my hat to all the girl crews that made names for themselves in the go-go's throughout the years- they know who they are.

What Up Babies!

Well, it's finally here! I have to say I'm truly excited about publishing this novel. I remember the day it was brought to my attention. I, Charisse, Jason Poole and Davida Baldwin were out celebrating the release of Victoria's Secret at Dave N Buster's when Jason hand delivered the novel to me personally. On his word, I was assured that I'd love the story. And I most definetly did.

Right off the back, I was immediately taken by the title. Those of you who know me, know how much I appreciate a hot title. In fact, the hotness of a title automatically let's me know how creative you'll be with your storyline. So there's no denying that Hell Razor Honey's screamed creativity!

So…I took the novel home, and from page one I was hooked! Eyone truly had me at…Hello! And if that wasn't enough, he took me on a journey from D.C., to L.A.! I felt like I was riding shotgun while looking at the lives of his characters. What an awesome writer! To make sure it wasn't just me, I gave the novel in its entirety *after* I was done, to Charisse, the V.P., of the Cartel. And she loved it too!!! So it was settled, I had to sign this literary genius and I'm glad I did.

I know beyond a shadow of a doubt that fans of the Cartel and of Eyone, will be proud to add this to their library. And I'm elated to add Hell Razor Honeys to the Cartel Collection. Eyone, your career will skyrocket from here.

Lastly, as always we must rep' an author we love and appreciate for his/her literary journey. So it is with great pleasure that we pay homage to:

Treasure stamped the urban world effortlessly with his fire novel, *Harlem Girl Lost*. And to be sure you knew he was here to stay, he delivered the phenomenal tale, *A Street Girl Named Desire*. Treasure, please continue to pen the hits and we will continue to read them.

Lastly we'd like to thank our Pep Squad. We're nothing without you!

"The Cartel Publications Pep Squad"

Jessica aka "Lyric" (Squad Captain), Ms. Toya Daniels, Erica Taylor, Shawntress, Kim "Bookbabe" Gamble, Lisa aka JSQueen625, Kim aka Kariymah, Miss Tori, Essence, Ms. Jazzy. Last but certainly not least, we want to give a shout out to our Street Team! They're growing and we appreciate everything they do.

Until I Hug You Later....
T. Styles, President & CEO

Chapter 1

"Girl, come on. Stop bein' scared. We gon' be back by the time lunch is over," Samara said, as she led her young protégé Vida through the crowded halls of Eastern High, in Northeast, Washington, D.C.

"I ain't scared, I just wanna know who we goin' wit'."

Vida was fourteen and in her freshman year of high school, but she was no fool. She knew that Samara's fast-ass had all kinds of niggaz chasing her—creep niggaz and all. At sixteen, Samara called it working what she had to get what she needed.

"Troy just takin' us to get somethin' to eat." Samara stopped at her locker, opened it, and grabbed her Polo jacket.

Vida seemed to trust Samara too much. After all, Samara was like a big sister to Vida. They had lived in the same apartment building for years.

"Nah, I'm cool," said Vida. "I don't like Troy. He be wit' all them 21st niggaz. Plus, I ain't giving up no pussy to ride to the store."

"Who said you had to give up some pussy?!" snapped Samara. She hated being questioned and always took such acts as a challenge to her position.

Samara was the queen bee of her little crew—The Come Back Honeys. She had started the crew a little over a year ago, after falling out with another crew of girls that she used to run with called The Polo Honeys—all they wore was top-of-the-line Polo gear. Samara told dudes that she and her crew, The Come Back Honeys, had that "come back" pussy. So far, they were living up to their name. Dudes as old as twenty-five were coming back for a shot at the young girls, who ages varied from fourteen to seventeen.

"Huh? Who said you had to give up some pussy?!" Samara repeated again in Vida's face.

Vida was getting tired of Samara's shit. Samara had damn near made her give up some pussy on more than one occasion. Running with Samara and the Come Back Honeys had cost Vida her young boyfriend; he'd told her that she let Samara turn her into a freak.

Vida sucked her teeth and said, "I said I ain't goin'." She took a stand.

"You little stank-ass bitch!" Samara put her hands on her wide hips. "You think you like that now?"

Vida rolled her eyes and looked around at all the eyes that were on her. The hallway seemed to go silent. Samara was trying to embarrass her in front of everybody and it was working. Vida's anger began to boil.

"Take off my jeans you little ungrateful bitch! I made your dirty ass!" Samara screamed on Vida.

Vida cocked back and stole Samara right in the mouth. She followed the first punch up with another to the eye that sent Samara slamming against the lockers with a loud bang. Samara screamed, grabbed a handful of Vida's hair, and began scratching at Vida's face. Vida used to be a tomboy; she could wreck for real, like a dude. She grabbed Samara by her Polo shirt and pounded her with countless uppercuts. The crowd seemed to be enjoying the fight; they all believed Samara needed her ass kicked. However, it was a surprise to see Vida doing it.

"Mr. Smith comin'. Break it up," said a young dude, as he stood between the girls to break up the fight.

Vida was hyped and ready for more. Samara was now the embarrassed one; her nose was busted.

"Act like you want some more, bitch!" Vida threatened with her fist balled up.

"You gon' pay, bitch! Watch!" Samara took off running down the hall.

Vida took advantage of the crowd and slid into the bathroom to check out the scratches on her cute face. Her reddish-brown skin had always made her look like she was mixed with Native American. Her long black hair was smooth and silky. At fourteen, her body was ahead of its time. She often told dudes that she was eighteen and they went for it. Her thick eyelashes and naturally arched eyebrows gave her an older beauty that made her stand out amongst the Come Back Honeys. As she looked at her face in the mirror she saw that she had a few scratches across her left eyelid and across her forehead.

"Bitch!" She sucked her teeth. She was still a smoker on any scale.

"You beat that bitch ass," a voice said.

Vida turned around and saw Tia, a cute light-skinned girl that was in her homeroom. They were cool, nothing more.

"She getting on my damn nerves," Vida said, fixing her hair.

"If she try to get them bitches to jump you I got your back, okay?"

Vida smiled. "Thanks, but I don't want you to get caught up in this bullshit."

"I don't like them fake-ass bitches anyway. I never understood why you was hangin' wit' them. Don't worry about me gettin' caught up in no bullshit." Tia pulled a straight razor from her little Gucci bag. "I'ma be okay regardless." She was from Southeast and could take good care of herself. Her red-bone looks could mislead a bitch, but she had sliced her fair share of bitches. "I'll slice one of them bitches up like it ain't nothing."

Vida laughed, she was feeling Tia. "If I need you I'll holla at you, okay?"

Tia put her weapon up and said, "Okay." She gave Vida five like a dude. "Watch your back, Vida," Tia said before leaving the bathroom.

Vida and Tia had always kicked it in homeroom, but now Vida had a new respect for Tia. Nevertheless, Vida wasn't trippin' off the Come Back Honeys. She ran with them and knew they couldn't fight. All they were good for was fucking and dressing good. Vida could beat any one of them into a coma. She checked the mirror one more time and left the bathroom.

The rest of the day went on without confrontation. Vida noticed that she had earned respect from some of the older girls at school. Some of them even commended her for beating Samara's ass. As school let out countless students flooded out of the doors, many of them headed for the bus stop.

A black 1994 Lexus Coupe pulled up at the bus stop and let down the passenger side window. A young brown-skinned dude that looked a little like Nas was behind the wheel. "Ay, girl," he called out.

Vida looked around like she didn't know who he was talking to. There were older and flyer girls at the bus stop with her.

"You in the Polo jacket, let me holla at you real quick," the dude said.

Vida liked the car, and the dude was fine, so she walked over and leaned inside the passenger window. The older girls were hatin'.

"What's up?" asked Vida, holding her notebook.

"What's your name, cutie?" the dude asked. He had spotted her from a block away and loved the way she was fitting her Guess jeans.

"Vicky," Vida lied, as Samara had taught her. "What's yours?"

"Scales." He turned down the Snoop Dogg CD that was blasting. "How old are you?"

"Seventeen, how old are you?"

"Nineteen." Scales looked around and said, "Let me give you a ride. You look too good to be standin' at a bus stop. If I don't grab you I know somebody else will."

Yeah right, Vida thought. She had heard better. "Is that right?" She smiled.

"Yeah, that's right."

Vida got in and they pulled off heading towards 19th Street.

"Where you from?" Scales asked, eyeing Vida's thick thighs.

"I live 'round Montana Avenue."

"Oh yeah, I used to come through there a lot to holla at Raff and Lil' Sean."

"I know them. They used to hang up the street from my house, but I really don't be hangin' out like that." Vida's grandmother had kept her in the house as she grew up, in an effort to protect her from the streets. In fact, Vida didn't start hanging out like that until she started hanging tough with Samara.

"So you a school girl, huh?" Scales smiled. "I like that."

"Yeah, you could say that."

"What's a pretty girl like you doin' wit' scratches on your face?" Scales softly rubbed her smooth cheek with the back of his hand.

Vida told him about the fight with Samara, but didn't really tell him what it was over.

"You got attitude too, huh?" he said as they cruised down Rhode Island Avenue.

"I guess you can say that."

During the short ride to Vida's apartment Scales laid his rap game down, and made plans to hook up with Vida at another time. He dropped her off in front of her building and rolled out. Vida walked up to her building, speaking to all the neighborhood dudes that were hustling out front. They all showed her love. She had big love for the hood.

Samara was inside her apartment looking out the window when Vida got out of the Lexus—that really pissed her off. Samara had two of her Come Back Honeys with her; they had a cake baked for Vida. *That little bitch ain't built like that,* Samara thought. She now had two ugly black eyes with the busted nose Vida had given her earlier. "Come on, let's get that bitch before she get to her door," Samara said to her followers.

Vida was coming up the steps when Samara and her crew stepped to her. "What's up now, bitch?" Samara hissed, as she grabbed a handful of Vida's hair.

Vida dropped her notebook and went to work, swinging nonstop punches. The two girls with Samara jumped in and started catching Vida with blows from all sides. Vida found herself on the floor being stomped out like a pipehead. She was close to blacking out when someone opened their door to see what was going on in the hallway.

"Sam! What the hell is goin' on?!" an old brown-skinned woman with gray hair came out into the hallway and said. Samara and the other girls ran down the steps and out the front of the building. "Lord, what have they done to my baby?" The heavyset woman knelt down beside her bleeding granddaughter and brushed Vida's hair out of her beat up face. "Come on, baby. Let me get you in the house." Ms. Green helped Vida to her feet and took her inside.

Ms. Green was all Vida had. At fifty-six, Ms. Green was a young grandmother. She had raised Vida since birth. Vida's mother was fifteen when she gave birth to her. Vida's mother, Angie, died in a car crash two months after Vida came into this world. Her father was a no-show that she didn't know. Since day one Ms. Green gave her all to Vida. She didn't have much money, but she had a lot of love.

Sitting on the old sofa in the living room with an ice pack on her face, Vida told her grandmother how she and Samara got into a fight because Samara tried to embarrass her by screaming on her in front of everybody in the hallway at school.

"Baby, I know you want to look good, and I'm sorry I can't buy you all them name brand clothes, but I want you to know that who you are is not what you wear," Ms. Green said. "I want you to go pack up everything Samara has ever given you. I'm going to sit it in front of her door. I want you to stay away from her, you hear me? I don't want you around her no more."

"Okay." Vida went to pack up all the gear she had gotten from Samara. As she cleaned out her closet she told herself that she wasn't going to let Samara get away with the stunt she'd pulled. It wasn't going down like that.

Ms. Green told Vida to stay home from school until her face healed. During the week that she stayed in the house all she did was plot on Samara. Scales called her a few times, and they talked on the phone for a while. He was trying to get the pussy and it was clear. Vida's story was always the same; she was sick and couldn't go out with him at the time. However, she promised him that they could get together as soon as she was feeling better.

The phone in Vida's bedroom rang and took her attention away from *The Young and the Restless*. "Hello," Vida said.

"Can I speak to Vida," a female asked. Her voice was all the way ghetto.

"Who is this?"

"Tia."

Vida wondered how the hell Tia got her home number, but didn't ask. "What's up, Tia?"

"I know you wonderin' how I got your number… you know how niggaz talk. I told your old boyfriend I was worried about you, and he gave me the number. I heard what went down. Them bitches been spreadin' a bunch of gossip about you all over the school, talkin' 'bout you scared to come back to school and all that shit. I know a real bitch when I meet one. I know you ain't goin' for that. I want you to know that I meant what I said when I told you I got your back."

"Damn, them bitches at school talkin' 'bout me and everything, huh?"

"You know how bitches act when they think they did somethin'."

"I ain't trippin'. I'll be back at school Monday. Then I'ma see what them bitches talkin' 'bout." Vida was pissed off that people thought that she was scared to come back to school. She thought about waiting for Samara at her door and beating her ass right there, but her other plan was far better.

"You don't even know why I told you I got you back, do you?" Tia asked.

"I was wonderin'."

"You don't remember when I was fightin' that bitch Amanda?"

"Yeah, I remember that," Vida said.

Vida remembered the situation like it was yesterday. On the first day of school Tia was beating the shit out of loud-mouth Amanda when Amanda's crew tried to jump Tia. Vida made sure Tia got a fair shake because she respected how Tia stood up for herself against the odds. Afterwards, Vida thought nothing of it. Tia beat the shit out of Amanda and thanked Vida later. That was it. Little did Vida know; she had just made a good friend.

"I never forget when somebody looks out for me, never. I'm all the way true to the game.

Vida laughed. "I hear that, girl. I'm glad you called, you made my day." Vida and Tia talked for a while. Vida put her down with the cake she had baked for Samara.

"I'm wit' you," Tia said.

Monday morning came quickly. Vida made sure she didn't run into Samara on the way to school. Once Vida saw Samara jump into some dude's white 1992 Nissan 300ZX twin turbo and head for school, she called Scales, who had already told her that he would give her a ride. Scales scooped Vida and at her request scooped Tia, too. He dropped both of them off at school. Vida gave him a kiss and told him that she would beep him later so they could hook up. She winked at him and went inside Eastern.

All eyes were on Vida and Tia, which was part of the plan. Vida had her hair braided to the back like a dude. She was wearing tight Polo jeans, a gray Polo sweatshirt and tan Timberland boots. They carried no books. It was clear that they came to kick some ass. Students whispered to one another about what was about to go down. Tension was thick.

Vida and Tia bent the corner and entered the hallway where Samara's locker was located. Samara was busy running her mouth about the dude that picked her up in the twin turbo; she had met him at the go-go Saturday night. Two Come Back Honeys were sucking up her every word. Samara was their role model. Vida slid right up on Samara, unnoticed, and punched her right in her face. She grabbed Samara's head and began banging it against the metal locker. Everybody stopped what they were doing to check out the situation. "You thought I was gon' let you get away wit' some shit like that?!" Vida growled.

Meanwhile, Tia had latched on to one of the other girls and had knocked her to the floor with the first blow. The third girl ran as Tia stomped her victim out with her Tims. After some good ass-kicking, Vida and Tia dragged Samara to the bathroom by her hair. Samara's bra was showing as she was dragged through the hallway kicking and screaming.

"Shut up, bitch!" Vida punched Samara in her mouth as she and Tia stripped her of her DKNY outfit right on the bathroom floor. Once Samara was ass-naked, Tia threw all of her gear out the second floor window and let the wind do the rest. Vida kicked and stomped Samara some more. "Stupid, bitch! Don't you ever think about puttin' your fuckin' hands on me again!"

Tia looked out the bathroom door and saw the security guard running in their direction. "We gotta go, Vee, the security guard comin'!"

Vida kicked Samara in the face once more. "Bitch, you ain't shit!"

Samara was balled up on the floor crying and moaning.

Vida and Tia took off running down the hallway through the crowd. Security tried to give chase, but the young girls were too fast. They were down the stairs, around the corner, and out the door in seconds.

Samara was beat up bad. She looked like she had been in the ring with Roy Jones Jr. The security guard had to send for a sheet to wrap around her naked body so he could walk her to the office where an ambulance was called for her. The police were called for Vida and Tia.

Thirty minutes later, Vida and Tia were getting off the train at the Rhode Island Avenue Metro Station. It was a cool March morning in 1995. The girls had established their bond by humiliating Samara and her fake ass Come Back Honeys. Vida and Tia knew they were in deep shit, but they didn't care. They had put their work in, as planned.

"What's up for the rest of the day?" Tia asked. "I know the school done already called my house by now. I ain't in no rush to get home and hear my mother bitch." She sighed as they stood on the high platform of the Metro Station overlooking the morning traffic flying up and down Rhode Island Avenue.

"Wanna hang out wit' Scales? I'm sure he got a friend for you. We can hit 'em up for a little money and smoke wit' 'em," Vida said.

"Cool," Tia said. She was going on fifteen, but she was already having sex. She had been taught to use sex as a tool by her older cousin, Green Eyes. However, just like Vida, she gave herself away for trivial things like tennis shoes, outfits and hairdos. It was what she called "workin' " her shit.

"Remember, you seventeen," said Vida.

"Girl, please. I got you… I ain't new to this. I told you my cousin Green Eyes been takin' me out wit' her since I was twelve," Tia said. Tia wasn't lying. At twelve she was telling dudes she was fifteen. Now, with her thick thighs, wide hips, and phat ass, she could pass for eighteen. Even if she didn't look eighteen most dudes would still go anyway.

At 5' 3", 135 pounds, she was already "healthy." She had the cute face of a young Mariah Carey—with a little mole on her cheek and all. She was a real red-bone. That alone had been the cause of a lot of drama in her life; that also made her tough and taught her how to fight. Bitches were always hatin' on her, claiming that she thought she was cute. She was. What the hell. Her Barry Farms, Southeast neighborhood also had a lot to do with making her tough and street-smart. She and Vida together could only spell trouble. For who? Only time would tell.

Vida beeped Scales from the pay phone and he got right back at her. She told him that she and a friend were trying to hook up with him and a friend of his. A short while later Scales pulled up on Rhode Island Avenue behind the wheel of a silver 1994 Range Rover. He had a nice looking dark-skinned dude riding shotgun.

Vida and Tia were psyched when they saw the ride. It was the first time they had hooked up with niggaz in a Range; the best they had done before was niggaz in 300 ZXs and Legends. A Range and a Lex Coupe were a big catch for them. Scales was Vida's first prospect after stepping out of Samara's shadow. The girls jumped in the Range. The dude Scales had brought along got in the back with Tia. His name was Shay.

Shay was eighteen. He and Tia got to know one another a little bit as they all rode around smoking weed and listening to Biggie Smalls. Come to find out, the truck belonged to Shay. Cuddled up under Shay, Tia could feel the effects of the strong weed as well as Shay's finger sliding in and out of her pussy. She was so wet and ready to fuck; she didn't care about anything else.

"Sssss, damn," she whispered in Shay's ear. "I'm ready to hit the hotel or somethin'."

Shay was rock hard. He smiled and asked, "is your girl wit' it?"

"Ay, Vee," Tia called up front.

"What's up?" Vida was higher than she had ever been; she had only been smoking weed for a few months. She was talking to Scales about going to get something to eat.

"I'm tryin' to get a room and chill for a while," Tia suggested.

Vida looked at Scales, who gave her a look that told her what was on his mind. "Yeah, me too," Vida said.

The hotel was the next stop. They ordered Chinese food and sat on the two beds in the Days Inn eating, while watching TV and making small talk. When they were done eating they sparked up some more weed and cut the TV off. Tia and Shay began to get real familiar with one another. Vida and Scales did the same.

Scales and Vida were lying on their sides facing each other while touching, feeling, and kissing in the dark. They smoothly eased their clothes off. Tia and Shay must have skipped the touching, feeling, and kissing. By the intimate sound of things coming from their side of the room they had jumped straight into fucking.

Scales wanted to get down to business as well. He rolled onto his back and pulled Vida on top of him. She reached down and grabbed his manhood with her soft hand; she was impressed by the size. She held it still while she slid down on it slowly, filling her insides with satisfaction. By the sounds Scales made she could tell that her young, tight, and wet box was doing the job. There was no way he could tell she was fourteen. She didn't know all the tricks yet, but she could ride a dick to the finish line. Even with the slight pain she felt, she put her hands on Scales' chest and rode him long and slow, taking him deep inside her.

"Aaahhh, it's so big, Scales. Ssssss, fuck me," Vida moaned. The weed had her in a zone of her own.

Scales began pulling her up and down faster as his breathing grew louder and faster. Vida began to moan and pant like she was in a competition with Tia. That was a losing battle; Tia sounded like she was being hit by two or three dudes at the same time. The fullness Vida felt, along with the sounds coming from Tia and Shay, made her wetter; then she exploded.

"Oh, shit... I'm cummin'. Ooooowww... I'm cummin'." Vida leaned forward, smashing her plump titties against Scales' chest and began bouncing her midsection up and down in a way that she had learned from fucking older dudes. She'd made it her patented move in the bed. She only used it when she was trying to throw the pussy on a nigga or hurry up and make him cum.

"Damn!" Scales wrapped his arms around Vida and began pounding up into her as far as he could. Her cream was pouring out. Every time he dug up into her, her moans became a sharp grunt. He knew he was hitting the right spot. He liked the sound she was making and kept hitting the same spot. "You like that?"

"Oh, yeah, don't stop. I'm 'bout to cum again, Scales!"

Damn, this little bitch can fuck, Scales thought. He felt her gush with cream again and knew she was cumming. He fucked her harder and deeper.

"Don't... cum... inside... of... me..." Vida forced out in between pants of ecstasy. "Aaaahh… yeah… ssssssshhhiiittt." Her whole body began to quake and quiver with sexual tremors.

With a quick jerk, Scales lifted Vida off of his dick and exploded all over her soaking wet pussy and stomach. She felt the warm nut hitting her skin and loved it. Vida got up to go to the bathroom when they were done. As her eyes adjusted to the darkness, she saw Tia on her hands and knees between Shay's legs, sucking his dick. *Damn!* Vida thought. *Homegirl don't be bullshittin'.* Samara had tried to get Vida to give a dude some head, but Vida didn't like the thought of putting a dick in her mouth. The dude ended up trying to force her to do it, but she wasn't having it.

Vida washed up in the bathroom. A few moments later, Tia came in the bathroom as well. Vida couldn't help but see that Tia's nipples were hard and pointing at her like little fingers. "I see you was takin' care of business." Vida smiled, drying between her legs with a towel.

Tia laughed. "You wasn't doin' too bad yourself." Tia grabbed a wash cloth and began cleaning herself at the sink.

"You let him get the top, huh?"

"Yeah," Tia said, "a nigga will let you do anything if you can suck a lil' dick. You don't fuck around?"

Vida shook her head. "I don't like it."

"You ever did it?"

"Nah, but a dude tried to make me before."

"Oh, I see. You'll get over that. Whenever you get over that you'll see how you can work magic wit' your top piece."

Vida opened the bathroom door to leave. "Bitch-ass niggaz!" She ran to the window. The Range Rover was pulling out of the parking lot. Scales and Shay had left them out Maryland, a good thirty minutes outside of D.C. "Them bitch-ass niggaz left us!" Vida was fired up.

"Fuck them niggaz," Tia said calmly.

Vida turned around and saw Tia holding a handful of cash. "Where you get that from?"

"I'm two steps ahead of them bamma-ass niggaz." Tia explained how she had clipped the $775 from Shay's jacket pocket inside the Range while he was playing with her pussy.

"That's right, girl!" Vida smiled and gave Tia five. "Let's get out of here."

The girls got dressed, split the money and caught a cab back to D.C.

Chapter 2

Everybody watched as Vida was brought out of her building in handcuffs and placed in the back of a waiting police car. It was just after 7:00 P.M. Ms. Green looked on from her bedroom window with tears in her eyes. The sight was painfully reminiscent of the first time Vida's mother was walked down the same walkway in handcuffs and placed in the back of a police car—Vida's mother had stabbed a young dude for feeling her ass. That was almost sixteen years ago.

Assault charges were filed against Vida and Tia. They were both arrested and went to court the next morning. No one showed up for Tia, so Ms. Green got her out; she understood the young girl's struggle. Tia also reminded Ms. Green of her late daughter. The two girls had been kicked out of all D.C. public schools.

In Ms. Green's old Cadillac, on the way to take Tia home, she spoke words of wisdom to the girls. She understood why they did what they did. Even though the girls were in trouble, she felt good that Vida had a friend that had her back. "I know how it is to be a teenager," Ms. Green said. "However, I don't want you girls throwin' your lives away and gettin' arrested. I don't want y'all gettin' hurt either. It's so many dangers out here for a young girl." Ms. Green's mind flashed back to her daughter's death—she'd died in a car crash while riding with a dude that was being chased by the police. Ms. Green seemed to talk for the whole ride.

Tia normally didn't pay adults any attention, due in part to not knowing any that really cared about her. Her whole household was on one drug or another. Her grandmother was the only adult she ever respected. She was nine when her grandmother died. From that point on Tia and her cousin, Green Eyes, did whatever they wanted to do. However, Tia was feeling Ms. Green, she liked her. The older woman reminded her of her grandmother.

Ms. Green pulled up in front of Tia's house in Barry Farms. People were everywhere doing everything. Police sirens could be heard in the distance. As Tia got out the car Ms. Green looked back and said, "You be good, baby. Make sure you come check on me soon."

"Yes ma'am." It was the first time Tia had said yes ma'am since her grandmother passed away. "I'll call you later, Vee."

Later that night, while sitting on the front steps of her building with a few neighborhood dudes, Vida laughed and joked like she was one of the fellas. She was comfortable around her homies. A group of six dudes were shooting dice on the walkway. Others were making hand-to-hand transactions, pumpin'. Two of Vida's homies, Tec and Kareem, were messing with her about what she did to Samara. Most of the dudes around the way didn't like Samara because she thought she was "like that" and wouldn't give the pussy up in the hood. Vida, on the other hand, got nothing but love from the hood. She had only given the pussy up to one of the homies, and that was Tec.

"I guess you got that fake-ass bitch Sam on house arrest since you beat that ass, huh?" asked Tec. He was wearing a black leather Hugo Boss jacket he'd robbed a nigga for last night and puffing on a blunt.

Tec was a fifteen year old stick-up kid that wouldn't think twice about firing his pistol. He was dark-skinned and real short, just over 5' 2", weighing about 125 pounds. He wasn't what most girls would call good looking, but he wasn't ugly either. Nevertheless, he was a young nigga that ate pussy. That alone got him a lot of pussy. He also had no problem spending a little cash on a broad.

"That's what that bitch get," Tec said. "I bet she won't jump out there wit' you no more." He laughed.

"I bet she won't either," Vida said, accepting the blunt from Tec.

Hell Razor Honeys

A pipehead walked up looking like he had been working on cars all day. He was carrying a brown paper bag. He called Tec over to the side. The two of them made a transaction, and Tec took possession of the paper bag. Tec returned to the front steps while the pipehead disappeared into the dark cut on the side of the building.

"What's that?" Kareem asked.

Tec flashed a beat up .38 revolver that looked like it had been put to work. "He ain't want nothin' but a fifty for it." Tec looked at Vida and said, "Put this up for me until I roll out."

Vida took the paper bag and said in a joking way, "That's gon' cost you." She smiled. She always hit Tec for a few dollars when she stashed something in her apartment for him, be it drugs or money.

Tec laughed and handed her a hundred dollar bill. "You good?"

Vida flashed a smile and went inside the building, switching in her tight black Versace jeans. As she was walking down the hallway Samara's door opened. Vida's heart seemed to skip a beat; she really didn't want to face Samara. Feeling the weight of the pistol in her hand, Vida stopped in her tracks. Samara stepped into the hallway. She looked bad. Her face was bruised like she was in an abusive relationship. Her eyes waved the white flag of defeat.

"Vee, I'm sorry." Samara was broken. Vida had made her respect her. "I don't want to beef wit' you."

"Yeah, okay." Vida gritted on her and rolled her eyes as she walked by without another word. She no longer trusted Samara and they could never be friends again.

Vida stashed the pistol in her bedroom and went back out front. A few minutes later a Yellow Cab pulled up and stopped in front of the building. All the dudes were checking out the bad little broad that was getting out. Vida stood up to get a good look. It was Tia. Vida walked down the walk, through her homies, to meet Tia.

"What's up, girl?" Vida said.

"I got ta' fightin' wit' my mother," Tia said, as she pulled her suitcase out the cab. "It's a long story. I'll tell you all about it, but I need somewhere to stay for the night. I'ma go over my cousin's house tomorrow. She's out of town right now."

"It's cool, my grandmother ain't gon' trip."

Vida led Tia into the building. All the dudes were trying to holla at Tia, but that would have to wait.

Ms. Green was watching TV when the girls came through the door. She saw the suitcase and knew something was wrong. "What's wrong, baby?" Her voice was warm and caring, as always.

"My mother put me out, Ms. Green," Tia said.

"What happened?"

Tia sat on the sofa while Vida took the suitcase to her room. Tia told Ms. Green that when she got in the house her mother smacked her in the face and began cursing her out. Tia ran out the front door to get away from her drunk mother. Her mother followed her outside and punched her in the back of the head. They got into an all-out slug-fest. Tia beat her mother down like she was just another bitch on the street; she took out years of pain and frustration on her. She then packed her things and left.

"I'm so sorry, baby." Ms. Green gave Tia's arm a warm rub. "You can stay here as long as you want. I don't have much, but you're welcome to all I have, baby.

"Thank you, Ms. Green."

"Don't worry about it. I understand. Make yourself at home."

Tia felt the urge to cry. She hadn't felt loved in a long time. She reached out and hugged Ms. Green. "Thank you so much."

Vida's bedroom was small, but comfortable. It had everything she needed. Posters of Tupac lined the walls. The little bit of fly gear that Vida had hung neatly in the closet. Her dresser was covered with cosmetics. A boom box sat on the nightstand. Her bed took up most of the room—it was a king size.

"Where can I sleep?" Tia looked around the tiny room and saw no space.

"Girl, stop trippin'. I ain't got no complex, you can sleep in my bed. It's big enough."

"Tia smiled and shrugged. "I'm cool wit' it."

The girls sat down and talked for a while. Tia told Vida how much she hated her mother, for reasons that went back to her childhood. She didn't tell Vida everything, not yet, but she did explain how her mother was very dark-skinned and her father was very light. Her mother seemed to have a problem with Tia being light-skinned like her father. She would call Tia names like red bitch, half-white and high yellow whore. For some reason, her mother felt that Tia thought she was too cute. What Tia didn't know was that her father left her mother for a red-bone years ago, leaving her mother's heart broken and feeling like her beautiful dark skin made her unattractive.

Vida listened and tried her best to understand. But Vida never got to know her mother and longed for such a bond. Inside, she couldn't see how a mother and daughter could hate one another.

Vida and Tia clicked like sisters. Their conversation eased on to other topics.

"So, what are you gon' do about school?" asked Tia.

"My grandmother gon' put me in Street Academy. I can't go no where else. What about you?"

"I'm tired of school. I get put out of every school I go to anyway," Tia replied.

"So what you plan to do? You gotta do somethin'."

"I'ma holla at my cousin, she always got some kind of scheme to get some cash."

"I feel you." Vida nodded her head and changed the subject, telling Tia about how Samara didn't want to beef any more.

Tia laughed. "Sucka-ass bitch. I knew she was a punk. She talks that shit but don't want no work." Tia got up and looked out the window at the dudes in front of the building. "We should start our own crew, just me and you."

"What would we call our crew?" Vida smiled, taking it for a joke.

Tia pulled her straight razor from her pocket and said, "We could call our crew Hell Razor Honeys." She laughed. "Bitches would know that we ain't to be fucked wit'."

Vida laughed. "Girl, you crazy as shit."

"Anyway," Tia nodded out the window, "what's up wit' your homies?"

Vida walked over to the window and began putting her on point about who was who. "That's Tec right there. I fucks wit' him tough, plus he eat pussy." She smiled.

"You fuck wit' him like that's your peoples?"

"Nah, not like that, we just real cool."

"Oh, I gotta holla at main man and see what his tongue skills like," said Tia. Both girls laughed.

Two weeks passed, and Tia was still staying at Vida's. She would have been at her cousin Green Eyes', but Green Eyes had gotten herself into some trouble with the law riding the Greyhound from D.C. to North Carolina carrying a brick of cocaine for a dude she dealt with. The FBI was waiting for her when she touched down. It looked like Tia would be staying with Vida for a while.

Today was Tia's fifteenth birthday. She and Vida were out riding around with Tec in his blue 1993 Ford Taurus Station Wagon, with black tints. Weed smoke filled the car as Nas' "It Ain't Hard to Tell" blasted through the speakers while they cruised down Georgia Avenue. The three of them had been hanging out all evening.

Tec was digging Tia, they had gotten cool. He had eaten the pussy and she had returned the favor. Vida was cool with it. When Tia told her about it, Vida said, "Ain't no fun if the homies can't have none." Now, for Tia's birthday, Tec offered to chauffeur the girls around, smoke with them and take them to get something to eat. His money wasn't long, so what he was doing was a kind gesture. Besides, he understood the importance of friendship and had grown to understand that females could be extremely loyal when treated right.

"Chauffeur," Tia called from the back seat where she and Vida were getting their trip on. "I'm ready to eat," she joked.

She and Vida died laughing. The weed Tec had smoked with them was top-of-the-line. They were smacked with blood-shot eyes.

"Where to, ma'am?" Tec played along. He was leaning hard behind the wheel with a black TEC-9 assault weapon on his lap. The air holes around the barrel and the long clip that held the thirty-two 9mm hollow tips made the weapon look as deadly as it was.

"I want pizza," Tia said. She was still laughing.

"Pizza it is, ma'am," Tec said like an English chauffeur. Moments later he pulled up in the parking lot of Pizza Hut on Georgia Avenue, near the Silver Spring, MD line.

"Look!" Vida pointed at the silver Range Rover at the far end of the parking lot. "That's that nigga's truck!"

Hell Razor *Honeys*

Tia looked around and saw Shay's Range sparkling in the night lights. "Sure is."

"What's up?" Tec quickly became serious. He had dropped two bodies during his time of running the streets—once at fourteen and then again just a month ago.

The girls told Tec how Scales and Shay had carried them.

"What y'all wanna do?" Tec asked.

"I'ma bus' his windows out," Vida said.

"I'm wit' it," Tia said. "Pull up on the side street, Tec."

Tec pulled into an alley right down the street. "Be careful." He looked back at the girls.

An idea came to Tia's mind. "Let me see that joint." She pointed at the TEC-9.

"Hell nah, you don't know what you doin' wit' 'dis joint." Tec shook his head no.

"Nigga please, I'm from the Farms, not Georgetown." Tia's homie, Lil' Ed, from Linda Pollin, had taught her how to fire a TEC-9 and a Glock. She knew what she was doing.

"You sure?" Tec raised his eyebrow.

"On my mother, young."

"What you gon' do?" asked Tec.

"I'ma light his shit up," Tia said.

Vida gave Tia a questioning look as Tec handed her the weapon.

Tia got out the car and looked back at Vida, saying, "Come on, Vee. Watch my back." She pulled her Polo sweatshirt over the TEC-9 as she and Vida jogged up the street. No one seemed to be in sight in the nice residential neighborhood.

When the girls got to the Range Rover, Tia pulled some red lipstick from her pocket and wrote on the windshield in big letters: HELL RAZOR HONEYS. "Back up, Vee," Tia said. She braced herself, holding the TEC with both hands. She then opened fire, pulling the trigger over and over, blowing out the side windows and putting countless holes in the doors. She shot the tires as well. Afterwards, the girls took off running and laughing.

Headed back around Montana Avenue, in the back seat of the car, Vida said to Tec, "You gotta teach me how to use that joint."

Tec laughed. "You should be askin' Tia. She emptied the clip."

"Yes or no!" Vida demanded.

"I got you," Tec replied.

"Tonight, I want you to teach me tonight."

"I gotta go get some bullets."

"I got a whole box of your bullets under my bed."

"Nah, them .45 bullets... I need 9mm for the TEC." Tec lit another blunt.

Vida saw the damage the TEC-9 did to the Range Rover and wanted to know how to use one just in case she ever needed to.

True to his word, Tec went and got some more bullets and then took Vida and Tia to a wooded area nearby. They all walked into the woods and Tec gave Vida the gun. Standing behind her with his arms around her, he helped her aim the joint.

"You gotta promise me somethin'," Tec said to Vida.

"What?" Vida looked over her shoulder at Tec.

"If I ever need you by my side, promise you'll be there," Tec said it like a joke, but wanted to see what Vida would say.

"That ain't even in the talk. You my nigga, you know that."

"Aight, come on." Tec raised her arms so the gun was aimed at the tree in front of her. As the chilly night wind blew and Tia looked on, he said, "Pull the trigga."

Vida did as she was told. With a light jerk the TEC-9 went off with a loud pop. She was surprised. She thought the gun would have a powerful kick, but she now knew she could control it. Pulling the trigger a few more times with Tec's help, Vida got the hang of it. She hit the tree five times in a row. The strong smell of gunpowder tingled in her nose.

"Go 'head and bus' it by yourself." Tec stepped back and put an arm around Tia.

Vida opened fire like she was trying to kill somebody. As a flame of fire jumped out of the barrel with every blast, countless shell casings were spit out of the automatic. It sounded like fireworks were going off. After twenty more shots Vida was satisfied. She turned to face Tec and Tia.

"I got the hang of it," Vida said with the smoking TEC-9 at her side.

"You need to know how to load it too," Tia said, ready to leave the woods. It was getting cold as the night grew old.

Hell Razor Honeys

Back in the car, Tia took the clip out the gun and flicked all of the bullets into her shirt, so she wouldn't have to touch them with her fingers when showing Vida how to load and cock the TEC-9. "You never wanna touch the bullets wit' your bare hands. Automatics spit shells. If the police find the shells wit' your prints on 'em they gon' lock ya' ass up." Using her shirt, Tia stuffed the bullets back into the long clip as she coached Vida through the process step by step.

Driving back around the way, Tec listened to Tia explain the workings of the weapon. He was impressed. Tia was his type of girl.

"Now you do it." Tia handed Vida the TEC-9.

Vida did everything just right and cocked the gun when she was done.

"You got it, boo." Tia smiled.

Later on, inside Vida's bedroom, she and Tia talked about how they had dogged Shay's Range Rover.

"Fuck that nigga," Vida said. "They shouldn't of tried to carry us."

"No bullshit." Tia was lying on the bed. "You know what? I really dig Tec, he a real nigga."

Vida had known him since she was old enough to walk. "That's my nigga. He cool as shit, if he trust you. But if you cross 'em he don't play no games. At the same time, if he fucks wit' you he gon' have your back til' your casket drops."

EYONE WILLIAMS

Chapter 3

Tia sat in History class daydreaming about the sex she'd had last night. She'd been living with Vida for over a month now. During this time she'd gotten very close to Ms. Green; she loved the woman like her own grandmother. Ms. Green enrolled both girls into Street Academy, a school where most cut-ups were sent from all over the city.

At Street Academy, Tia met a dude by the name of Ellis who was seventeen. He was a good looking dude that didn't mind hitting her off with a few dollars, plus he could fuck. He bent Tia's little body into all kinds of back-breaking positions when laying the pipe. She loved the dick. There was only one problem; she and Vida had vowed not to fall for a nigga, at all. She had only been seeing Ellis for about three weeks. She thought he was so smooth. Tia was dealing with a few other dudes, but Ellis had her attention.

Tia met Ellis outside of Street Academy one afternoon when she and Vida were trying to buy some weed to go home with. A dude they knew directed them to Ellis, who had some of the best weed around. Tia bought two $20 bags from Ellis, and at his request she gave him her phone number. Two days later they hit the movies, went out to eat and hit the hotel. All Tia had gotten out of the deal at the time were a pair of Air Jordans, a Polo outfit and hard dick. However, Ellis was still after her, even after he hit it.

He had taken her to New York with him on a "business trip" two weeks after he'd met her. Balling up the highway at dangerous speeds in his BMW 740i, Ellis had his mind on the few things he had to do once he got to Brooklyn, where his cousin Sonny lived. Tia had never been to New York, which is why Ellis took her for the ride. Looking out the window at the beautiful scenery, Tia thought about how good the dick was and turned down the Scarface CD.

"Why you do that?" Ellis asked.

Tia smiled, taking off her clothes. "Just enjoy the ride, nigga."

"Roll that other Wood. Let's make it a party."

With nothing on but a black bandanna tied around her head gangsta-style, and a pair of Gucci shades, Tia rolled and lit a Backwood stuffed with weed. Behind the tinted windows, she puffed the smoke a few times and then passed it to Ellis. Undoing his pants, Tia held his thick, erect manhood in her small hands. She then took off her shades and said, "Don't crash."

"I got us." Ellis took a long pull on the Backwood and held the strong smoke in his lungs for a moment. "Handle your business."

Tia went to work. Up and down, she took him deep in her warm throat. She came up and licked all over the head and then went back down to his balls and back up around the tip, before easing it back into her mouth. Her slurps were loud and wet, followed by popping sounds. As she took her fill, she looked up into his eyes and knew she was driving him crazy, sucking the shit out of his dick. She continued to suck and pop while jerking him off at the same time.

"Aaaahh, shit!" Ellis came all in her mouth.

She wasn't ready for the explosion; she quickly grabbed the base of his dick with both hands and held on as she let him empty his thick, creamy load in her mouth. She swallowed it all and then licked all over his dick until he went limp.

"You like that?" Tia asked, as she took the Backwood from him and took a long pull.

Looking at the curves of her sexy body, with her nipples pointing straight ahead, Ellis said, "You the best that ever did it, boo." He smiled and reached over to rub her long nipple between his thumb and index finger.

"Ssss…" Tia's pussy gushed with another surge of wetness as chills ran through her body. Her nipples were her hot spots. They were like a switch that when flicked on made her pussy gush like the Nile River.

Ellis and Tia got their freak on all the way up I-95. Like most red-bones, Tia had a lot of freak in her. But she only let it out when she wanted to and not with just anyone.

Once in New York, Ellis went to holla at his cousin in Marcy Projects, where he copped a pound of weed for dirt cheap. He hid the weed in the stash spot that was customized into the trunk of the used BMW that he had bought from his cousin as well. He then took Tia shopping and bought her a few outfits and a gold chain.

When Tia got back to D.C. she talked Vida to death about the trip and gave her two Prada outfits.

The rush of students leaving the classroom snapped Tia out of her daydream. She got up in her black, skin-tight, Versace jeans and headed out into the hallway looking for Vida. Vida bent the corner in a short blue Polo jean skirt, a black Polo T-shirt, no socks and a pair of colorful track Nikes. Her shoulder-length haircut framed her cute face, while the gloss on her sexy lips only added to her sex appeal.

Vida gave Tia five and said, "What's up, girl?"

"Ain't shit, young."

"How we gettin' home?" Vida smiled.

They were above catching the bus now. One way or another they got a dude to give them a ride home everyday. Ellis hardly came to school so that wasn't an everyday thing.

"It's your day, bitch." Tia laughed as students brushed by her in the loud, crowded hallway. She had gotten a young dude to give them a ride yesterday in his old Cadillac bucket with black tints. Vida joaned on the car for a good hour after they got home, talking about how niggaz were going to think they were about to do a drive-by if they ever got in that car again. Needless to say, Tia threw dude's number in the trash.

"Come on, let's go outside. I'll see what I can do. After all, I ain't got on this little ass skirt for nothing," Vida said.

Vida and Tia headed for the door. At the end of the hallway the sound of someone crying caught their attention. Two straight ghetto bitches were pressin' a white girl that looked like a hood rat wannabe in her tight blue Versace jeans, white Versace T-shirt and white Reeboks. The white girl even had a phat ass. Her long blond hair was

Hell Razor *Honeys*

even done in a stylish around-the-way-girl hairdo.

Her name was Magen, but all the black students she went to school with didn't like the rich Georgetown girl; they called her Vanilla Ice. They had no reason to dislike her, it seemed like they disliked her because she wasn't one of them. Tough black girls took her earrings and name brand handbags, along with anything else they wanted. Vanilla Ice never fought back, but she never told either.

Vida had been watching the white girl for a month, just checking her out. She felt sorry for her and wondered why she was going to such a school when it was known that her family had money. "Look at that shit, poor girl." Vida nodded in Vanilla Ice's direction.

Tia laughed. "She better learn how to stand up for herself or them bitches gon' keep takin' her bad."

Vanilla Ice was doubled over in grave pain from a hard punch to the stomach. Her oppressors were two sixteen year old Southeast bitches. Vanilla Ice was crying and covering her face protectively as she leaned against a locker. The two Southeast girls had taken her earrings, her Prada bag and were demanding her gold Gucci watch. Vanilla Ice wasn't giving up the watch for some reason. The taller of the two Southeast girls began punching Vanilla Ice hard in the back. It sounded like a kick drum was being beat. Vanilla Ice cried out in pain and fell to her knees, balling up on the floor. The other girl, a fat brown-skinned bitch, began kicking the hurt white girl, still demanding her watch.

"That's enough!" Vida stepped on the scene. She didn't like what she was seeing; she hated to see the weak being taken advantage of. Tia, on the other hand, didn't give a fuck one way or another. However, she was rolling with Vida. regardless.

"Bitch, you better mind your business!" the fat bitch warned Vida.

"Who the fuck you callin' a bitch?!" Tia stepped up and got in the fat bitch's face.

Vanilla Ice was still moaning in serious pain.

"Bitch, you heard what th—"

In one flashing motion Tia swung at the fat bitch, and everything seemed to stand still. No one moved. The fat bitch seemed shocked that Tia had smacked the shit out of her. However, in a few seconds, it was clear that Tia didn't just smack her. The fat bitch grabbed her

26   EYONE WILLIAMS

face and screamed. Blood began to seep between her fingers. From her right temple curving all the way to her chin was a nasty, fine and deep slice wound from Tia's straight razor.

"Now what, bitch?!!" Tia boldly challenged, still holding the bloody straight razor.

The two Southeast bitches took off running. A dotted trail of blood followed behind them.

Vanilla Ice, now safe, was no longer a concern. Vida grabbed Tia's arm and said, "We gotta get the fuck outta here!" They took off running as well.

Minutes later, Vida and Tia were blocks away from the school, out of breath. They were standing by a pay phone where Tia had just beeped Ellis. The girls looked at one another and busted out laughing.

"You crazy as shit." Vida pointed at Tia, who seemed to be watching her back for the threat of police.

Tia had felt how deep she cut the bitch and knew what kind of damage had been done. "Shhhhhiiit, you crazy. You the one that turned into Captain Save-A-Ho," Tia joked.

Both girls died laughing again.

"The poor girl was cryin'. I felt sorry for her. Excuse me for havin' a heart."

"Fuck that white bitch, blue-eyed devil!" Tia rolled her eyes. "If a bitch ain't woman enough to stand up for herself, fuck her. I done got my ass beat a rack of times, but I always fought back. I ain't saying she gotta win, but she gotta fight back. If she woulda fought back I wouldn't have mind helpin' her, but that bitch just balled up and cried like a baby."

"Yeah, but for some reason she ain't give up that watch," Vida said, watching the busy traffic fly by.

Moments later, a big, green 1991 Mercedes Benz 420SEL pulled up at the curb. Vida and Tia were taken off guard and looked startled. Vanilla Ice was behind the wheel with a black eye.

With the push of a button she lowered the passenger window, leaned over and said, "Can I give y'all a ride?" She sounded black, effortlessly.

Vida and Tia looked at each other with surprise. Together they said, "Hell Yeahhhhh!"

They jumped in the Benz. Vida got up front. The car eased back into traffic.

"Thank you so much," Vanilla Ice said to both girls.

"Ain't no thing," Vida said.

"Who car is this?" Tia asked, looking around while rubbing the leather seats and wood grain. She was impressed.

"It's my mother's," Vanilla Ice said.

"Why you go to Street Academy if your peoples got money?" Vida asked, picking up the car phone.

"It's a long story." Vanilla Ice sighed and explained her situation. She was sixteen years old. Her mother was a federal judge in D.C. Her father was a defense attorney that cheated on her mother and she couldn't stand him. She grew up in private schools, but was put out for smoking weed in the bathroom. Her parents were angered like never before. They sent her to boarding school in Arizona for a year, where she developed a desire for black dudes. She got pregnant by a black dude at fourteen and was sent back home to D.C. Her parents forced her to have an abortion and put her in public school in Georgetown. She ended up stealing the keys to her math teacher's car and called herself running away to Arizona to be with the young dude that got her pregnant. She was arrested in Oklahoma on the highway. Her mother pulled some strings and got the charges dropped for the stolen car. In an attempt to scare Vanilla Ice, her parents sent her to Street Academy with the tough inner-city kids. However, she like going to school with blacks. Even with the hardships, she wouldn't break.

"Well," Tia said with a laugh, "you sure can't fight, but you can take a mean ass-whuppin', you one tough white bitch. I'll give you that much."

Vida laughed, thinking that Tia was a trip.

With no shame, Vanilla Ice laughed as well and then said, "I never said I was tough. I ain't grow up in the hood."

Vida looked at the gold Gucci watch Vanilla Ice was wearing and said, "I see you ain't give the watch up. What's up wit' that?"

"My grandmother bought it for me before she died. I'd die before I let somebody take this from me."

"It looked like you was about to die before Captain Save-A-Ho stepped on the scene," Tia joked. All three girls laughed.

"Let me give y'all some money for helpin' me out. I know y'all ain't have to do that," Vanilla Ice said.

Tia didn't waste any time. "Hell yeah, the police probably lookin' for me right now."

"Where y'all live at?"

"You know where Montana Avenue at?" Vida asked.

"Nah, but you can show me, and I can stop at the ATM on the way," said Vanilla Ice.

On the way to Montana Avenue Vanilla Ice stopped at the ATM and withdrew $300. She gave Vida and Tia $150 each. When the Benz pulled up in front of Vida's building Vanilla Ice was amazed; she was really in the hood. It was like on TV to her, she saw the pipeheads, the hustlers, even the police cruiser coming down the block. Something about the "hood" excited her. Her Georgetown neighborhood was boring.

"I'll see y'all later, maybe we can hang out sometimes," Vanilla Ice said.

Vida laughed. "Maybe," she said as she got out the car.

Tia just laughed and shut the door behind her.

Tec and Kareem, along with a few other dudes, were sitting in front of the building when Vida and Tia got out of the Benz. Tec and Kareem questioned the girls about the white girl.

"What, you like white girls or somethin'?" Tia asked Kareem, as she took a seat between him and Tec.

"I just wanna fuck a white girl—"

Vida cut him off, "You just wanna fuck anything, pipeheads and all."

Everybody died laughing.

"I trick here and there, but that's only on the late night, when I can't find no pussy," Kareem said.

Kareem was fifteen years old, 5' 10" and 160 pounds. He was a brown-skinned dude with wavy hair and a nasty scar on the side of his face where a bullet had grazed him in a shoot-out in the Brentwood section of Northeast. According to the ladies, he was still good looking. He and Tec were the closest of all their homies. They lived in the same building, a few buildings up the street from Vida's.

"Besides," Kareem said. "I heard white bitches take it anywhere."

He smiled.

"How you know?" Tia asked.

"That nigga got all them damn porno tapes in his house." Tec laughed. "He be watchin' *Debbie Does Dallas* and shit, tryin' that shit on bitches. Now he wanna find a white bitch that take it in the ass."

"Ain't nothing wrong wit' that, is it?" Kareem shrugged with his hands in the air. "White bitches just do shit black bitches don't do."

"If you ain't never been wit' a white girl how do you know what they do that a black girl don't do?" Vida asked, watching Tec roll a Backwood.

"If you get me that phone number I'll find out what a white girl do." Kareem looked down at his vibrating beeper.

"You just don't know how to get a black girl to do what you want. Your game is lackin'," Vida said.

"Whatever, what make you think that?"

"I'm just sayin'. If your talk game right you should be able to get what you want. Not to mention that your pockets gotta be right too," Vida said.

Tia giggled while smoking the Backwood Tec had just lit. "I guess your dollars ain't right," she said to Kareem, blowing smoke into the air.

"Oh yeah, is that right?" Kareem pulled a thick $1,800 knot from his pocket and waved it in Tia's face. "What can I get for this here? It gotta be about two Gs."

Tia said confidently, "I ain't gon' let you put it in my ass, but I'll milk you dry for your two Gs. Bet that, playboy. But you cool peoples so I ain't gon' take your money."

"I'll get the white girl's number for you," Vida said, reaching out to grab the Backwood from Tia.

One of Tec's homies came running from around the side of the building with his gun in hand, breathing hard. He told Tec and Kareem that the same brown Cadillac that had been riding through earlier was riding through again. Tec and Kareem hit the cut with their homie, leaving Vida and Tia with the Backwood. The girls knew it was time to go inside. A few moments later, gunshots tore through the air like the 4th of July.

Vida went to school the next day without Tia. Tia didn't know if the police would be looking for her or not. Fortunately, the girl that got her face sliced didn't go to the police so Tia was cool for now. Vida saw the girl that was with the one that got her faced sliced; they walked right by each other in the hallway. The girl didn't want any trouble, although she did give Vida a cold glare as she walked by. Vida didn't trip; she had a box cutter in her pocket.

Vanilla Ice was in most of Vida's classes. She followed Vida around like a lost puppy. The shit got on Vida's nerves, but she put up with it for the time being.

As weeks passed by, and Tia returned to school, Vida and Tia started to like the white girl. It was from the heart with Vida, she found Vanilla Ice to be real good peoples—very loyal. At first, Tia was just using the white girl. Vanilla Ice had her own Visa card and spent money on Vida and Tia. However, Tia began to really like her as time went on. Just like Vida, Tia respected the fact that Vanilla Ice was loyal.

The girls accepted Vanilla Ice as a Hell Razor Honey. They dropped the Vanilla and began calling her Ice. They started taking her to the go-go with them, where Ice carried a box cutter as well. Dudes began chasing the new white broad on the scene. Vida and Tia schooled her every step of the way. Ice even grew a little heart as a Hell Razor Honey.

On a number of occasions at the go-go, the Hell Razor Honeys got into beefs with crews of girls that were deeper than them. Ice stood firm with Vida and Tia. The first time Ice sliced a girl's face with a box cutter she couldn't believe how much blood hit the floor of the Black Hole. The Hell Razor Honeys made a name for themselves, almost overnight. They got a lot of attention due to the fact that there were only three of them, and one of them was white.

By the summer of 1995, dudes from other parts of the city were coming through Montana Avenue to holla at the Hell Razor Honeys— the crew that had the white girl with them that could fuck like a porno star.

On the D.L., Tia was falling for Ellis. She would never admit it, but Vida could see the writing on the wall. Vida didn't care, as long as the nigga did right by Tia, and that he was doing. Ellis started getting more money as he started fucking around with cocaine along with the weed. He spent more and more money on Tia and took her to different places like Atlanta and Miami. He knew she was a Hell Razor Honey, but he wasn't trippin'. He was doing his thing on the side as well. Tia didn't know that, she never gave that any thought either.

Sitting in front of her building on Montana Avenue, Vida enjoyed the summer time with Tia and Ice by her side. They looked like they were in a Luke video, with their short shorts that allowed their ass cheeks to hang out when they stood up. They all wore top-of-the-line gear. They were on the come up. Tia had gotten Ellis to give them a few ounces of weed to get on their feet. They now sold weed out of the third floor apartment that Ice rented with her fake ID. The apartment was also a hang out for them and the homies Vida grew up with.

"Ice," Kareem called out from behind the wheel of his dark blue 1991 Park Avenue with black tints. Geto Boys' "We Can't Be Stopped" blasted from the speakers. Tec was riding shotgun. Two other homies were in the back, hidden behind the tints. Kareem was turned out on Ice and couldn't get enough of her. He was amazed that the hair on her pussy was as blond as the hair on her head. But the way she took it in the ass had him wrapped around her finger. It was nothing she couldn't ask him to do for her or the crew.

"What's up, Reem?" Ice walked over and leaned in the driver's side window. Combing her long blond hair out of her face with her fingers, she spoke to the crew in the car. She knew it made Kareem jealous. He wanted to be the only homie that could fuck Ice. However, after he talked about what Ice could do in the bed, Tec had to see if it was true. It was true!

Kareem handed Ice a hundred dollar bill and said, "Let me get two of them bags."

Ice said, "I'll be right back." She walked back to the building swinging her black-girl ass for the eyes in the car. She got two $50 bags of smoke out of a brown paper bag that was stashed by the side of the building. Returning to the car she gave Kareem the bags. "Can I see you tonight?" she asked, licking her lips. "I got somethin' I want us to try."

"No doubt, I'll be waitin'." Kareem got hard just thinking about what she had in mind.

"See you later then." Ice stepped off.

Getting tired of sitting out in the heat, the girls went up to the apartment that they sold weed out of, where they could chill in the AC. They had some of the best weed around and had dudes and broads coming through to cop.

Tia's beeper vibrated. She got on the phone and called the unknown number back. "Who is this?"

"Green Eyes."

"Damn, bitch, where the fuck you been? I ain't heard from you in forever." Tia was excited to hear from Green Eyes. She looked up to Green Eyes and had always wanted to be just like her. "I miss you. How the hell you get my beeper number?"

"I saw Lil' Ed around the way, he gave me your beeper number. I just got back in town. I jive ran into some trouble, I'll holla at you about it though. Anyway, I hear you doing your thing, got yourself a little crew and shit. Niggaz talkin' 'bout y'all all the way on the Southside."

Tia smiled, she was proud that Green Eyes was talking to her like an equal. She had always wanted to run with Green Eyes and her crew—The G-String Honeys. Now Tia had her own crew and she wasn't somebody's little tag-along. "I live around Montana wit' my girl now. Come holla at me."

"Cool. I gotta make a few runs, put some things in order, I'ma slide through there later on," Green eyes said.

While Tia was on the phone, Vida looked out the window and saw Samara and two Come Back Honeys pull up out front in a big, white, 1992 Lexus LS400 with chrome rims. The Come Back Honeys were stepping their game up as well. They made it a point, however, to stay out of the Hell Razor Honeys' way. Samara jumped out of the Lex and ran toward the building. A few moments later there was a knock at the door.

Vida answered the door and said, "What's up, Sam?"

"You got some smoke?" Samara bought all her weed from Vida and tried to act like nothing had ever gone down between the two of them.

"Yeah, what you tryin' to get?" Vida checked Sam out. She was looking good, working that Toni Braxton look.

Hell Razor Honeys

"Can I get two for $85?"

"Cool." Vida looked over her shoulder and told Ice to bring her two $50 bags of smoke. Ice brought her the smoke and she handed the bags to Samara and got the money.

"Thanks." Samara put the bags in the pockets of her Guess jean shorts. "Catch you later."

As Vida shut the door Ice was just popping in Tupac's *Me Against the World* CD in the boom box. Vida smiled and said, "Do you listen to anything other than 'Pac?"

"Sometimes, but that's my nigga. You know that." Ice was in love with Tupac. "I feel like 'Pac sometimes, me against the world. I always been on the outside lookin' in. I'm a white girl that loves everything black people love. People always look at me like a wannabe, not knowing this is really me. I am what I am, I'm real."

Just getting off the phone, Tia said, "You ain't on the outside lookin' in no more, we the baddest bitches in the city."

All the girls laughed.

"For real, niggaz talkin' 'bout us all over the city, like the old Hechinger Mall bitches." Tia had another cousin that used to run with a notorious crew of girls called The Hechinger Mall Honeys. Their name was kicking real heavy in the late-80s and early-90s.

"We need to step it up like them," Vida said, counting the money they had made for the day—they had hustled up $965. Vida put the money up. Their stash was almost $4,000 now.

CARTEL PUBLICATIONS PRESENTS

Chapter 4

Behind the black tinted windows of Tec's Taurus Wagon, Vida
listened to the instructions he was giving her. Tec had sicked
Vida on a dude named Los who was getting a nice piece of
money in the city. Los had just bust out with a new Infiniti Q45 and
was rumored to be handing out a lot of weight Uptown. Vida had been
working her shit with Los for a few weeks now.

Junior M.A.F.I.A.'s "Player's Anthem" played down low as they
cruised through 18th and D Street just after 6:00 P.M. "However shit
go," Tec said. "I don't want you to tell nobody about this move, not
even Tia. Feel me?"

"I got you."

"That's why I fucks wit' you." Tec looked at Vida's thick, sexy,
reddish-brown thighs. Her pussy print was clear as day through her
tight cutting Polo jean shorts. Her nipples could be seen slightly
through her tight, grey Polo tank top. Her plump titties filled the tank
top well. "You before your time," Tec said.

"You know you fuckin' wit' the realest." Vida was popping gum
and looking at her hairdo in the side mirror. "Make sure I get my
break down." Vida was now fifteen and playing a deadly game of setting niggaz up. Tonight was her first time. For some reason she was
very calm about it, as if she'd done it before.

Tec smiled and said, "You know I got you. I'ma break you off real
nice." He rubbed his hand up her smooth thigh and caressed her pussy
print.

Vida didn't mind. Tec could still hit if he wanted to.

Hell Razor Honeys

Meanwhile, around Montana Avenue, the other two Hell Razor Honeys were terrorizing shit. Tia and Ice had just beat a bitch down and sliced her face with box cutters. Their victim had called the police on Kareem and lied saying he beat her up; all because Kareem wasn't fucking with her no more. Kareem paid Ice and Tia $200 each to punish the bitch. Tia and Ice went on the move in all black, wearing ski masks like it was a real caper.

Sitting on the steps in the hallway of their building, a short while after they had punished the girl for Kareem, Tia and Ice were smoking weed and joking about the work they had put in. Ice's beeper vibrated, it was her mother.

"I'll be right back; I gotta see what my motha want." Ice went upstairs to their clubhouse apartment and called her house.

"Your father says he's sick of you hanging out in the ghetto. He said he wants you home right now or he's taking everything. I tried to talk to him, but he's not bending." Ice's mother sounded worried; her father could be heard in the background yelling. Ice's father blamed her mother for the way Ice was.

"Mom, I'm sick of him. I'm not comin' home. Matter fact, I'ma bring the car back and wash my hands of his no-good, cheatin' ass. He's not a father anyway."

"Baby, don't talk like that, just—"

"Mom, I love you, but I can't live in that house wit' him anymore." Ice hung up the phone. She then walked into the living room looking like Pamela Anderson with a phat ass and a "hood" makeover. She was rocking a black Gucci bodysuit that clung to every curve of her body and cut into her pussy.

Kareem was sitting on the sofa counting a handful of cash with a burning blunt handing from his lips. *Damn this bitch look good,* he thought.

"Reem, I need to use your car real quick." Ice sat beside him, taking the blunt from his lips and puffing it a few times.

"I can't do it right now. I gotta go meet Tec in a minute." Kareem was waiting for Tec to beep him and let him know what was up with

Los. "What's wrong wit' the Benz?"

Ice told him about her conversation with her mother. "I'ma be livin' here from now on. I like it better in the hood anyway." She rubbed his crotch, making his dick hard. "It's me against the world. That's how I'm carryin' it from here on out. Whoever ain't down wit' me, fuck 'em."

"I'm glad you on my team, young," Kareem said as Ice unbuckled his shorts and began licking all over his dick. Looking down at her all he could see was a lap full of blond hair going up and down. He loved what she could do with her tongue while his dick was in her mouth.

Outside, coming down Montana Avenue in his repaired Range Rover, Shay was looking for the bitches who called themselves the Hell Razor Honeys. Since the name was now kicking in the streets, Shay knew who had destroyed his Range Rover and cost him thousands of dollars in repairs. When he pulled up in front of Vida's building fate was on his side; Tia was leaning in the driver's side window of an old Caprice Classic serving a dude some weed.

Shay threw his truck in park and jumped out just as the Caprice pulled off. Leaving his door open and the music playing, Shay called out, "Ay, bitch!"

Tia turned and saw him; she took off running for the building. Shay gave chase and grabbed her by her black Versace T-shirt, ripping it off of her little body and causing her to fall to the ground with only her bra covering her titties.

"You don't know who you playin' wit', bitch! I should blow your fuckin' brains out!" Shay kicked Tia in the face and chest a few times and then bent over and started punching her in the face. She screamed and tried to fight back.

Samara and two Come Back Honeys pulled up in a gold BMW and saw Shay punishing Tia brutally. Tia's whole face was bloody. Samara jumped out of the car and ran to help Tia; she didn't know why, but it felt like the right thing to do. Samara's two cronies followed her lead.

"Get off her, muthafucka!" Samara yelled as she jumped on Shay's back, scratching at his face in her fresh Dolce & Gabbana outfit.

Shay slung her to the ground in one quick motion. Samara hit her back hard on the rough sidewalk and let out a painful grunt. The two Come Back Honeys that were with her attacked Shay. Samara got up quickly and rejoined the fight. Shay was fighting off the girls like they were wild dogs.

Ice stepped outside with a cold Coke in her hand and saw the drama. Tia was on the ground knocked out, with blood all over her face; the Come Back Honeys were all over Shay, yelling and screaming. Enraged, Ice threw the soda to the ground and went for the Glock 19 the girls kept stashed by the front of the building—Tec had given it to them. Ice fired twice in the air. Shay saw yet another girl, this one with a gun, and knew it was time to get the fuck on about his business. He took off running for his truck, where his pistol was.

"Don't run, muthafucka!" Ice screamed, as she held the Glock with both hands, firing shots repeatedly, running after Shay.

Bullets flew by his head as he jumped in the truck and pulled off. Ice kept blazing, blowing the windows out as the truck flew down the street. Standing in the middle of the street surrounded by empty shells, Ice was still pulling the trigger of the Glock after she had fired the whole nineteen rounds.

Vida's beeper had been vibrating over and over for more than an hour but she didn't know it. Her beeper was on the hotel floor with the rest of her clothes, while she was riding Los like a pro. With her hands on his chest, her head back, and her titties bouncing wildly, Vida was throwing the pussy on him, taking her fill at the same time. *Might as well enjoy the dick,* she thought. Every time she came up and down on Los it felt like he was deep in her stomach.

She knew he was close to cumming by the way he was pulling her back down on his dick, hard and fast, with his hands around her small waist. She moaned like he was killing the pussy. The dick was good, but not that good. She'd learned to exaggerate her sexual pleasure, knowing what it did to a nigga's ego. Knowing that Los was about to cum, Vida began flexing the muscles in her tight pussy, massaging his dick better than his hand ever could. She didn't care if he came inside

EYONE WILLIAMS

her; she made every nigga wear a rubber now.

"Say my name, Vicky." Los was breathing hard and fast.

Nigga please, Vida thought. "Los... oh, Los... Los, aaahhhhhh! It's so big! I... I can't take it no more," she went into her act, although she had got her nut already. "Don't stop, it feels so good!"

"Ahhhh... the pussy is so tight," Los declared as he came. If the twenty-one year old Los knew he was fucking a fifteen year old, then maybe he wouldn't be so surprised the pussy was so tight. "Uuuhhh...." He came with the force of a rushing waterfall.

When they were done with the first round, Los got up and walked across the room ass-naked. He grabbed one of his weed-stuffed Backwoods and returned to the bed, sitting next to Vida as he lit the smoke. He looked down at Vida's sexy body as she lay on her stomach with her phat ass in the air. He softly rubbed her round ass and squeezed it, sinking his fingers into her flesh like warm clay. "I want some ass, Vicky."

"Huh?" Vida's mind was on how she was going to get to the phone and give Tec her location. "You just got some ass." *I know this nigga don't think he gon' fuck me in my ass,* she thought. *It ain't goin' down like that.*

Still rubbing her ass, Los blew smoke in the air and said, "I wanna feel how tight the asshole is."

Vida smiled. "The pussy is tight enough, young. We ain't movin' that fast."

Los spent a few more minutes trying to talk her into the anal action, but Vida wasn't going for nothing at all. Her big break came when Los went to the bathroom. Quickly and cautiously, Vida got on the phone and called Tec. Her heart was pounding; she didn't want Los to catch her on the phone. She whispered her location to Tec and hung up the phone. She was back in the bed before Los returned. He had no idea what had been set in motion.

"If my baby's mother could fuck like you maybe I'd keep it at home," Los said as he lay down.

"You askin' a lot, ain't you?" Vida smiled as she slid toward his dick and began licking it to life. She went to work sucking on him, going all the way down; deep throating him, like Tia had taught her using a ten inch dildo.

Los was loving her mouth. He closed his eyes and let her take him to the promise land. He had no idea that Vida had left the door unlocked when they first entered the room.

Five minutes after Vida began giving Los head Tec let himself in wearing a ski mask and carrying a smoke grey TEC-9.

Los heard the door open and opened his eyes. "Oh shit!" He almost shitted on himself.

Vida got up and began grabbing her clothes.

"You set me up, bitch!"

Tec smacked Los in the face with the gun. "Shut the fuck up, bitch nigga."

"Ahhhhh… that bitch set me up!" Los grabbed his eye.

"Charge it to the game," said Vida, as she got dressed and left the room, as planned.

An hour later Vida learned about Tia. Inside Tia's hospital room with Ice and Samara, Vida had tears of anger in her eyes. Ms. Green was out in the hallway talking to the doctor. Vida couldn't believe what had happened to Tia; Tia's jaw was broken and had to be wired up. Standing at Tia's bedside holding her hand, Vida listened as Samara and Ice told her what had went down, step by step.

Vida rubbed Tia's forehead while looking at her bruised face and wired up jaw. "That bitch nigga gon' pay for this shit… I swear to God," Vida said.

Tia weakly nodded and struggled to whisper through the wires, "I know… I know."

"Don't you worry about nothin' you gon' be just fine," Vida said, then got up and told Samara to let her holla at her in the hallway. In the hallway, as nurses walked back and forth, Vida gave Samara five and said, "I respect what you did. You didn't have to do that." Vida paused for a second and looked at the busted lip Samara had suffered in the altercation. "If you ever need me, I got your back. Okay?"

"One hand washes the other, right?" Samara smiled. "Even wit' our situation, I know you wouldn't have let a nigga beat me up like that. But on the real, the white girl that be wit' y'all put that work in."

"Yeah, I'm hip. That's my girl." Vida looked at her Gucci watch. It was almost midnight. "I gotta go. I'll holla at you tomorrow."

Back in Tia's room, Vida said to her, "Grandma gon' stay here wit' you. Me and Ice gon' get on top of this situation."

"Be careful," whispered Tia.

Rolling in the big Benz, headed back around Montana Avenue, *Thug Life Volume 1* was pumping through the speakers as Vida and Ice discussed what was going on and what was to be done. Vida respected how Ice had emptied the clip on Shay. Ice had handled herself like a thoroughbred under pressure.

"You put that work in tonight," Vida said.

Ice was proud. She had already felt the love of being accepted by Vida and Tia, but now she really felt like she had paid her dues and earned her keep. "You and Tia are family to me, Vee. I'll never let anything happen to y'all if I can help it."

"I know, Ice," Vida said.

Vida picked up the car phone and beeped Tec a few times. When he didn't call back by the time they got around the way she figured he still had his hands full. "It seem like Tec ain't gon' call back no time soon."

"So what we gon' do?" Ice asked.

They were sitting in front of their apartment building. A few pipeheads were walking up the street. Further up the block a few neighborhood thugs were posted up in front of another building.

"We gon' raise hell 'til we catch up wit' Tec and Reem," Vida told Ice.

"Cool."

"I'll be right back, I'ma go get one of them joints out the house."

"One?" Ice looked at Vida like she was crazy.

Vida smiled. "I mean two."

Just as Vida was getting out the car, the car phone rang. It was Ellis. Ice gave the phone to Vida.

"What's up?" Vida asked.

"I just left the hospital. Tia told me what's up. Don't worry about shit. I got this, okay?"

"Okay," Vida said. It was better that somebody who really knew what they were doing put in the work.

"I'll holla at you later." Ellis hung up.

"I guess the dude Ellis really fucks wit' Tee," Vida said as she hung up the phone.

"We might as well chill for the night," said Ice.

The night turned out to be a murderous one. Ellis and one of his homies caught Shay, Scales and one of their homies in a white BMW and aired the car out with AR-15 assault rifles on Benning Road, Northeast. Everybody in the BMW died. It was all over the news the next day.

Tec slumped Los and left him in the trunk of his Infiniti Q45 in the parking lot of a Capitol Heights, Maryland apartment complex. Things didn't turn out as he had planned. He only got a quarter key of coke and $18,000. He and Kareem split the coke and gave Vida $6,000—the most money she'd ever seen at one time. The $6,000 changed her understanding of "working niggaz." She told herself that she would want for nothing, never again.

Chapter 5

The Black Hole was a notorious go-go spot uptown on Georgia Avenue; it was also a dangerous spot to party. Morton Street— 640 Lorton Morton—ran along the side of the Black Hole and it was home to some known killers. Other crews from across town also played the spot real heavy, some of which were at war. As of lately, the Hell Razor Honeys were always in the spot, carrying razors of some sort. It was known that they would use 'em too.

The summer passed quickly and fall took over. During this time the Hell Razor Honeys began to grow in numbers. They began going to the go-go with the Come Back Honeys, but people saw the group as the Hell Razor Honeys being as though Vida, Tia and Ice were amongst the group. If those three were in the group it was automatically the Hell Razor Honeys. Tia's cousin, Green Eyes, had started hanging with the crew. Green Eyes was the oldest at eighteen.

Tonight the Black Hole was packed and jumping. The famous go-go band, Rare Essence, was crankin'. All the honeys in the spot were freakin' and dressed to impress. There was a little tension in the air between the Hell Razor Honeys and another crew of low-budget bitches called The Hotel Honeys. Green Eyes was fucking a nigga that had a baby by one of the Hotel Honeys and this was the source of the tension between the two crews. However, most broads tried to avoid the Hell Razor Honeys in the darkness of go-go spots, due to the fact that it was almost impossible to defend themselves from razor attacks in the dark.

Dressed in a black Versace sweatsuit and black Air Jordans, Vida was grinding against the dude behind her; they moved to the rhythm of the loud and thumping go-go music that had them both sweating like they were in the bed fucking. The dude was feeling all over Vida as they danced. He was also hard, and Vida liked the size of what she felt.

The dude leaned forward and shouted into her ear, "You leavin' wit' me?"

Vida looked over her shoulder and shouted, "Yeah, we can do that."

"Cool."

In the middle of the crowd, with Hell Razor Honeys all around, Vida and the dude Daddieo kept doing their thing.

Outside the Black Hole, sitting in his BMW, Ellis was getting head behind the tinted windows—bomb head, too. The broad was going hard, making all kinds of slurping sounds as she did her deep-throat routine. She was a man eater, working her magic until Ellis came all inside her mouth.

"Aaahh… damn, girl." Ellis rubbed the back of her head as she sucked the last out of him. "Swallow it."

"You like that?" Green Eyes asked.

Back inside the Black Hole things were heating up. One of the Come Back Honeys was face-to-face, arguing with a broad that had accused her of fucking her man. Tia walked up; her jaw was fine now and she was still looking good. She grabbed the Come Back Honey by her arm and shouted over the go-go music, "Stop arguin' wit' that bitch; it ain't shit to talk about." Tia already had her box cutter cuffed in her hand. She gave the opposing broad a vicious glare and added, "You got a problem?" The broad just walked away. Tia looked at the Come Back Honey and said, "That's all it is to it. Fuck all that rappin', either she want some work or not. Cut them bitches up if they get outta line. Simple as that."

"I feel you." No Draws nodded. No Draws was one of Samara's new recruits. She was a cute red-bone, just like Tia. At seventeen, she was phat to death like she was twenty-five. No Draws had earned a name for herself for obvious reasons. Even now, under her Gucci jean skirt, she had on no drawers. All the dudes that were trying to get between her legs knew how she got down.

"Let's go party," Tia said.

Tia seemed to take a liking to No Draws, not to mention the fact that No Draws was one of the girls that came to Tia's aid with Samara when Shay broke her jaw. Rare Essence changed the grove of the go-go and started calling out the names of crews that were in the spot tonight. Rittenhouse Street, Kennedy Street, East Gate, 18th and D, Montana Avenue and First Street were just a few. Tia heard the loud chant from the Hell Razor Honeys. About twenty teenage girls were waving their hands in the air and screaming "Awww Hell Razor, awww Hell Razor."

Tia and No Draws made their way to the front where the rest of their crew was. As they made their way through the thick crowd, a dude grabbed No Draws' ass. It was bad timing on his part; No Draws was still thinking about the talk she'd just had with Tia. With no talking, No Draws pulled her straight razor out the inside of her cheek and went across the nigga's face in one swift motion, cutting him to the white meat. Blood went everywhere. Out of shock the dude didn't even swing on No Draws, he just grabbed his face and yelled out in pain.

Tia wasted no time; she attacked like a pit bull, slicing at any part of his body she could get to. No Draws did the same. A huge rift in the crowd opened quickly. The music stopped. Security rushed the floor. The rest of the Hell Razor Honeys noticed what was going down and swarmed like killer bees. People began to rush the door in the midst of the madness. A security guard tried to grab Vida, but like a female lion defending her cubs, she spent around and sliced his face wide open in one quick slash. He grabbed his bloody face and tried to rush her, but found two more girls attacking him from the back. As the chaos ensued, two gunshots went off. No one knew where they'd come from. Everybody began to make a run for it.

Ten minutes later, inside Tia's white 1991 Ford Escort, she, Ice, No Draws and Samara were flying through the D.C. streets, headed back around Montana Avenue. Tia pulled onto a side street just off of New York Avenue and pulled into a dark alley. Putting the car in park, she looked back at Ice and said, "Give me that joint." Ice gave her the .380 she'd snuck into the Black Hole. Tia quickly wiped the prints off the burner as she got out the car and then threw it in a big green dumpster. She jumped back in the car and pulled off.

Ice sat in the back seat and thought back to the very moment she saw the flash of gunfire in the darkness of the club. As the dude that grabbed No Draws' ass was fighting off three Hell Razor Honeys, Ice aimed the .380 at his back and fired twice. She watched him hit the floor and wondered if he was dead. For a second, the thought of killing somebody scared the shit out of her. She snapped out of her daze when she felt No Draws grab her arm and pull her toward the door with everyone else that was rushing out of the club.

"I wonder if you killed that nigga," Samara said. She was sitting next to Ice.

Before Ice could say a word, Tia spoke up, "Ain't no sense in talkin' 'bout that shit. It's done." She didn't want it to even be a conversation. "We don't know shit. Y'all hear me? If anybody ask about that shit we don't know a muthafuckin' thing. Feel me?" Everybody agreed.

When they pulled up around Montana Avenue, Vida's white 1992 Ford Taurus was already parked in its normal spot. The girls went inside the building and headed up to the apartment that was in Ice's name. Vida, Green Eyes and two other girls were already inside, smoking weed and watching *Juice* on video. Tia called Vida into the bedroom along with Ice. They put Vida on point about who'd done the shooting. Even though Green Eyes was the oldest and had the most street smarts, Vida was the unofficial queen bee; she was a leader the girls loved and trusted.

"As dark as it was in there don't nobody know who did the shootin'," Vida said, looking at the huge poster of Tupac on Ice's bedroom wall. "Ain't shit to worry about right now, we just gotta chill out for a while."

The next day, just after noon, Tia heard a knock at the door that woke her up. She'd been asleep on the sofa, knocked out cold. Ice was in the bedroom, Green Eyes was in Tia's bedroom, and Vida was downstairs in the apartment that she still shared with her grandmother. Tia got up and answered the door. It was Kareem, dressed in all black, carrying a Washington Post and a bag of McDonald's.

"Y'all gangsta-ass bitches done made the paper." Kareem walked past Tia and sat down on the sofa. "You hungry?" he asked.

"Nah." Tia sat beside him. "Let me see the paper."
He handed her the paper. "Look at the Metro."

Tia did just that and it read:

Female violence is on the rise. Among known female gangs, the Hell Razor Honeys, the NWA Honeys, the Knock out Honeys and the 100 Honeys rank among the most violent. The Hell Razor Honeys are said to be behind the shooting of a young man in a Northwest night club last night. Four other men were also attacked, one being a security guard, by teenage girls slashing them with straight razors and box cutters. D.C. Police say the female gangs are becoming a major problem in a city that already has a dark reputation for murder and drugs...

"Our name kickin' like shit," Tia said, somewhat proud and somewhat afraid of the heat.

"I'm hip," Kareem said as he stuffed his face. "Y'all better chill out."

"Me Against the World" began to blast from Ice's bedroom.

"Looks like your sex kitten just woke up," Tia joked.

"Go 'head wit' that bullshit." Kareem laughed, almost chocking on his food. "We just sparrin' partners. We get each other ready for the ring."

"Yeah right." Tia laughed as she stood up and stretched. All she had on was a long white T-shirt and a black thong.

"I'm tryin' to get wit' your cousin, that's who I'm tryin' to get wit' for real."

"I told you what to do but you keep bein' cheap," Tia said. "It ain't trickin' when you look at it from my point of view. She got somethin' you want and you got somethin' she want, fair exchange ain't no robbery, no matter how you look at it."

Kareem laughed. "Ain't you somethin'?"

Tia went to the bathroom to get herself together. Moments later, Green Eyes came strolling into the living room in matching panties and bra, looking phat to death. Excluding her green eyes, she could pass for an eighteen year old version of Salt, from the female rap group Salt-N-Pepa.

Hell Razor *Honeys*

Green Eyes saw Kareem sitting on the sofa looking at her perfect body like he wanted to rip her panties off and fuck her right on the hardwood floor. She put her hands on her wide hips and said, "You like what you see? You look like you havin' a wet dream. What's up Reem?"

"When you gon' stop fakin' on that pussy and let a nigga test that box?" Kareem was staring at the fat knot bulging out of her panties like a small fist.

"I ain't fakin'. I'm tryin' to get my own apartment and shit, so I'm tryin' to save up a little cash. You ain't tryin' to pay to play. I told you, $250 gon' get you all the pussy you can handle."

Kareem really didn't mind giving up the $250, but his money had been fucked up for the last month or so. The police had run up in Tec's apartment and arrested him; they found five ounces of coke and $8,500. Half of the $8,500 belonged to Kareem. Tec was sent to Oak Hill—a juvenile detention center. Since Tec's arrest, Kareem had been fumbling, only making enough money to get by.

"Check this out, why don't you give me a taste of that thing first, then we can talk money." Kareem rubbed his chin.

Green Eyes smiled and rolled her eyes. "You runnin' thangs now, but watch this…" She got on the floor and put both of her legs behind her head with no problem. "I can take it like this, anywhere you wanna put it."

"You got a deal!" Kareem said.

A short while later, Tia was downstairs in Vida's bedroom watching Samara do Vida's hair. "Where you goin'?" Tia asked, sitting on the bed with the newspaper in her hand.

"This dude 'bout to come pick me up." Vida told Tia about meeting the dude Daddieo last night. He had called and still wanted to get with her. "Why you walkin' around wit' a newspaper?"

Tia showed Vida and Samara the article about female gangs. They all agreed that they needed to chill out for a while. After all, Vida and Tia just had their assault charges dropped for what they did to Samara months ago.

EYONE WILLIAMS

"We just need to lay back, we gon' be okay," Vida said.

Kareem and Green Eyes left and went to Kareem's apartment to do their thing. Ice was in the apartment alone. She'd just gotten out the shower and was in the bedroom getting dressed. She was not totally on her own. Her mother told her that she could always call upon her, but Ice took pride in being able to take care of her self. The phone rang and she answered it. It was Tec calling from Oak Hill.

"Ice, where Reem at?" Tec sounded frustrated.

"He ain't here right now." Ice knew something was wrong with Tec by the sound of his voice. "What's wrong, you need me to tell him somethin' for you?"

"Yeah, tell slim I said why the fuck he keep tellin' me he gon' send me some money and don't do that shit? Tell 'em I thought we was better than that." It was clear that Tec was pissed off.

"I'll tell 'em when he come back through here. I told 'em what you said last time. He keep sayin' he gon' do it. How much you need? I'll send you some today."

Tec respected the offer and made a mental note of it. "A hundred dollars will hold me. I don't need a lot, just enough to get a few things I need until I go back to court."

"I got you, don't even trip." Ice pulled her tight Polo jeans up and looked at her ass in the long mirror on the door. She was proud to have a phat ass like a black girl. "Did you get the pictures of me and the girls?"

"Yeah, I got them." Tec laughed. In one of the pictures Ice was bent over with her skirt pulled up showing her ass. The white panties she had on had "Thug Life" written across her ass cheeks in big black letters. "You love you some 'Pac, don't you?"

"That's my nigga. I just wrote him a letter and sent him some pictures, the same ones I sent you." Ice got Tupac's prison address out of the VIBE Magazine. She was high when she wrote him and sent him the sexy pictures of her and the Hell Razor Honeys; she didn't even expect to hear back from 'Pac.

Laughing, Tec said, "You wrote 'Pac, huh?"

"Yeah."

Ice and Tec spoke for a few more minutes and then got off the phone. Ice finished getting dressed and began bagging up the weed she and the girls had left.

Later on, both Vida and Tia were hopping into BMWs. Vida was rolling out with Daddieo while Tia was rolling out with Ellis. Green Eyes was walking down the street as the BMWs rolled by. Her heart was full of jealousy and envy. She felt like she was supposed to have dudes picking her up in fly cars and spending money on her like she once had it. She once was a broad that niggaz were chasing morning, noon and night. Now she was a witness in a drug case against a dude she use to transport coke for. She was laying low, hanging with the Hell Razor Honeys over Northeast because no one could connect her to the area.

She knew Tia loved her and looked up to her, so she could always count on her little cousin to be down for her. Tia had no idea that Green Eyes was a snake. Green Eyes had been fucking and sucking Ellis for over a month. The first time she got him to fuck her he was drunk, but after that he just couldn't get enough of the freak in her. Once she got her mouth on him he had to go back for more. She now had dirt on him.

By evening time, Vida found herself digging Daddieo. He was twenty years old, tall and slim. He had light brown skin and curly hair that he wore in a temple taper. He had a Will Smith look to him. Daddieo took Vida out to eat at a top-notch Italian spot in Fairfax, Virginia and to the movies. Over dinner they talked about all kinds of things from past relationships to music. They even talked about a little black history after Vida found a Howard University newspaper in his car and saw an article that Daddieo had written about Harriet

Tubman.

As it turned out, Daddieo had a thing for black history and often wrote articles for the school paper about strong black people of the past. Daddieo was surprised and impressed to learn that Vida was in the know about Harriet Tubman and was interested in his article. She was also impressed by his writing skills. Vida told him that in the 4th grade she won a black history contest for a report she'd written on Harriet Tubman—her report was published in The Washington Post.

Daddieo was intrigued; he'd taken Vida for a regular hoodrat, but was quickly learning that it was more to her. Vida was surprised to learn that Daddieo didn't sell drugs; he was a student at Howard. He was from New York—Harlem. His family had a little money and sent him to school to study communications. As far as Daddieo knew, Vida was eighteen.

Cruising along the beltway in his BMW, taking Vida home, the conversation was smooth as Daddieo continued to flirt with Vida. A heavy rain was pounding on the car as D'Angelo's *Brown Sugar* CD played at a low volume. Vida was still amazed that Daddieo didn't know she was a part of the violence in the Black Hole last night. She was also amazed that he wasn't trying to take her to the hotel.

"Did you have a good time?" Daddieo flashed a smooth smile.

Vida jive blushed. "Yeah, you cool peoples." *I'd give this nigga the pussy if he would just ask,* she thought.

"I can't believe you don't have a man."

"Believe it, most dudes I run into just want the pussy and that's it. I don't even open up to niggaz no more."

"Is that why you don't like talkin' 'bout your personal life?" Daddieo cut his eyes at her.

"Kinda, but on the real, it's not too much goin' on wit' me. I sell a little weed and party, that's all." After the words left her mouth she realized how shallow her statement sounded, but didn't try to clean it up.

"Well, from talkin' to you I can tell that there's more to you than that. You got a good head on your shoulders. Not too many young ladies know about their history."

Vida wasn't dumb at all; she was just caught up in a lifestyle. In school she'd always made A's. She even had dreams of going to college.

Thirty minutes later they pulled up in front of Vida's building. She leaned over and kissed Daddieo on the cheek. "Make sure you call me."

"You know I'ma do that," Daddieo said.

On Friday, Ice was picking up the mail. There was a letter from Tec and another big brown envelope. When she flipped it over to see who it was from she screamed and almost jumped out of her skin with excitement. The envelope was from Tupac Skakur. Ice couldn't wait; she tore the envelope open right in the hallway. Inside was a letter and a paperback book by someone she'd never heard of; Niccolo Machiavelli. The book was called "The Prince."

Ice read 'Pac's letter right in the hallway; she was shocked that he wrote her back. In the letter he thanked her for the letter she'd sent him as well as the pictures. He told her that his fans meant the world to him. He also told her that he would be out soon and that he was signing with Death Row Records, where he was going to make history. The book "The Prince" was what he'd been studying; inside of it was a signed picture of him just for Ice. She kissed the picture of 'Pac in his prison clothes. On the back of the picture were the words, "All Eyes On Me." Ice ran upstairs to share the news with her crew.

Chapter 6

few days later there was pure madness going on inside the apartment. Small sums of money had been coming up missing over the last couple of weeks. At first the girls blamed it on the in-and-out traffic that came through the apartment. However, for some reason, Ice felt that Green Eyes was the one doing the stealing. This morning she stepped to her about it. They were standing in the middle of the living room, face-to-face, arguing loudly, on the edge of fighting.

All the yelling and screaming woke Tia up. She had been out all night with Ellis and was dead tired. Looking at the alarm clock on her nightstand she became angered when she saw that it was 8:14 A.M. Pissed off, she stormed into the living room in her bra and panties. "What the fuck is goin' on?" Tia yelled. Her face was already turning red.

"This white bitch gon' step to me 'bout some bullshit! You better get her before I beat her ass," Green Eyes said.

"You ain't doing shit to me!" Ice gave Green Eyes a hard shove.

Tia stepped between them before they could lock ass. She couldn't believe Green Eyes was stealing, but she knew for a fact that Ice wasn't the type to start shit. Tia looked at Ice and said, "Why you say Green Eyes stealin'?"

"Check her purse, Tia. I'm missin' $195. It was in my jacket. I saw her fuckin' wit' my shit last night, but ain't think nothin' of it until I got up this mornin'."

"You check my purse, bitch!" Green Eyes barked at Ice.

"Check her purse for what?" Tia asked, wanting to put out the fire between the two.

"I had a hundred dollar bill in my jacket wit' a phone number on it in red ink. I know she got it," Ice said, looking Green Eyes dead in the eyes.

"Let me see your purse." Tia looked at Green Eyes, who was

burning with anger.

You gon' believe this white bitch over me?" Green Eyes was fucked that Tia asked to see her purse. "Fuck that, ain't nobody checkin' my purse."

"Watch me." Tia headed for the bedroom to get the purse. She felt that her cousin was hiding something.

Green Eyes tried to stop Tia by grabbing her arm. Tia had a very short fuse. She snatched away from Green Eyes and they got into a shoving match. Tia then stole Green Eyes in the mouth. They got into an all-out fist fight. Tia quickly took control and began beating the shit out of her older cousin. She beat her all over the bedroom, tearing up everything. Ice stayed out of it and let Tia handle business.

"Okay, you got it, you win! You got it!" Green Eyes was on the floor balled up, trying to protect herself from Tia's violent wrath.

Fired up, breathing hard and standing over her cousin with her fist balled up, Tia looked at Ice and said, "Check the purse."

Ice checked the purse and found the hundred dollar bill with the phone number on it in red ink.

Tia kicked Green Eyes in the stomach. "Get out, petty ass bitch!"

"Please—"

"Fuck that!" Tia grabbed Green Eyes by her hair and dragged her through the apartment and threw her out into the hallway in nothing but a long T-shirt covering her bra and panties. There would be no stealing where Tia laid her head, cousin or not.

Ice had a shocked look on her face; she didn't expect Tia to go so hard on her own cousin.

"Why you lookin' at me like that?" Tia asked.

"You jive went hard on her," Ice said.

"We family, all of us, family don't steal from family. If we can't trust each other, who can we trust? If somebody cross one of us, they cross all of us and they gotta pay. If she wasn't my cousin I woulda put that razor on her ass." Tia walked pass Ice, going back to bed. "Wake me up whenever you leave out."

"I got you," Ice said.

Vida was awakened by her grandmother, who got on her about not going to school. Vida had lost interest in school. Wiping the cold out of her eyes, Vida said, "I'm goin' grandma."

"Okay, now I'm going to work, I'll see you later on. Don't go back to sleep." Ms. Green left the apartment and went to work.

Vida had all intentions of getting up. However, she closed her eyes and dozed back off to sleep. Three hours later, she was awakened again, by the phone. "Hello," she answered sounding irritated.

"Vee, what's up?" Tec said.

"What time is it?" Vida was still sleep for real.

"Almost noon."

"Damn, I was supposed to go to school," Vida said as she sat up in the bed. "What's up wit' you though?"

"I'm trying to catch that nigga Reem. That nigga keep tellin' me he gon' do shit and don't do it." Tec was getting fed up with his man. "He was supposed to send me some tree, but the nigga ain't come through."

"Why you ain't just holla at me, you know I keep that now. Reem can't sit still. Plus, he ain't doin' too good since you been gone. You know how niggaz play anyway—out of sight, out of mind. Whatever you need just let me know, I got a few dollars," Vida said.

"I fucks wit' you, Vee, you my nigga, for real."

"Nigga, ain't shit changed wit' us." Vida looked at the clock and said, "I gotta go. Call me later on. I'll get that to you."

A few nights, later Ice was leaving the hotel with a dude she was dealing with when a BMW 740i pulled into the parking lot. "Dirty ass bitch," she said under her breath when she saw Ellis and Green Eyes together.

"What you say?" J-Rock asked.

"Nothin'," Ice replied.

An hour later Ice was telling Tia about what she'd seen. Sitting on the bed in Ice's room, Tia was on fire inside. She was hurt, at the same time she was mad at herself for catching feelings for a nigga. She was fucked up at Green Eyes and would deal with her as well, but first she wanted to deal with the bitch-nigga Ellis.

"I can't believe he tried to play me and fuck my cousin, like I wasn't gon' find out," Tia said. Her whole face was red; she didn't understand. She had opened up to this nigga and he said fuck her. "It's okay. I can play games too." Tia looked like she wanted to cry, but she didn't. She wouldn't dare cry over a nigga.

"What's wrong?" Vida asked as she walked into the bedroom, sensing something was up.

"That bitch-ass nigga Ellis fuckin' my slut-ass cousin," Tia said. She told Vida what Ice had seen. "He fuckin' wit' the right bitch though. I got somethin' for both of they asses."

"What you tryin' to do?" Vida asked. She sat beside Tia and rubbed her back, seeing that Tia was hurt.

"Let's rob that nigga," Tia said.

Vida and Ice looked at each other like Tia was lunchin'. Vida laughed a little bit and said, "You don't mean that, you just mad. You not gon' feel like that in the mornin'."

"I'm dead serious. Niggaz can't be trusted. The minute you start diggin' one of 'em, they cross you. I ain't goin' for that. I know where his money at and everything. We can take everything he got."

"You serious? You really wanna rob 'em?" Vida asked.

"Fuck yeah, I'm dead serious."

"What happens when he finds out we did it?" asked Vida.

"He won't do shit about it." Tia was going to show him just how hateful she could be when crossed.

"What make you think he won't do shit?" Ice asked, remembering what Ellis did when Tia got her jaw broken.

"'Cause a dead nigga can't do shit when he six feet deep," Tia said with a straight face.

Vida and Ice just looked at Tia for a moment, saying nothing. They both believed Tia was talking out of hurt and pain; they all knew that she loved him.

"If you really want to get the nigga we don't have to do it ourselves," Vida said. "We can get Reem to get 'em and get a break down. That way, we ain't gotta get our hands dirty."

"Fuck that. We ain't gotta break down wit' nobody. We don't need no nigga to help us. We can do the shit ourselves," Tia said.

"I ain't tryin' to kill nobody," said Vida.

"You was ready to kill somebody when I got my jaw broken."

"That was different."

"Why?"

"Because the nigga broke your jaw; he jumped his ass out there and deserved a good killin'."

"This nigga jumped his ass out there, too. He crossed me, he gotta pay, Vee. We said that whoever crossed us would pay, right?"

"You right," Vida sighed.

Tia kept pushing the idea. Out of loyalty, rather than desire, Vida and Ice agreed to roll with Tia.

"So, y'all sure?" Tia asked.

"Yeah, I'm wit' you," Vida said.

"It's whatever wit' me," said Ice.

The girls plotted the move out for a little while and vowed to keep it between the three of them.

A few days later, Vida was standing in the hallway of her building waiting on Daddieo to come pick her up. She was digging him heavy. They hadn't had sex yet and it was cool with Daddieo, so far. He liked spending time with Vida and saw more in her than she allowed most people to see.

Kareem walked into the building in a blue over-sized Eddie Bauer Bear, with the hood pulled over his head. "What's up, Vee?"

"What's up, Reem?' Vida said flatly. She had nothing against Kareem, they were homies. However, she didn't like the fact that he was not keeping it real with Tec. That fact alone was changing the way she felt about Kareem. Even though she'd just sent Tec $200 and some weed, Vida still said, "You know Tec need some money, right?"

"Yeah, I'm hip. I just sent him some money last week."

"Stop lyin'. Tec just called me this mornin' and told me you been fakin' on him and ain't sent him shit. That's supposed to be your man. That's some fucked up shit, young," Vida snapped and rolled her eyes. Before Kareem could respond Vida heard Daddieo's horn blow. "I gotta go. You need to stop fakin'," Vida said, as she stepped off leaving Kareem with those words to think about.

Inside Daddieo's warm BMW, Vida asked, "Where we goin'?"

Hell Razor Honeys

"It's a surprise," Daddieo said, driving up Rhode Island Avenue. He smirked, thinking about what he had up his sleeve.

"Come on, tell me where we goin'." Vida began pressing Daddieo, but he wouldn't bend.

Daddieo forced the conversation in other directions as he jumped on US-50 East heading toward Annapolis, Maryland. A short while later, they crossed the Choptank River and continued on until they entered Dorchester County. Vida saw a huge sign that read: Home of Harriet Tubman… "The Moses of Her People," Harriet Tubman of the Bucktown District found freedom for herself and some three hundred other slaves whom she led north.

Vida smiled and looked at Daddieo. Dudes had taken her shopping, out to eat, to the hotel and many other places around the D.C. area, but never to the actual hometown of the legendary black woman that put the Underground Railroad on the map—even though there were a well-established system of safe houses and secret passageways that pushed hard across hundreds of miles of America heading north to Canada some time before Tubman made a name for herself.

Sitting in the car on a rural road, gazing out at endless farmland on a clear winter afternoon, Vida said, "This is original." She laughed and rubbed Daddieo's hand.

"I thought it would be a nice getaway. It's a lot of history down here in the country." Daddieo pointed at the green farmland and said, "That's the Brodess Farm right there. It was the plantation that Harriet Tubman was born and raised on. The old estate is gone, but that's where her struggle started back in the 1800's."

Vida gazed out the window, and even though it had been years since she had read about black history, all the stories she'd read about Harriet Tubman came back to her mind. She could feel the history in the air.

Daddieo then took her on a tour of Dorchester County, pointing out historical landmarks of Tubman's life. He drove to the county seat in Cambridge as they took in the beautiful countryside of small farms and an occasional breathtaking view of the Chesapeake Bay. They

EYONE WILLIAMS

drove by the old courthouse where Reverend Samuel Green was given ten years for helping Harriet Tubman escape time and time again. With every landmark, Daddieo educated Vida, making her feel loved and special.

Never having a father; Vida felt like a little girl out on a field trip with a loving dad. They even drove by the still standing Bucktown Village store, where one day a young Harriet Tubman was out buying food for her master's dinner when she saw a runaway slave being chased into the store by an overseer. The overseer told Tubman to help him tie the slave down. Tubman refused and became the subject of the overseer's anger; she was bashed in the head with an iron weight. The blow left her incapacitated for months.

As night fell, Daddieo and Vida got on US-50 West headed back to Drama City (D.C.). Vida couldn't believe they had spent half a day in such a way. "I had a good time today, learned a few things as well. You are so smart," Vida said, leaning back in her seat as Notorious B.I.G.'s "Juicy" came through the speakers.

"I read a lot." Daddieo nodded his head to the beat. "Knowledge is power, Vee. You know that? You should really think about goin' to college. You got a good head on your shoulders."

"I really can't afford it."

"You sellin' weed, where all your money goin'?"

"I got bills, plus I gotta look good." She smiled.

"You gon' look good regardless." He smiled.

A short while later they pulled up in front of Vida's building. It was dark and cold outside around Montana Avenue, but dudes were still outside on the grind. Vida thought about what she'd committed herself to with Tia and had no desire to go inside at the time. Vida leaned over and kissed Daddieo on the cheek. "What you gon' do for the rest of the night?"

Daddieo shrugged. "Go back to the dorm and chill out. I gotta go to New York tomorrow to check on my moms. What's up wit' you for the night?"

"I'm tryin' to spend the night wit' you."

"Cool wit' me."

Twenty minutes later they were in his dorm room sitting on his bed watching *Poetic Justice* on video. Vida wondered how Daddieo could dress so well, drive a BMW and keep cash if he wasn't selling drugs. She didn't want to get all in his business so she never asked. She just took what he was willing to give at the time—his peoples had a little money. However, as the night went on Daddieo began to tell her more about him.

Daddieo was the youngest of four brothers. All of his older brothers were products of the streets of Harlem. One was dead, one was doing twenty-five years in the Feds and the other one was a big boy on the New York drug scene—that's where the "family money" came from.

His brother Tonio, the big boy, was only two years older than him, but had kept Daddieo on the straight path from his early teens on up. Daddieo looked up to Tonio. Tonio's mindset was for Daddieo to break the cycle that all the other males in their family had fell victim to since the 70's. Daddieo's future was set; Tonio had a stash of money put away for Daddieo and all Daddieo had to do was finish college and make plans for the future. Daddieo had vowed to his mother and Tonio that he would make the best of himself.

Rubbing Daddieo's hair, Vida said, "You got a lot goin' for you."

"I'm grateful. My brother makes sure I'm taken care of. Shit, he makes sure everybody is taken care of; he got a lot on his shoulders. Everybody depends on him. Nevertheless, I guess you can call me the great black hope of the family."

Vida kissed his sexy lips. "You the great black hope, huh?" She began rubbing his chest.

"Yeah."

Daddieo put his arms around her and began kissing her passionately as he laid her flat on her back. They kissed and rubbed all over one another. Slowly, they undressed, licking on each other and exploring body parts. Daddieo took a good look at Vida's sexy body. *Damn, she looks even better naked,* he thought. He slowly licked around her nipples while sliding in and out of her tight, wet pussy with his fingers. With his tongue he went down her flat stomach until he was between her legs, licking all the right spots, taking his time to

please her.

Vida began to moan as she climbed the walls, getting wetter with every move he made. He worked his head game in ways that Vida had never endured. She came and began to shake as she wrapped her legs around his head, rubbing her fingers through his curly hair. He knew what he was doing and kept the press on, driving her crazy and higher and higher into sensations of ecstasy.

Vida felt him fill her with slow, satisfying, erotic pleasure and moaned, "Aaaahhh... ssss...." She tightly wrapped her arms and legs around Daddieo, and with every long and wet stroke she tried to pull him deep into her soul. As she answered his rhythm by pushing her midsection up at him, she was telling him with her body that she was willing to give him just as much as he was giving her, and more. Daddieo was slow and precise with his love making. Vida was lost in a utopia of pleasure, making sounds she'd never made before; she had never been with a dude that made love to her.

As she came again, stronger and harder than the first time, she said, "Don't stop, please don't stop, Daddieo... aaahhhhh, don't stop. I'm cummin'."

"You like that, baby?" Daddieo felt her gushing and pulled one of her legs up over his shoulder, hitting her spot from different angles, making her cum again in minutes. The wetter she got, the deeper he got. Minutes later he had both of her legs up in the air, sliding in and out of her soaking wet pussy. "It's so tight, Vee." Dripping with sweat, breathing like an exhausted boxer, he began to pound inside of her.

"Oh yeah, fuck me!" Vida enjoyed the love making, but she got off on being fucked nice and hard. "Fuck me harder!" Her legs were damn near behind her head at this point. She was loving it. "Oh shit." Her eyes rolled back in her head. "Sssssss...."

Daddieo was digging in and out of her at a violent pace, racing to his climax. As he came inside the rubber he continued stroking her, slowing down like landing a 747 airliner. "Uurrgggghhaa...."

Hell Razor *Honeys*

Later on, Vida felt so good laying her head on Daddieo's hard chest. She really felt loved. He rubbed her ass and said nothing for a while; they were both lost in thought. *Damn I love this nigga,* Vida thought. There was only one problem; Vida had been lying to Daddieo, telling him she was older than she really was. *I gotta do something, I can't keep lying to him,* she thought. Serious feelings were growing inside of her heart. She had to address the situation and tell him the truth.

"Daddieo, I need to tell you something," said Vida.

"What's up, baby?"

Vida sat up a little bit; her titties were right in his face. "I'm really feelin' you…" She paused, trying to pick her words carefully.

"What's wrong, Vee?"

"I'm… I'm fifteen," she just spit it out.

"Aww, man, shhh…" Daddieo sighed and shook his head. He didn't need or want the drama or the trouble of having sex with a minor. "Why you just tellin' me some shit like that?" He got out of bed and grabbed his boxers.

He was pissed off, but he kept his cool, although Vida could see his anger and hear it in his voice.

"Don't you know they will lock my ass up for this shit?"

Vida didn't say a word. She was crushed, feeling as though she'd lost him.

"Come on, Vee, you gotta get dressed. I'm takin' you home. We can't do this."

Vida wanted to cry, but refused. "I'm sorry. I didn't mean to lie to you. I… I just didn't want to tell you my real age because I knew you wouldn't mess wit' me." She began to get dressed.

"Vee, you good peoples, I really dig you. But we can't be doin' this. I know other dudes might not care, but I do. I got nieces your age."

Fully dressed and ready to roll, Vida said, "I knew you would feel like that. You woulda found out sooner or later, so I just wanted to put it out there before my feelings grew too strong."

"Come here." Daddieo hugged her, trying to comfort her. He knew she was hurt. "You gotta find a dude your age, Vee."

Savoring the moment in Daddieo's arms, she looked up into his eyes and said, "I don't want a dude my age. I want a man, like you."

"We can't do that, Vee. I'm sorry. We can only be friends, nothin' more. I'm sorry."

Hell Razor Honeys

Chapter 7

"Let's go." Tia led Vida and Ice out the door on their mission. Ellis had called Tia a little while ago and asked her to come help him bag up some weed; he had just copped his re-up. Tia's young heart was hard and vengeful. She vowed that she'd never be crossed again. She was full of bitterness for anyone that made her shit list. It was no second guessing in her heart about what she planned to do tonight. She was going to put a bullet right between Ellis' eyes, with no regrets at all. Fuck him.

In the back seat of the car with a .380 in her hand, staring out the window, Vida was lost in thought. She still didn't feel good about the move. She felt butterflies in her stomach, her palms were sweaty and she was nervous. However, her heart was still hurting from the pain of losing Daddieo. She regretted telling him the truth about her age; now she felt numb inside, almost emotionless. That alone helped her deal with what she was about to do. She didn't care about anything at the time.

Ice checked the chamber of the TEC-9 she was riding with, it was ready to go. She was ready to fire all thirty-plus rounds in the clip. Simple as that.

"Make sure y'all put them gloves on. We gon' go straight to work," Tia said. She was behind the wheel with a .380 in her hand and a black bandanna hanging around her neck. She'd set a few niggaz up for her homies so she felt she knew what to expect. If dudes could do it she could, that was her mindset. She'd stolen the keys to Ellis' apartment so she could let herself and the others in. Once they were inside it was curtains.

"You sure he in the joint by himself?" Vida asked in a calm voice, rubbing the trigger of her pistol.

"Yeah, I'm sure." Tia pulled into the dark parking lot of a Silver Spring, Maryland apartment complex and parked on the far end by the woods. Looking around the car with an evil sneer, she said, "Let's do this."

The girls masked up and ran across the parking lot to the back of the building. Tia let them in and they made their way up the back stairs to the third floor. Dressed in all black and ski masks, they looked like teenage dudes. The third floor hallway was clear. With their guns in hand, they crowded around Ellis' door. Their hearts pounded with apprehension as Tia stuck the key in the door and flung it open. The girls rushed inside, guns raised. Ice slammed the door behind them.

"Oh shit!" Ellis screamed, standing in the middle of the living room. He took off running for the bedroom.

Vida was the first to react, fearing he was going for a gun. Pop! Pop! Pop! Vida fired, lighting up the apartment with gunfire. The other girls followed her lead and began blasting. Hit in the back six times, Ellis tumbled to the floor. Tia ran up and shot him in the back of his head twice. The sight made Vida's stomach turn. It all happened so fast.

Suddenly, out of the bedroom came a dude firing a .45 Automatic. He tried to take Tia's head off, but she jumped out of the way and fell to the floor. The .45 slugs flew by Ice's head and crashed into the front door. In a panic, Vida and Ice unleashed a hail of bullets that cut the dude down. Silence took over the apartment. The only thing the girls could hear was the loud ringing in their ears and the pounding of their hearts. For a few seconds they were frozen with fear. They had come within inches of losing their lives and they knew it.

Thinking quickly, knowing that someone had to hear the gunfire; Vida took control and directed the search of the apartment. In less than two minutes they went to work and grabbed what they came for—five pounds of weed and $15,000.

Swiftly, they made it back to the car carrying the goods in two pillowcases they'd taken from Ellis' bedroom. Just as they were about to get in the car, police cars with flashing lights and blaring sirens came from out of nowhere. Fear attacked the girls.

Vida looked into the darks woods and said, "Fuck the car, lets hit the woods." She ran into the woods followed by the others.

Five minutes later, still running, the girls were deep into the woods and could still hear the police sirens. However, they were far enough away to stop and catch their breath. It was bone-chilling cold outside. Steam came from their noses and mouths as they all bent over sucking in air with their hands on their knees. Out of the blue Ice let out a small but odd laugh. The other girls looked at her from behind their ski masks like she was crazy.

"What the hell is so funny?" Vida asked. Her legs were shaking with nervous jitters that only she was aware of. Her heart was pounding like a speed bag in motion. It would be a bold-face lie to say she wasn't scared to death. After all, they had just murdered two people and the police were surrounding the area. A helicopter could be heard nearby.

"I'm shakin' like shit," Ice said.

A flashback of Ellis' brains blown all over the white carpet came back to Vida's mind. Without warning, she snatched off her ski mask and spit up.

"Damn, you okay, Vee?" Tia stepped away from the warm spit up that had steam coming from it.

Still catching her breath, Vida said, "Yeah, I'm okay. I just never seen no shit like that close up before."

"Me neither," Ice said.

Tia was still shaken up by the fact that she almost got her brains blown out. But she'd seen murder victims with their brains blown out more than once.

"Let's keep movin'," Vida said.

Twenty minutes later, they had gotten rid of their ski masks and murder weapons. Standing on the side of a busy gas station waiting for Samara to come pick them up, the girls tried to look normal. They'd calmed down, but were still very nervous. They had placed the weed and money in Safeway bags so they wouldn't look suspicious with the pillowcases.

"We can't tell Samara about what just went down," Vida declared.

"I'm hip," Tia said.

"As far as she's concerned we went to the hotel wit' some niggaz that was trippin' so we left they ass," Vida said, holding one of the Safeway bags.

"What if she asks what's in the bag, Vee?" Ice asked, knowing how nosy Samara could be.

"She won't ask me about it, so we cool on that," Vida said.

Samara arrived shortly driving a red BMW and picked the girls up. The ride home was smooth. Samara was more concerned with the dudes the girls told her about than anything else.

Inside Tia's bedroom, Vida, Tia and Ice counted up the money. "We got fifteen Gs. That's five Gs apiece," Vida said, sitting on the bed with Tia and Ice. They each took their portion of the money. "This what we gon' do." Vida laid out a plan. They were to do whatever with the money, but the weed was to be sold and the money from that was to be saved and put up for them all. "Y'all cool wit' that?" she asked. Everyone agreed.

"I got one request." Ice was flipping through her money.

"What's up, Ice?" Vida smiled, still feeling the affects of what they'd done—but she blocked it out. It was something she would have to live with.

"Can we have some fun now? Let's go out of town or somethin'," Ice said.

"No bullshit," Tia said. "Let's spend this nigga's money."

"I'm wit' it," Vida said.

Days later, Vida, Tia, Ice, Samara and No Draws were in Tec's station wagon on I-95 smoking weed, laughing and listening to music as they headed for New York to go shopping and hang out a little bit. Vida was keeping Tec's car for him since he no longer wanted Kareem to have it while he was down Oak Hill.

"I'm tryin' to pull one of them big money New York niggaz," No

Draws declared.

Sitting behind the wheel, Samara said, "We goin' to the Big Apple, anything is possible."

Tia whispered into Ice's ear, "We might run into a move up here. If we catch a nigga slippin' we gon' get 'em." Tia smiled and nudged Ice with her elbow.

Ice giggled. "It's whatever," she whispered.

"What you gon' do if you meet a big money New York nigga?" Samara asked No Draws.

No Draws laughed. "It ain't even in the talk, I get down for mines. My name ain't No Draws for nothin'."

All the girls laughed and continued joking all the way up the interstate. Vida was laughing and trying to have a little fun, but she kept thinking about Daddieo. She couldn't get him off her mind. The double murder was still bothering her as well. However, she told herself that she was going to do her best to clear her mind while in New York.

In their Manhattan hotel room, the girls sat around talking about what they wanted to do. They all had fake IDs that would get them into any club in the city. Samara had met a dude from Fort Greene, Brooklyn on her last trip to New York that had showed her around, so she was to get the girls to all the spots they wanted to hit.

Vida stood at the window looking down at the city lights from twenty-four floors up. The sight was one of a kind. She turned around and said, "What's up for the night?"

Changing into her sexy gear, Samara said, "I'm 'bout to make a few calls and see what's up here right now."

No Draws went to the bathroom and returned in a white bodysuit that showed everything—EVERYTHING! She could pass for a high-class hooker. "I'm ready to hit the town," she stated.

"I see." Tia looked her up and down. *The bitch looks good,* she thought. "Lookin' like that you gon' get a lot of attention." Tia laughed.

"You ain't hip? I'ma do my thang," No Draws said.

In the bathroom, Ice loaded her .25 Automatic and slid it in her Prada bag just as Tia walked in. "You strapped?" Ice asked Tia.

"No question." Tia looked at herself in the mirror. She was looking good.

Later on, the girls found themselves in Club West surrounded by a few ball players, rappers and New York ballas. Samara's Fort Greene friend had directed them to the club. It was dark and packed inside. The drinks were flowing. The DJ had the dance floor grooving. Vida wasn't a drinker, but Samara had her sipping a little Remy that had her real laid back and easy going when dudes tried to holla at her. Ice and Tia had worked their way into VIP with No Draws; they had the attention of dudes in the music industry. A video director saw how No Draws moved her sexy body on the dance floor and sent for her. Just the two of them sat in a private booth with curtains around it.

"So, you from Chocolate City, huh?" Nigel asked. He was sipping Cristal in Versace gear with gold and diamonds around his neck, on his wrist and pinkie. He was a smooth brown-skinned dude that reminded No Draws of Puff Daddy. In fact, when Nigel first sent for her she'd actually thought he was Puffy. "I like it down there. D.C. is a town that knows how to party."

"Yeah, that's my hometown. I love it." No Draws was sipping her drink and feeling real loose.

"I'm always at Howard's homecoming." Nigel slid around the booth and put an arm around No Draws. They got to know one another a little bit better. Nigel had directed videos for Biggie, Snoop Dogg and Kool G. Rap, just to name a few. He was thirty-two and had connects throughout the industry—he made that fact known. He was about to direct an L.L. Cool J video and wanted to know if No Draws was interested.

"Yeah, but I never did anything like that before," she said, as he rubbed her cheek with the back of his hand in a way that sent chills through her body and made her wet between the legs.

"You were doing just fine on the dance floor."

"If you say so," she blushed, playing the shy girl role.

"I'm not playing, Michelle. I'm dead serious." Nigel handed her his card. "Don't lose that. Stay in touch with me if you want to try out some new things."

"I won't lose it." No Draws tucked the card inside her Prada bag. "So what's up wit' you?!" No Draws had no cut cards. She undid his pants and pulled out his erection. She licked it one long time, leaving a long wet trail. "Let me show you what I do best." She put it on him in high fashion. He was cumming in minutes.

Downstairs, Tia walked up behind Vida, who was taking pictures with a dude that played for the New York Jets. "Vee, me and Ice 'bout to slide, we gon' meet y'all back at the hotel."

"What y'all up to?" Vida saw a devious look in Tia's eyes and knew she was up to no good.

Tia smiled. "We got some rap nigga name Cees or Zees, some shit like that... he said he never been wit' two girls at once and never been wit' a white girl at all," Tia winked at Vida. "so we gon' make his dreams come true."

Vida smiled and shook her head. Her two comrades were growing more vicious by the minute. "Y'all better be careful up here bullshittin'."

"We cool, Vee." Tia looked around the crowded club and saw Ice, who was with the rap nigga; they were waving for Tia to come on. "I'm gone. Catch you at the hotel." Tia stepped off.

Moments later, a tall, slim, brown-skinned dude walked up to Vida as she sat alone at a table in the back waiting on Samara to come out of the bathroom. "Can I sit wit' you, ma?" the handsome dude asked. He was dressed in top-of-the-line casual Hugo Boss gear and had a drink in his hand.

"Yeah, but my girlfriend will be back in a minute." Vida was feeling the stranger; he had a serious pretty-boy look going on.

"My name is Tonio, what's yours?" He took a seat.

"Vickie."

"I been checkin' you out. Why you ain't dancin' or nothin'? What's the deal, ma? You ain't havin' a good time?"

"Nah, it's not that." Vida saw Samara coming through the crowd. She introduced Samara to Tonio and the three of them had a few drinks.

"I feel like an odd ball so I'ma let y'all two get to know one another," Samara said, about to leave.

"You don't have to leave. My brother is supposed to meet me here in a few. We can all hang out," Tonio said.

Vida was staring at him. She felt like she had seen him before. While she was thinking, the DJ stopped the music and got on the mic saying, "We got my man Daddieo in the house, yo! Show my man some love." When Vida heard Daddieo's name everything came together. It all made sense. Out of all the Tonios in New York City, she had to attract Daddieo's brother.

"What's wrong, Vickie?" Tonio saw the look on Vida's face.

"Nothin'… I gotta go." Vida grabbed Samara's arm and pulled her through the crowd. Tonio didn't understand what was up. Halfway through the crowd Vida ran into Daddieo. They locked eyes.

"Vee, what you doin' in here?" Daddieo felt a sense of overprotective love. He didn't like the fact that Vida was all the way up New York in a night club at fifteen years old.

Vida wasn't in the mood to be questioned by a nigga that wasn't trying to be with her. "You not my man or my father!" She tried to rush pass him.

"Hold up!" Daddieo grabbed her arm. Samara, Tonio and a few others looked on.

"Get off me!" Vida snatched away.

"Calm down! Let me holla at you!" With a little smooth talking, Daddieo got Vida up to the VIP section where they got their own booth and pulled the curtains closed, leaving Samara with Tonio.

Rolling her eyes Vida said, "Who do you think you are? You said we can't be together and now you want me to explain myself to you. I don't think so." She was heated and really wanted to blow on him. However, she still had strong feelings for him and couldn't see herself carrying him like a sucka.

"You right. You don't have to explain nothin' to me, but that don't mean I'm not supposed to care about you."

Vida stood up. "If you care about me you should realize that I'm a woman. Niggaz always say age ain't nothin' but a number; I ain't no little girl." She stepped off on that note.

Hell Razor Honeys

Tia and Ice were in a plush suite on the thirty-seventh floor of the Le Parker Meridien Hotel in Manhattan. They were with a baby-faced rapper that was acting like he was a superstar—but they had never heard of him before.

After a little drinking the rapper seemed to be out of it. In a slur, he said, "Let's do the damn thing." He flopped back on the huge bed, undoing his pants.

"That's what I'm talkin' 'bout, playboy." Tia pulled her .380 and Ice pulled her .25 at the same time.

"What the fuck is goin' on?" the rapper slurred.

"You know what it is, daddy." Ice smiled. "Run your shit, chump."

"Don't move too fast either, or I'ma pop your good rappin' ass. Now throw that jewelry over here nice and slow." Tia didn't smile at all, she was dead serious, and the look in her eyes made it clear that she wasn't playing games.

Their victim got right with the program and began tossing over the jewelry. "Who put y'all up to this? It was them Red Hook niggaz, wasn't it?"

"You askin' too many questions," Tia said and then handed Ice her pistol. "If he try anything bus his ass." Tia snatched off the dudes Timberlands and yanked out the strings. "Strip!" she barked.

"What?!" the dude asked in disbelief.

Ice laughed.

"You heard me, nigga! Take off your clothes and don't make me say it again!" Tia demanded. The dude did as he was told. In his pocket, Tia found $1,900. "Roll over on your stomach."

"Fuck that. I ain't—"

In a flash Ice smacked him in the face with the .380, cutting his forehead. Blood began to ooze. "She wasn't askin', she was tellin' you. Now roll your bitch-ass over before I let loose in this muthafucka!" Order had been established.

Tia tied the dude up nice and tight with the strings from his boots. She kissed him on the cheek and said, "At least we ain't kill you."

Tia and Ice got away with the cash, a $10,000 gold chain, a $30,000 diamond ring and a $120,000 diamond encrusted Rolex. They had no idea how much the jewelry was worth, but they knew for sure they had come off with a nice lick.

EYONE WILLIAMS

Early the next morning, Vida was on the phone with Daddieo. Samara and Tonio had left the club together last night while Daddieo and Vida were in VIP together. Daddieo got the hotel number from Tonio and surprised Vida with a phone call. Vida was pleased to hear from him. She couldn't fake about it either; she had a huge smile on her face.

"Vee, I'm feelin' you, I can't front. I didn't like seeing you in the club last night. I didn't like how you stepped off either. I don't want to see you wit' nobody else, Vee." Daddieo was still in bed at his mother's house.

"So what does that mean?" Vida was smiling, lying in bed with Tia sleeping beside her. No Draws and Ice were in the other bed.

"That means I got the pussy on lock."

Vida laughed. "Is that right? You must plan on puttin' in work."

"You know what I do. I take care of business."

Vida and Daddieo stayed on the phone for more than an hour.

Tia woke up after hearing Vida laughing. "What got you laughin' like that?" she asked Vida.

Vida had just hung up the phone. She told Tia what was up with herself and Daddieo. Tia was happy for her.

"Either you got some good pussy or you steppin' your game all the way up," Tia said. Both girls laughed and gave each other five.

"I think it's a little bit of both," Vida said. "You know how it go, I need what he got in my life." She laughed. "So what you and Ice get into last night?"

Tia let out a loud laugh as she thought about the robbery. She put Vida down with how it played out. They both laughed so hard their stomachs started hurting. "You shoulda seen the look on that nigga's face when Ice smacked him wit' the pistol. We coulda fucked him in the ass if we wanted to, Vee. No bullshit. The nigga was sweet."

"Y'all crazy as shit. Y'all come up here and rob a rap nigga. Let me see what y'all took from the nigga." Vida stretched.

Tia showed her the jewelry and asked, "How much you think this shit is worth?"

Vida checked out the expensive jewelry and had no idea what it was worth, although she knew it was worth a pretty penny. "I don't know how much this stuff cost, but I tell you what, I'll go to some different jewelry stores and check out the prices of shit like this. That should give us an idea. Daddieo gon' pick me up around noon. I can do it then."

"Cool."

No Draws woke up and went to the bathroom in her bra and panties. She returned and said, "Where y'all get that jewelry from?"

"We came off wit' that lil' nigga that was talkin' 'bout he rap and shit," Tia said. "What happened wit' you and that director joker?"

No Draws smiled. "I put it on 'em. He want to put me in an L.L. Cool J video."

"Oh yeah?" Vida asked, impressed with No Draws' catch. "Y'all bitches up here makin' moves, huh?"

"Nobody move!" Ice woke up joking, holding two pistols, pointing them at the girls.

"Stop playin' wit' them joints," Vida said, laughing.

They all sat around laughing and joking for the rest of the morning. The Hell Razor Honeys were on the come up.

Chapter 8

The girls got $50,000 for the jewelry Tonio took off their hands. Tia and Ice split the money with the others, and they all went crazy in New York City shopping spots, dropping thousands of dollars on Fendi, Gucci, Armani, Prada, Versace and jewelry. They returned to D.C. in style, on a new level, putting other crews to shame.

The girls had one problem; they spent money like it grew on trees. By mid-January, 1996, they had run through all their money and were down to a few hundred dollars each. They didn't have a weed connect anymore and were trying to correct that. Nevertheless, they still looked like a million bucks.

Vida and Daddieo were past the age issue; they were fucking with each other tough. Daddieo didn't understand what was up with Vida and Tec—she went to see Tec on the regular. However, Tia and Ice went to visit as well, so Daddieo accepted the homie thing Vida was pushing when it came to Tec.

No Draws got $1,500 and a free weekend in Miami for gracing the L.L. video with her beauty and phat ass. Two weeks later, she was getting calls to be in other videos. The calls were due to the fact that there were a few industry dudes that knew what her name really meant.

Whatever Samara did to Tonio in the bed after they left the club, it worked. He had sent for her more than once since that night. Every time he sent for her he paid for her trip. He would spend big money on her and she would return the favor in the bedroom.

Hell Razor Honeys

Tia and Ice were on the move, coming out of Wheaton Plaza with Hecht's bags full of Ralph Lauren gear. It was a cold winter evening so they rushed to Tia's Escort and threw their bags in the trunk. Inside the car, Ice pulled her Ruger 10mm and checked the chamber. It was loaded. "Where them bitches at?" she asked Tia, who had already grabbed her .380 and got back out the car, looking for the two girls that had caught their attention. It was the same two girls that were strong-arming Ice the day Vida and Tia came to her aid in the school hallway. Ice was a different person now.

"Remember me?" Ice smacked one of the girls with her heavy 10mm. The girl cried out in pain and fell to the ground, begging Ice not to shoot her. "Shut up, bitch!" Ice snatched the shopping bags the girl was carrying. Tia took the shopping bags the other girl was carrying. "Take off them coats and that jewelry," Ice demanded.

"Hurry up, bitch!" Tia pistol whipped the girl she had at gunpoint.

A few bystanders saw what was going down and began to rush in the other direction. They were sure to go to the police. The girls had to hurry. They robbed the girls of their $500 coats, their shopping bags, $600 in cash, jewelry and their Gucci bags.

Tia and Ice jumped in the car and got ghost. Twenty minutes later they pulled up in the parking lot of a Northeast McDonald's.

"Which one of these watches you like the best?" Ice asked Tia, holding two gold Gucci watches in her hand.

"I like the one wit' the black band," Tia said, going through the Gucci bag she had taken.

"I'ma give Vida this one then, she loves these Gucci watches."

"Yeah, she gon' dig that joint." Tia smiled, looking in the mirror as she tried on the diamond earrings she'd taken. "I like these joints."

A metallic-silver 1995 BMW 850CSI pulled up and parked beside the girls. The dark tined window on the driver side came down. Biggie's "Me & My Bitch" was playing. Ice looked at the cute dude that was telling her to roll her window down. She did and got a good look at the attractive dude that reminded her of Method Man.

"What's up?" Ice smiled.

"Ain't too much, what's up wit' y'all? I see y'all lookin' good," the dude said.

"We 'bout to get somethin' to eat, but we ain't never said no to a good time, feel me?"

"What's up wit' your girl?" the light-skinned dude in the passenger seat of the BMW sat up, smoking a blunt.

"I got a mouth," Tia said with sexy sass. "You can ask me what's up wit' me."

"That's right. So what's up wit' you?" the light-skinned dude shot back with a smile, as he passed the blunt to his man.

The girls felt the dudes out with a little small talk. The dude pushing the 850 was Chris and his man was Zach. Numbers were exchanged and then they all went inside the McDonald's.

On the highway coming back from seeing Tec, Vida and Tia discussed the move he needed them to pull off for him. Tec had been committed for two years on the drug case, and he had no plans on staying down Oak Hill for two years. That was out. He'd tried to get his homies to come get him, since Oak Hill was a juvenile detention center without armed guards. However, none of his homies would come get him, except for Vida and Tia. They agreed to go get him with no hesitation.

"Them niggaz make me sick." Vida sucked her teeth while driving. "They supposed to fuck wit' him, and they keep fakin' on him like he some kind of off-brand." She was pissed. "Them niggaz always talkin' that keep it real shit. That shit just talk."

"He don't need them niggaz, he got us," Tia said.

"He fed up wit' them niggaz anyway."

"I could see it in his face," Tia agreed.

"Shit, I'd feel the same way." Vida turned off the highway, heading into D.C. "Them niggaz used to be together every damn day, now they done forgot all about a nigga, and he only been gone a few months."

"Well he ain't gotta worry 'bout them niggaz no more," Tia said, as she turned the Back Yard tape up and let the go-go sound fill the car.

Hell Razor Honeys

Around Montana Avenue, inside the building hallway, Ice was down on one knee shooting dice with a few of the homies. She was winning at the time.

"Bet another fifty, I ain't never been scared to bet," one of the homies said to Ice.

"I like your spirit." She rolled the dice and hit her point. "Bet back?" She winked at him.

"Fifty she throw a seven," Malik called a side bet with Lil' D.

"Bet," Lil' D said.

Ice struck on her first roll and kept the hot hand for five more rolls. Money exchanged hands left and right for a good thirty minutes as the dice went around in a circle. Out of the blue two plain clothes police came inside the building. In a panic everybody grabbed their money.

"We ain't come for the crap game," one of the officers said, as he grabbed Ice by the arm. "We came for you."

"Get the fuck off me." Ice was stronger than the officer had expected. She snatched away from him and dashed out the building. Both officers gave chase. Ice hit the cut beside the building and was ghost. Minutes later she was jogging up 20th Street. She ran up to No Draws' door and knocked.

"What's wrong?" No Draws asked, seeing the look on Ice's face when she opened the door.

"The bodeans on my back," Ice said, as she rushed by No Draws. No Draws shut the door in a hurry. They both went up to No Draws' bedroom where Ice told her what had just went down.

"You don't know why they was lookin' for you?" No Draws asked, sitting on her bed in a pair of tight Guess jeans.

"I don't know," Ice said. It was no telling why the police wanted her. She had been in so much shit since she started running with the Hell Razor Honeys. "I gotta holla at my mother, she can find out what's up for me." Ice feared she was wanted in connection with the murder of Ellis and his man. "Let me see the phone."

A short while later, Vida and Tia were in No Draws' bedroom listening to Ice tell them what she'd learned from the conversation with her mother. Through her resources, Ice's mother had found out that Ice was wanted for the Black Hole shooting. The shocking part for the girls was who the police got the information from—Green Eyes—

EYONE WILLIAMS

she had been caught shoplifting down Georgetown and told the police everything. Ice was wanted for assault with a deadly weapon. The only up side to the situation was the fact that she was being charged as a juvenile. Her mother had begged her to turn herself in, but Ice wasn't going for that. They would have to catch her when they caught her.

"I don't believe this shit." Tia was pissed that her cousin had snitched on Ice. "I can't wait 'til I catch that bitch." Tia felt no love for Green Eyes at all. In fact, she would have been punished her about the Ellis shit, but no one had seen her.

"You said the dude not even pressin' charges, right?" Vida asked, standing over No Draws' desk, looking at her CD collection.

"Yeah, but my mother said Green Eyes sayin' she saw me shoot the bamma, so the police is pushin' the shit. My mother said she tryin' to get the shit dropped, but I gotta turn myself in, and I ain't doin' that." Ice shook her head.

"Green Eyes ain't gon' remember shit when I catch her ass," Tia said, looking out the window.

The phone rang and No Draws answered it. The call seemed important because she stepped into the hallway. "Say that again," she said, not believing her ears.

"You heard me right the first time. We want you to come out to L.A. for the shooting of the 'Pac video. You hot right now and I want the hottest girls in the video," Heat Wilson said. He was directing the "California Love" video. "It's two Gs in it for you for everyday we shoot. All expenses are on Death Row." You'll have a good time and meet some new people, too."

No Draws loved the idea and loved the thought of meeting new people even more. She'd just met Heat a few weeks ago in Miami and he was calling her already. The head she gave him must have kept his attention because he had surely kept his promise about putting her in his next video. "When do I have to be in L.A.?" she asked.

"Two weeks. Is that cool for you?"

"Yeah, it's fine for me." No Draws wanted to jump up and down she was so excited.

"I'll send you some travel money this week, okay?"

"Okay. Thank you so much," No Draws said and then put a sexy tone to her voice and added, "I'm gon' make sure I let you know that I appreciate you lookin' out for me."

"I can't wait."

No Draws went back into the bedroom and screamed, "Guess what, y'all!" The girls stopped talking and looked at No Draws. "They want me to come out L.A. for the shootin' of Tupac video!"

"For real?!" Ice jumped to her feet, disregarding her troubles. The mention of Tupac snatched all of her attention. "When... when are you goin'?"

Vida and Tia looked at each other and laughed. No Draws put the girls on point.

"You steppin' it up, huh?" Vida asked.

"I'm goin' wit' you to L.A. I gotta meet 'Pac," Ice said.

"You ain't got no L.A. money," Tia joked. "All your money is in the closet on hangers." Everybody laughed.

"I got a pistol and a pussy." Ice flashed her 10mm Ruger. "As long as I got these, I got money," she joked, dead serious at the same time.

"Why don't we all go out there together?" No Draws said. Everybody was with it but Vida. She spent most of her time with Daddieo, not to mention the fact that she was scared to fly.

"Come on, Vee. It'll be fun," Tia said.

"Yeah, you right. I'd love to see L.A. anyway," Vida said.

Later on, Ice was at the hotel with the dude Chris. She'd been fucking with him for a while now. He was getting a nice piece of money and Ice had no problem working him for it. After they'd fucked for over two hours and were just lying in bed naked, smoking weed, Ice told him about the trip to L.A and cracked on him for some money.

"How much you need?" Chris asked. Ice was lying on his chest as he rubbed her ass.

Sliding her hand between his legs and softly stroking his long and think manhood, Ice said, " 'Bout four or five Gs. I know that's some-thin' small to a giant."

Chris laughed. "You got game, girl. But I fucks wit' you. I got you."

"That's why I fucks wit' you." Ice went down and started licking his dick. She then put it in her mouth and began to deep-throat him.

Just after noon on Saturday, Vida woke up in the bed beside Daddieo. She was still worn out from their night long session of love making. She thought about the things she needed to take care of for the day. She and Samara had a money scheme to work some stolen credit cards Samara had gotten her hands on. After that, later on in the night, Vida, Tia and Ice were to go get Tec from Oak Hill.

Daddieo woke up with a throbbing erection. He looked over at Vida, who was in a daze of thought. They were both under the covers naked. "What's on your mind, sexy?" He rolled over and kissed her cheek.

"Nothin', just thinking 'bout how you made me feel so good last night." Vida rolled onto her side to face him, and her hand brushed against his erection. "Damn." She smiled as she began to stroke him with her soft hand. "You wake up ready to hurt somethin', huh?"

Enjoying the sensation of her hand going back and forth around his manhood, Daddieo began rubbing her hair back. "The way you throw it on a nigga I ain't got no choice but to wake up hard." Slowly but surely he was growing closer and closer to Vida; she was one of a kind. She was all about him and he could tell; he loved that about her. His alarm clock went off. It was 12:30 P.M. He had some business to take care of as well. "Damn, I gotta take a shower... owch!"

Vida gripped his dick as if she was going to rip it off if he tried to get out of bed. "You ain't goin' nowhere 'til I get some more of this. You know how we get down, nigga," she hissed.

"Okay, Vee." Daddieo laughed. "Don't castrate me."

"Act right then."

"It's all yours," he said, rolling onto his back, his dick standing straight up.

Vida threw the covers off of them and took a position between his legs. *Damn, I'ma be late*, he thought. But as he looked at Vida he didn't care. He loved the way she deep-throated him. Vida loved to please him and he loved to do the same to her. In fact, she loved him, period.

On her hands and knees between his legs, with her tongue between her teeth, Vida waved his dick side-to-side across the tip of her tongue, driving him crazy. "I won't be long," she said, putting him in her mouth and unleashing the animal in her, doing all the things he had taught her—things that would make him cum in her mouth in seconds. She didn't have to warm up, once she put her mouth on him she was in rare form, licking, sucking, deep-throating and looking him in the eyes at the same time. She knew she was turning him on.

Daddieo couldn't take it. He didn't want to cum before he got her to ride him. He got her to climb up on his dick. She sat down slowly, with him deep inside her and teased him for a second.

"Stop playin', Vee. Ride this dick for me, baby," he said, squeezing her ass. She leaned over and began licking his ears as she moved her pussy up and down, riding him with style and grace.

"Oh, yeah, I love this big dick, Daddieo." She began to grind her pussy down on him, loving the way it felt when he smacked her ass. "I love it… ssssssss. Yeah, I love it deep inside me."

"Whose pussy is it?" Daddieo grabbed her hips and began pulling her down on his dick a little fast and a little harder.

Vida let out a moan that sounded like he had hit a spot that had never been hit before. "Oh shit! It's your pussy, it's all yours, it's your pussy, it's your pussy… oh God, it's your pussy!" she panted, breathing hard and riding him fast and hard. With a big explosion of cream, and a violent tremble of her body, she started cumming. "I'm cummin'… I… I…" She threw her head back and rode him like a massive mustang.

Daddieo couldn't control her; she was working the pussy in overdrive. He had been in lots of pussy, but Vida brought great pussy and a mean fuck to the table like no other. Daddieo couldn't imagine anybody else getting inside her sweet pussy. She was his, and he planned to keep her all to himself. He had in her all that he could ask for in the bed. She was before her time. Whatever he asked, she did, and she did it in unimaginable positions that could last as long as he could stay hard.

By the time they satisfied their appetite for one another it was 1:17 P.M. They jumped in the shower and got dressed.

Inside Daddieo's car, Vida asked him about his trip to Baltimore.

"Remember when I was tellin' you about the publishing company me and Tonio was tryin' to start?"

"Yeah, so what y'all gon' do? Publish books?"

"Nah, Tonio got some friends in the music business that turned him on to the publishin' game. He gave me the run-down on it and wants me to start the company."

"How you gon' put it in effect? You don't deal wit' music," Vida asked.

"That's the catch, I don't have to deal wit' music in that sense." Daddieo turned onto North Capitol Street. "Once I start the company, me and Tonio will own a piece of the publishin' royalties of artist signed to the company. It's almost like gettin' paid for nothin'. All we gon' have to do is market the music and make sure royalties get paid and split up the right way.

"I see. You gon' be dealin' wit' the business side of things," Vida said.

"Yeah, we'll be issuing licenses for songs to be used for things like TV shows, movies and anything else that has somethin' to do with the song in question. The way Tonio broke it down to me, we can't lose. All I gotta do is follow the blueprint. I'ma meet him and his man Puff today so we can go over the plans."

"Puffy? Puff Daddy?" Vida asked.

"Yeah, him and Tonio came up together." Daddieo explained the history between Tonio and Puffy.

"So what you gotta do to start the company? You need a lot of money?" Vida liked the idea of starting a business.

"Nah, ain't nothin' to startin' a business. It's easy for real. You can start big and incorporate your business off the top, or you can just get your business certificate and start from the ground up. It's as easy as going downtown and fillin' out the application. Follow the instructions, pay the fee and it's done. You'll get what's called a DBA— Doing Business As—license; some call it fictitious name certificate. It's as simple as that, Vee. Once that's done you can open a bank account and you're in business. In D.C., I believe you can start with fifty dollars."

Later on, under the darkness of nightfall, Vida, Tia and Ice were in Tec's Taurus Station Wagon parked on a dark rural road surrounded by woods. It was 11:27 P.M., they were on schedule. The plan was simple, Vida and Tia were to sneak up to the fence and cut a hole in it. Tec had already paid one of the staff members to let him out the back door of his cottage so he could run across the dark field, slide through the hole in the fence and dash into the woods, where the girls would be waiting for him in the ride.

It was bitterly cold outside. Snow had begun to fall. Vida pulled on her thick winter gloves and grabbed the wire cutters. "Let's do this," she said. She and Tia got out and hit the woods, leaving Ice behind the wheel. They navigated through the dark, thick woods as the snow fell and the bone-chilling wind blew. Tia led the way with a small flashlight. For a while they thought they were going the wrong way, until the detention center appeared at the edge of the woods. Wearing all black, Vida carefully crept up to the fence and went to work. After she cut the hole in the fence she dashed back into the woods and threw the wire cutters to the side.

After about five minutes Tia became concerned. "You think somethin' went wrong?" she whispered to Vida. "Tec stressed the point that everything had to go down at 11:30 P.M. on the dot."

"Nah, everything should be cool. He gon' come." Vida was staring across the dark field. Minutes later she saw someone running across the field. "There he go. Flash the light."

Tia flashed the light twice. Tec saw it and smiled. His real comrades had come through for him. As he ran for the hole in the fence the patrol van that circled the detention center came around the corner. Tec dove to the ground and lay in the snow for a moment, hoping the van wouldn't stop. Vida and Tia were both afraid that the man in the van would see Tec lying in the snow. The van began to back up, flashing a light at the hole in the fence. The whole move was now in danger. Something had to be done.

POW! POW! POW! POW! Vida fired her 13-shot .380 at the back of the van as she stepped out of the woods. The van sped away. Tec wasted no time; he made a run for it. Time was running out. He slipped through the hole in the fence and together they ran through the woods at top speed.

Ice had the car ready. Police sirens were already in the air. Tec, Vida and Tia jumped in the car and Ice took them flying to the highway, somehow avoiding all law enforcement. They didn't try to make it back to D.C., instead they checked into a Maryland hotel with Ice's fake ID.

Inside the hotel room laughing and smoking weed, Tec was glad to be free—even if on the run. He let the girls know that he had nothing but love for them and that there was nothing he wouldn't do for them; his loyalty for them was eternal. Laying on the bed in his institution clothes, he said, "I fucks wit' y'all, on everything. It ain't shit I won't do for y'all; y'all my niggaz. When I get on my feet y'all ain't gon' want for shit." He blew smoke in the air. "That's from the heart." Looking at Vida, he said, "Vee, you wasn't fakin' wit' that pistol, huh?" He laughed.

"You ain't seen shit," Tia said, rolling up more weed. "Your girl fire that hammer."

"Is that right?" Tec said, looking at how phat Ice was in her Guess jeans. While he was locked up she had been sending him naked pictures, money and books to read. She wrote him a few letters telling him how she would make sure she made up for all the pussy he missed while he was gone.

"I'm the same ol' Vee." Vida smiled. "They the ones that's goin' hard."

"Thuggin' 'til the casket drop." Ice laughed.

Tec laughed. This was his crew.

Hell Razor Honeys

Chapter 9

Los Angeles was everything the girls thought it would be—palm trees, fast cars, movie stars and dreams come true. The only down side to the trip was that Vida changed her mind and stayed home with Daddieo. However, No Draws, Ice and Tia checked into the L'Ermitage, a luxury hotel on Burton Way in Beverly Hills. Heat had set them up in class on behalf of Death Row.

The girls had never seen such style. They felt like they were part of the rich and famous. From the plane ride in first class, to getting to meet Dr. Dre and Suge Knight, who were with Heat at the airport, everything about the trip was off the chain. Vida didn't know what she was missing. The girls really got to play big when Heat let No Draws hold his rented Mercedes Benz 500SL. They hit the town. The weather was great, far warmer than it was back in D.C.

All afternoon on their second day in L.A. the girls rode around hitting all the spots and meeting people. They ran into actor Chris Tucker at the Beverly Center Mall where they ate lunch. Chris Tucker had them laughing the whole time as he made countless jokes about No Draws' nickname. After lunch the girls hit Rodeo Drive, where Ice tried her hand at the credit card move Vida and Samara had started working. Acting as white as she could, dressed like the daughter of a rich Hollywood socialite, Ice walked into the Gucci shop with a stolen American Express card and came out with $5,000 worth of bags and shoes. She was just testing the water. All went well. The girls hit the Versace shop next. Tia spent a few hundred dollars to take the attention off of Ice, who broke 'em off for $10,000. That was enough for the day.

They then drove down Sunset Boulevard and took in the scenery.

EYONE WILLIAMS

Larenz Tate flew by them in a blue, convertible Ferrari 348 Spider; he even gave them a wave. Tia blew him a kiss. The girls were really feeling themselves and sucking up the California love.

Back at the L'Ermitage, in their four floor suite, the girls got ready for the night. They threw on gear that made them look sexy and wealthy. Black revealing gowns and sexy heels is how they were doing it.

On the phone with Vida, Tia was bragging about how much fun the crew was having on the Westside. "We 'bout to hit the club; you shoulda got your scared ass on the plane wit' us, Vee."

"Maybe next time." Vida laughed. She was over Daddieo's watching *Dead Presidents* on video. "Y'all ain't meet 'Pac or nobody yet?"

"We met a few people." Tia told her who they met. "We gon' hit the video shoot tomorrow. 'Pac gon' be there."

"I want an autographed picture," Vida said.

"I got you, Vee. You know that," Tia replied.

Ice jumped on the phone and kicked it with Vida for a second. "You know that move you put me down wit'?"

The credit card move came to mind. "Yeah, what's up?" asked Vida.

"It's sweet out here. No bullshit." Ice laughed.

"Be careful, y'all ain't out Landover Mall."

Ice laughed. "What's up wit' Tec?"

"He still layin' low, playing the hotel real tough."

"Tell 'em I said what's up."

"Cool, I'll catch y'all later," Vida said.

The girls hit the Orchid night club, a club Heat recommended. It was also in Hollywood. There was a long line to get in, but the passes the girls had allowed them to sidestep that problem. Inside the club was packed, with the party in full swing. The old 1988 hit, "It Takes Two" by Rob Base was pumping over the system. The whole vibe was perfect, nothing like the go-gos the girls were used to. Black balloons that read: ALL EYEZ ON ME lined the top of the walls. The girls were impressed. It was by all means a Death Row party.

Dressed in a black blazer, blue jeans by Hugo Boss and a pair of black Ferragamo loafers, Nigel watched No Draws and her crew come through the door. He hadn't seen No Draws since the video shoot in Miami. He wondered what she was doing in Hollywood. He stepped to her, grabbed her hand and said, "What's up, Michelle?"

Caught off guard, No Draws said, "Oh, Nigel. What's up? How you doin'?"

"What brings you out West?" he asked, glancing at Tia and Ice, who gave him looks like he was holding them up. They hoped he didn't trip; they had straight razors on them.

"I'm here for the Tupac video."

"Oh yeah?" Nigel was jealous. *I'm the one that discovered her. Now she on another nigga's dick,* he thought. "Damn, you get around, don't you?"

No Draws felt disrespected, but before she could say anything Tia spoke up. "Yeah, we get around, nigga!" Tia grabbed No Draws' arm and the girls disappeared into the thick crowd. They made their way up to the VIP section. It was full of the Death Row Family. The girls had never seen so many niggaz in red. There were a number of private booths, pool tables and two bars.

Heat saw the girls and made them feel at home. He introduced them to important figures in the Death Row family. Most importantly to Ice, he introduced them to Tupac and Snoop Dogg. Ice played it smooth. She wanted to fuck the shit out of 'Pac, but she was not about to play the groupie role, it wasn't her style. The girls took a few pictures with 'Pac and Snoop and then made their way to the booth Heat got for them. Heat had two of his comrades with him. There was some high priced bubbly sitting in a bucket of ice on the table. The girls got to know the dudes at their booth as they drank and made small talk.

Heat put his arm around No Draws and whispered in her ear, "You said you was going to let me know how much you appreciate me bringing you out here, right?"

No Draws giggled, the drinks were adding up. She slid her hand inside his pants and began giving him a mean hand job. "You don't have to remind me. When you treat me good I treat you better."

Loving her work, Heat said, "Is that right?"

"You hip to my work, we been together before."

"I was telling my man about you. You think you can treat him like you treat me?"

Working her hand up and down his manhood, No Draws licked his ear and whispered, "Your man gotta treat me good like you treat me if he wants me to treat him like I treat you."

Tia wasn't feeling the bamma she was kicking it with. He came off like an industry off-brand that was trying to play the gangsta role. Tia wasn't buying it, she could see right through him; she knew gangstas when she met them. She was thinking about robbing the bamma; he had to have on at least $250,000 worth of jewelry. However, Tia didn't want to fuck up what No Draws had going on with Heat. Tia excused herself and Ice did the same moments later; they hit the dance floor to see what they could get into.

Alone with three dudes, No Draws was still at ease.

Heat closed the curtains and said, "It's a closed party now."

Still at work with her hand, No Draws said, "A girl got needs now. I know y'all pockets ain't hurtin'."

"No doubt, I pay to play," the light-skinned dude said—he was the one Tia wasn't feeling. He sat $1,000 on the table.

"What about you?" No Draws looked at the other dude that could pass for Caine in *Menace II Society*.

"I wanna see what all the hype is about." The Caine look-a-like threw a G on the table as well.

No Draws had no shame in her game; she loved the attention she got when she really let her hair down. She looked at Heat and said, "It's your call. What you want me to do?"

"Show 'em why they call you No Draws," Heat said.

No Draws looked at the ceiling. The curtains went up high enough for her to stand on the table. She was about to get down to business when Tupac's "California Love" hit the air, blasting. In her high heels, No Draws got up on the table, looking into the lustful eyes of the three men. She was feeling the song and moved her body to the beat like a striper. She unzipped the back of her Versace gown and let it fall on the table. It was clear why her name was No Draws. She had on nothing under her gown. In nothing but her heels, she dipped and worked her hips seductively. Her thick, red-bone body captivated her three-man audience. She squatted in front of each man and opened her thick thighs, showing the full view of her trimmed pussy, as she licked her fingers and rubbed her clit.

After the little freak show, No Draws put ice cubes in her mouth and began to give each man head, milking them like cows, one by one. She had the first two coming in no time, but she took her time with Heat. She wanted him to crave more in the future. Under the table, naked, she gently put his dick in her ice-filled mouth and began doing her thing. By the way he was moving she knew she had him by the balls. As the ice melted she went up and all the way down on his dick. As Heat came in her mouth, filling the condom she had rolled on with her mouth, he put $1,500 on the table for her. What she did with a dick deserved a place in the history books.

Meanwhile, Back in D.C. it was 1:10 A.M. Kareem, Malik and Lil' D were in front of Vida's building pushing coke hand-to-hand. A small rush of sells was coming as coke and money exchanged hands in a blur.

From behind the building came a masked stick-up kid in all black with a short, sawed-off pump shotgun. Sliding up on Kareem, Malik and Lil' D like a ghost, the stick-up kid hissed, "Get on the fuckin' ground!"

Kareem and his two comrades were caught with their pants down, not to mention scared shitless by the sight of the pump. There was no way they could get their pistols out. They quickly lay facedown in the snow.

"Spread your fuckin' hands out! Move and I'ma murder you niggaz out here!" the stick-up kid declared.

Everyone did as they were told. However, Kareem knew who was behind the mask. He'd known Tec all of his life, he knew how he walked, how he thought and damn sure knew how he talked. Tec's voice was unmistakable. Kareem didn't dare act as if he knew who was robbing him.

CARTEL PUBLICATIONS PRESENTS

Standing over his homies with the pump, Tec searched them one
by one. In all he took $2,100, close to three ounces of coke and a .45
automatic that Kareem had on him. Tec then disappeared just as fast
as he'd come. No one was safe anymore.

Out in the crisp air of El Mirage Desert Lake Bed, one hundred
miles of north of L.A., No Draws, Tia and Ice were on the set of the
"California Love" video. Helicopters flew overhead and dirt bikes
zoomed by kicking up sand. Everyone had on black leather shirts,
vests, gloves, hats and pants with metal spikes. It looked like a scene
out of Mad Max.

Chronic filled Tupac's trailer. 'Pac and a few Thug Life members
were smoking weed with Ice and Tia. They had hooked up with the
Thug Life members at the club and had spent the night with them.
'Pac was the life of the party; he and Ice got to kick it. She tried to get
him to remember that he had written her back from prison and sent
her a picture along with the book "The Prince" by Machiavelli. Ice
even had the picture with her. She couldn't believe it when 'Pac
remembered sending her the book.

"Did you read it?" 'Pac held in the strong weed smoke as he
spoke.

"From front to back; like five times. I know most of it by heart."
Ice had given 'Pac a little bit of her background, she let it be known
that she was thuggin' for real.

'Pac smiled. "Would you rather be feared or loved?"

Ice had studied that chapter—so did Tec when she sent him the
book down Oak Hill. "For the life I live," Ice said. "I'd like to have a
little bit of both, love and fear. I know it don't go like that all the time
though, just like Machiavelli said. If I gotta pick one over the other,
muthafuckas gon' fear me. It's too many cruddy niggaz in the game,
they be on some snake shit. You treat 'em good and they still cross
you when they claim to love you, but when they fear you they dread
what you gon' do if they play you fifty."

'Pac passed her the blunt. "You got it down. Men don't care about

91

Hell Razor Honeys

crossing the ones they love when it is for their own gain. Whether it is better to be feared or loved is easy to answer. We all want to be loved, and feared, too, at times. But on the real, it's far better to be feared in the streets. Niggaz in general can be ungrateful, liars and deceivers that run from danger. They get greedy. When you spoil them they are at your disposal; they will risk their lives for you as long as they know it's safe, but when shit really hits the fan they leave you standing alone. Only your true comrades stand with you when the heat is on. Seeing is believing. Promises blow in the wind and if you depend on them you set yourself up for ruin. Love is built, many times on a bond of gratitude. A bond niggaz break when it is to their advantage. You gotta watch your homies." 'Pac spoke with great energy, as if he was rapping.

"I feel you." Ice blew smoke in the air. "Just like when it talks about Hannibal in the book. When it was time to put that work in he didn't give a fuck about using cruelty and it made him feared and respected. I want to be respected all the way around the board."

"Some niggaz love as they please, but fear when the right nigga is on the scene; that makes the game what it is. A lot of people think they have respect, but for real, they are feared. Aside from all that, niggaz gon' hate you for whatever you do."

"I feel you," Ice said.

Chapter 10

Vida rushed to see who the fuck was banging on her door like the police. Looking through the peephole, she snatched the door open ready to curse a muthafucka out, but found a huge .44 revolver in her face.

"Where the fuck Tec at, bitch?" Kareem and his cousin Johnny forced their way into the apartment and slammed the door behind them.

Vida was scared to death and instantly began to sweat. "I don't know where Tec at. Why the fuck you come up in her wit' that damn gun in my face?!"

Kareem smacked her in the face with the pistol, splitting her shit. Vida screamed out in pain as she grabbed her face and fell to the floor, bleeding. Out of the blue, automatic gunfire ripped through the small apartment. Pop! Pop! Pppppppppppop! Tia came out of the bedroom blasting at Kareem and Johnny with a TEC-9. She hit Johnny in the back as he and Kareem ran for the door. Vida covered her head and balled up on the floor as the gunfire rocked the apartment in the early morning hours. In a dash, Tia jumped over Vida, running after Kareem and Johnny with the TEC-9 blazing.

Tia saw Johnny tumble and fall at the top of the steps. He was hit bad. She hit him with seven more slugs as she ran down the steps blasting at Kareem, who had made it out of the building. Tia didn't chase him; instead, she hit Johnny in the head two more times and looked down at him with contempt. She then ran back upstairs to check on Vida.

Holding a towel on her forehead to stop the bleeding, Vida said, "You gotta get out of here, Tee." Vida snatched the smoking TEC-9.

Hell Razor Honeys

"Go down Sam's apartment and wait 'til I come get you. The police gon' be here any minute."

Tia broke and ran down to Samara's. Vida wrapped the gun in a Polo sweatshirt and ran up to the roof where she slung it over to the next building. Police sirens were rushing in the direction of Montana Avenue.

A short while later; Vida's apartment was covered with cops. Homicide detectives questioned Vida and knew she was lying about what happened. Her whole apartment was destroyed by the gunfire. Nevertheless, her story stayed the same—someone was banging on her door, she opened it and Johnny ran inside her apartment being chased by two masked gunmen. The shooting exploded inside her apartment and spilled over into the hallway. Vida said she didn't see much after she was smacked with a pistol. The detective that questioned her threatened to take her in, but she stood on her story. She was taken to the hospital and got stitches for the gash above her eye.

Later on, when Vida returned to her apartment, her grandmother was hysterical and couldn't believe what had gone down while she was at work. Vida told her grandmother the whole truth; she couldn't stand lying to Ms. Green.

"Lord, ha' mercy. What you children done got into?" Ms. Green shook her head, feeling faint.

"Grandma, I gotta get you outta here. I don't want you up in here like this until I find out what's goin' on," Vida said.

"What are you mixed up in, Vida?"

"I think Lil' Timmy is beefin' wit' Kareem. Since me and Lil' Timmy are close I think Kareem was trying to use me to get to him."

Ms. Green sighed. "I don't understand how you children just kill one another like it's nothin'. God ain't put you here for that."

Later on that same night, Kareem, Malik and Lil' D were over

Lil' D's girl's house out Kentland, Maryland. They were planning murders—Tec's, Tia's, Ice's and Vida's. Kareem was fucked up about his cousin and blamed himself for the way he was gunned down. He would have never guessed Tia would come out of the blue blasting a TEC-9. Kareem's manhood was also crushed—he let a girl chase him away from the scene after he ran out of bullets. However, there would be hell to pay. There was an up side to the situation; Kareem had the hood on his side. He'd told everybody that the girls were a part of the robbery Tec had pulled.

Loading rounds into a banana clip for an AK-47 assault rifle, Lil' D said, "All we gotta do is snatch one of them lil' bitches that be wit' Vida and them. They'll tell us where they at." Lil' D popped the clip into the chopper.

Malik never liked Tec when they were growing up, but he now had a reason to hate his ass and to take him out. "Let's do somethin', we doin' too much talkin'. That nigga Tec and them stank-ass bitches outta control." Malik cocked a MAC-10.

Kareem was sitting on the sofa in a bulletproof vest. He knew Green Eyes didn't fuck with the Hell Razor Honeys anymore. He had still been fucking her; she could be used. "Look here, y'all see what's up wit' any of them other lil' bitches. I'ma see if I can get some info out of the bitch Green Eyes.

Inside a Maryland hotel room, Vida was cursing Tec's ass out. On the strength of the love he had, Tec took it in stride; he felt bad for putting her and the girls in danger. He didn't think Kareem would take the beef to them. Ice and Tia watched Vida vent; when she was mad she released the fury of hell and wasn't to be fucked with.

"Vee, you right." Tec got off the bed and walked to the window. He checked the parking lot. "I didn't think that nigga would bring y'all a move like that. I got his ass."

"Fuck that! When you do some shit like that you gotta let us know what the fuck is goin' on! You can't just have us out there like that! Everybody know we fucks wit' you!" Vida yelled, full of fire. "Them niggaz coulda killed me!"

"She right, Tec," Tia added. "Kareem know we fucks wit' you tough, everybody know that. If they can't get to you they gon' come for us."

"Y'all right. That's my bad. It won't happen again, y'all got my word on that," Tec said. The crew worked everything out. They all came to terms; they were in it together. Tec pulled a gym bag from under the bed and took $3,000 out and gave it to Vida. "Find two apartments, one for your grandmother and one for us; somewhere out Maryland."

"What we gon' do about Kareem and them?" Ice asked, ready to bus' some ass. She was fucked up that Kareem had come up in Vida's apartment with that bullshit.

"We gon' clean house." Tec pulled a pump from under the bed. "Whoever stand wit' Kareem and them gon' get it."

"How we gon' do it?" Vida wanted Kareem's dick in the dirt.

"We gon' do what they think we won't do." Tec laid down the game plan. The Machiavelli book had given him some mean ideas. The girls were down and ready for whatever.

The Metro Club was a well known go-go spot in Northeast, D.C. It was jumping. Rare Essence had the crowd hyped. Most of all, they had the honeys freaking. Tec was at the bar rapping to a bad-ass broad that was friends with Malik's baby's mother. Malik's baby's mother was also in the club.

Over the loud music the cute dark-skinned girl said, "Where you been? I ain't seen you in months."

Sipping his drink, watching everything closely, with a Glock in his waistband, Tec said, "I was locked up for a minute, some light shit."

While Tec was talking to the girl different dudes that he knew came up to him asking him about the situation between him and Kareem. The streets were already talking and watching. Tec played everything off like it wasn't shit; it was nothing to talk about.

On the sneak tip, Malik's baby's mother slid to the bathroom and got on her cell phone. "Malik, that nigga Tec up here in the Met."

"Keep an eye on him. I'm on my way." Malik hung up. He and Lil' D headed for the Metro Club, ready to put that work in. They couldn't believe Tec was hanging out at the go-go, out in the open, when he knew he was marked for death.

A short while later Malik slid in the Metro club strapped with a .40 caliber. It was dark inside so it took a while for him to locate his baby's mother. From afar, Tec spotted him and smiled. Malik found his baby's mother at the bar with the broad Tec was rapping to. Tec knew what time it was, he pulled his hood over his head and began to creep through the crowd like a panther, watching Malik intensely. Tec was sure Malik had come to kill.

However, everything ain't always what it seems. Little did Malik's baby's mother know, she'd done exactly what Tec wanted someone to do—tell Kareem, Malik, or Lil' D where he was so they would come to him. That's why Tec went to the Metro Club in the first place; he wanted to be out in the open so he could be seen. He wasn't slipping; he had Vida, Tia and Ice out in the parking lot.

Out in the parking lot, Vida, Tia and Ice were in a stolen Dodge Caravan. Vida had a .45 automatic in her hand, Ice had Tec's pump and Tia was rolling with a TEC-9. They were dead serious. Parked where they could see everything, they'd seen Malik, Lil' D and another dude named Derrell arrive in a red Pontiac Firebird. Malik got out and went inside the Met, leaving Lil' D and Darrell in the car.

The girls knew Tec could handle himself inside, so they masked up and got ready to do their part. Hunched down, creeping behind parked cars, the girls slid up on the Firebird. Wasting no time, Ice fired the pump through the passenger side window, blowing Lil' D's brains all over the driver's side of the car, killing him instantly. In unison, Vida and Tia opened fire on Derrell in the back seat, riddling his body with slugs. Ice pumped the shotgun four more times, blasting the car with buckshots.

"Let's go!" Vida called out. The girls took off running.

Inside the club someone must've informed Malik about what had just gone down outside, because Tec saw him rush toward the door. *It couldn't get any sweeter,* Tec thought. With the hood still over his head, Tec tied a black bandanna around his face and fired his Glock in the air twice. The go-go band stopped playing. In fact, everything seemed to stand still for a second. Then, in a wild rush for the door, the crowd began to stampede. It was just what Tec needed for cover. Glock in hand, he fell in with the crowd, not far behind Malik. Once outside, still mixed in with the crowd, Tec let loose. He hit Malik in the back at least ten times before Malik fell. The crowd scattered. Standing over Malik, Tec emptied his clip into the back of his head. Running off into the night, popping another clip into his Glock, Tec knew that his plan had worked. Kareem was next.

Inside a Riverdale hotel, Kareem was trying to get some information out of Green Eyes about the Hell Razor Honeys.

"I know how you can get close to Vida." Green Eyes was hitting the Backwood Kareem had just fired up. She told him about Daddieo. "You know she fuck wit' that nigga real tough. Lay on his ass, and Vida gon' walk right into your arms."

"Damn, you right," Kareem said. "That's what I'ma do." He looked at his watch and back at Green Eyes. "Well, we might as well have a little fun since we rented the room."

"No bullshit." She smiled.

They undressed without another word.

"Turn around and bend over the bed," Kareem said as he smacked her phat ass.

"Oh yeah." Green Eyes looked over her shoulder as she placed her hands on the bed and braced herself.

"You know I love this pussy from the back." Kareem slipped inside her wet pussy and made her let out a deep moan. He grabbed her waist and began to stroke her nice and slow for a while. The wetter she got, the better the pussy got. She began pushing the pussy back at him as she moaned and groaned.

As Kareem fucked her nice and long from the back, Green Eyes looked over her shoulder with a fuck-face and moaned the words, "Put it in my ass. Fuck me in the ass, Reem." He pulled out of her soaking wet pussy and slid his cream covered dick right in her tight asshole. "Oh shit," she moaned. "Oh yeah, fuck me... fuck me, daddy. Mmmmmmmmm... sssssss... cum in my ass, Reem. Fuck me." Kareem started fucking her hard and deep, banging the ass like the whore loved it. "Fuck me harder, Reem. Make it hurt. Aaaaaahhh... yeah, yeah, yeah, yeah," she panted as he banged the ass like a jackhammer. "Ooooohhh shit, I'm cummin'... I'm cummin'... don't stop... don't stop!" She felt him yank her head back by her weave and let out a little yell, but loved it. She felt like she was being sodomized with a broomstick and continued to throw her ass back at Kareem while she came. "Oh yeah, I love it." She began to shake violently. "I love it... I love it... I'm cummin' so hard! Don't stop! Don't stop! Sssssss... aaaaaahhhhhhhh yeah!"

Kareem loved the whore in her; it's what kept him coming back. After they were done fucking Kareem noticed that his beeper was vibrating. He checked it and saw that Malik's baby's mother had beeped him seven times with code 9-1-1. He called her without another thought.

"They did what?!" he snapped.

"They killed Malik, Lil' D and Derrell," she sobbed.

Kareem felt pure fear shoot through his body. "Who did it?"

"Tec!" she screamed.

"Where you at?"

"Wit' Malik's mother."

"Did the police question you?" Kareem asked.

"Yeah, I told them everything."

Kareem was pleased. Now Tec also had to worry about the police. That would be another distraction.

"I didn't really see Tec do it," Malik's baby's mother said. "But I know he did it." Her sobs grew louder and stronger.

"Stay put. I'll be over there in a minute." Kareem hung up and looked at Green Eyes. "Put your shit on, we gotta go."

Hell Razor Honeys

Chapter 11

A week flew by like seconds on a stopwatch. Tec was wanted for murder and Vida was wanted for questioning. The police had information that connected Johnny's murder to the Metro Club murders. The stakes had been raised manifold; No Draws and Samara weren't cut out for the gunplay, so Vida warned them about the situation and told them to stay on point. In an effort to protect her grandmother, Vida got her an apartment in Greenbelt, Maryland. She also got the crew an apartment in Capitol Heights, Maryland. Kareem was still the only focus of the crew, but Tec and the girls couldn't seem to locate him. They had laid on him everywhere, even in front of his mother's house in Fort Washington, Maryland.

Vida and Daddieo had been having little spats back and forth over the phone about the way she'd been acting. She'd stayed away from him while the beef was in the air, for his sake. It did look funny; she'd gone from not being able to go a day without seeing him, to not see-ing him for a whole week. He had no understanding of the situation and believed Vida was fucking Tec; he'd seen them together the night of the Metro Club murders. Vida tried to tell him that she was in a bad situation and that she didn't want him to get caught up in her drama. However, he wasn't trying to hear that. Daddieo's feelings were in too deep at this point.

In the nearly empty apartment, Vida was sitting on the thick, light-brown carpet watching *Boyz N the Hood* on HBO while eating steak-n-cheese with Tec. Ice and Tia were in the bedroom sleep; they'd been out all night with Tec, stalking Kareem. Vida stayed with her grandmother last night, taking care of her. Ms. Green hadn't been doing too well lately.

EYONE WILLIAMS

"You really on this college nigga, huh?" Tec said; his mouth was full of food. In a T-shirt and boxers, he was at home and at ease around the girls. He couldn't care less that he was wanted for murder. "I never thought you'd fall for a New York nigga." He laughed, washing down his food with a big gulp of Pepsi.

"Don't even go there again, nigga." Vida waved him off. She was dressed in a gray Polo sweatsuit. "We done already had this conversation. I told you Daddieo cool peoples."

"What kind of name is Daddieo, anyway?" Tec laughed.

"Oh, you got jokes? What kind of name is Tec? You named after a gun and shit," Vida shot back, all in fun.

"That ain't my fault, you know Lil' Sean gave me that name before he got locked up. But on the real, I never thought I'd see you in love wit' a square." Tec liked messing with Vida about her relationship with Daddieo.

"It be like that sometimes. You gon' meet a bitch that's gon' throw the pussy on you, and you gon' fall in love. You ain't gon' know what to do."

"Picture that," Tec said with no nonsense.

"Yeah, whatever. Talk that rough shit to me, but all you niggas fall for a bitch sooner or later." Vida rolled her eyes.

"You know what? I'm jealous." Tec lit a Backwood and filled the room with weed smoke. "I go away for a few months and you start givin' my pussy to a New York nigga."

"Your pussy?" Vida exploded with laughter. "All the bitches you put your dick in, what makes me so got-damn exquisite?"

Tec choked on the weed smoke as he burst out laughing. After recovering from the laughing fit, he said, "You know we been like Bonnie and Clyde since 2nd grade."

"Yeah, right, you just liked rubbin' your lil' dick on me back then. And getttin' me to beat bitches up for you."

"Lil' dick?!" Tec twisted up his face as he passed Vida the Backwood.

She playfully punched him in the chest. "I was talkin' 'bout back then, nigga. Stop trippin'."

"Be clear now. I ain't got no problem whippin' this muthafucka out for you."

Hell Razor Honeys

Vida died laughing. She and Tec clicked so well, like brother and sister. As they continued smoking and joking, Vida's cell phone rang. Still laughing, Tec answered the phone. "What's up?"

"Where Vida at?" a male voice snapped.

"Who the fuck is this?" Tec snapped back, matching the bass in the dude's voice.

"Daddieo... put Vida on the phone."

Tec sighed and handed Vida the phone. He didn't want to get into anything with Daddieo, out of respect for Vida.

"Hello." Vida got on the phone.

"Oh yeah, it's like that?" Daddieo asked.

"Nah—"

"You playin' games now that your lil' boyfriend home. I got you." Daddieo hung up.

"Where you goin', Vee?" Tec asked, seeing her going for her coat.

"I gotta go see slim. I gotta explain this shit to him." Vida walked out the door.

The tantalizing smell of seafood filled Samara's nose as she and Tonio dined at Philip's down at the Baltimore Harbor. They were enjoying lobster tails, Alaskan king crab legs and steamed shrimp. Tonio was growing addicted to Samara. On the other hand, he was her "Big Fish." Since Tonio was in B-more on business, he decided to take Samara out to eat. He was getting into real estate in New York, Philly and B-more and already had a number of run-down houses and apartments.

"You sure got a lot of time for me these days." Samara smiled, knowing she had her claws in Tonio.

"You know how it is... some people get a whole lot better with time." Tonio winked at her. "You never fail to surprise me. I like that." Aside from that, he also loved the fact that Samara went the whole nine yards and more when it came to pleasing him. He loved whores and freaks so much that good girls didn't even turn him on.

"It's always two sides to a coin, though."

"What's that supposed to mean?" Tonio raised his eyebrow.

"When you flip me you get a different look every time." She blew him a kiss. They both laughed. "Besides, I gotta keep my shit tight. I know its a million bitches chasin' you, and I need you comin' back to me as long as I can keep you happy."

"That's what I like about you." Tonio felt a bare foot rubbing up his leg under the table. "You don't do no pretendin'."

"For what? It is what it is; supply and demand." She pulled no punches.

While Samara and Tonio were enjoying each other, No Draws and Nigel walked in. Nigel was sprung. Since running into No Draws in L.A., he'd been pressing her for some of her time. She knew she had him wrapped around her finger and that was enough to spend a little time with him. After all, he was still an asset. No Draws saw Samara and Tonio, she and Nigel went over to speak. Nigel knew Tonio; the two had met at a Puffy party. They spoke for a second and went on about their business. No Draws and Tonio had made eye contact in a way that made Samara jealous. *I know this bitch ain't tryin' to step on my toes,* Samara thought.

"You know No Draws from somewhere?" Samara asked as she and Tonio left Philip's.

"Ain't that your homegirl that was in that L.L. video?" he asked, as they stepped out into the cold evening air.

"Yeah, that's her." Samara had an attitude of suspicion. "Do you know her?"

"Nah, I just remember her from that video. I couldn't remember where I'd seen her before," Tonio said, as they walked up on his silver 1996 Porsche 993 Cabriolet. He'd heard stories about No Draws. Good stories, too. It was no question about what he wanted to do.

Vida had a hard time explaining everything to Daddieo, but she finally got him to understand. He couldn't believe what she was caught up in, as a female at that. He didn't want her around Tec anymore; he blamed Tec for the whole situation.

"Promise me you'll leave Tec alone. He's going to get you

killed." Daddieo was rubbing her hand as they sat on the sofa in his dorm room.

"I can't do that. Me and Tec like family. We all we got, in a sense, I can't let nothin' happen to him. Besides, these dudes after me too, so it's no easy way to take care of this shit," Vida said.

Daddieo sighed. "Let me holla at Tonio. He got people down here in D.C. that can take care of things like this. They can clean this mess up for you, baby."

"I don't want you or your brother to get caught up in this shit. We got it under control. Trust me, boo."

Putting an arm around Vida, Daddieo said, "I'm worried about you, Vee, for real. I don't know what I'd do if somethin' happened to you behind this bullshit."

Vida felt safe and loved with Daddieo. "I'ma be okay, don't worry about me. Everything will be taken care of in a minute. I'm cool. Please don't worry." She kissed him, expressing what she felt with the kiss. They began to melt into a passionate embrace. His hands rubbed her back as they continued to talk. Passion began to overtake them. Vida's soft moans encouraged him to explore her body and he did, smoothly. He planted soft kisses all over her face, down her neck and back up.

"I love you, Vee." Daddieo laid her flat on the sofa, gracefully." He took off her colorful Nike track shoes and her socks, admiring her pretty toes. Looking in her eyes, he kissed her foot. "I wanna take you away from all this madness, Vee." Next he smoothly eased her out of her sweats and panties. His eyes locked in on her pink wetness. She still smelled like Dove soap.

Closing her eyes, Vida leaned her head back, knowing what kind of pleasure she was in store for. Daddieo always set out to please her. Babyface could be heard on the stereo. He softly licked up her sexy, reddish-brown leg until he was upon her sweet spot. Rubbing it with his finger a few times, he began to suck her clit, sending chills through her body. He stopped and went up to her beautiful breast.

Looking at her perfect nipples while he took off his gear, Daddieo said, "I love you." Going back down on her, he spread her thighs. Her breathing went from slow and smooth to heavy panting. The whole room seemed to heat up. As his tongue went to work on her clit, licking and sucking, she wrapped her legs around his neck, trying to pull his face into her pussy.

"Daddieo… sssssss." She bit down on her bottom lip and began to moan with lust and passion. Her body began to shake and writhe from the effects of the licking, sucking and biting on and around her swollen clit and pussy lips. "Ooooo… sssss, damn… I'm cummin'." She began to shake convulsively as she called out his name over and over again, feeling the urge to cry. It was that good.

A short while later they were walking to Vida's car, hugged up together like sweethearts. It was dark and cold outside. A few students were outside, some walking back and forth through the parking lot. Standing beside Vida's car hugging and kissing as the cold wind blew, Daddieo and Vida made a public display of their love.

"I'll catch you later on, okay?" Vida said as they broke their embrace.

"Call me as soon as you get home," Daddieo said.

The sound of a passing car caught Vida's attention. "Yeah, I'll hit you as soon as I get home," she said sounding distracted.

"What's wrong?" Daddieo looked over his shoulder and saw a masked gunman jumping out of an old station wagon.

Vida shoved Daddieo to the ground just as the gunfire exploded. In a flash, she was bussin' her Glock 19 with no fear. The gunman was blasting at her from less than ten feet away. Firing her pistol with two hands, Vida dashed behind her car. People began to scream and run in all directions. The gunman tried to get a better shot at Vida, but caught slugs in the chest that knocked him backward.

Seeing that she'd hit the gunman, Vida stepped from behind the car and fired five more rounds. The gunman fell; his gun fired no more. The station wagon pulled off burning rubber as Vida fired shots at it. She couldn't believe who was behind the wheel—Green Eyes! With her pistol empty and smoking, Vida tried to check on Daddieo, but felt her head spinning. Slowly, everything started to go black and she passed out, falling to the cold ground.

The scene at the hospital was so out of control that the police had to restore order and make some people leave. Tonio and three of his men got the news of Daddieo being shot and rushed to Washington Hospital Center. Tension was thick. Daddieo had been shot once through the arm pit. The bullet had tore through a vital artery and had him clinging to life. Tia met up with Samara and rushed to the hospital to find Vida clinging to life as well. Vida had been shot five times with a 9mm. In surgery she had to have a lung removed. The doctors doubted if she would pull through now that she'd slipped into a coma. Ms. Green almost had a stroke when she got to the hospital and saw Vida in such a state. Also clinging to life was Kareem, who had been shot nine times in the chest and arm. He was on the same floor as Vida and Daddieo.

As they stood in the lobby Samara told Tonio who Kareem was and what the beef with Tec and the girls was about. Tonio's men were standing around him like bodyguards.

"So this nigga shot my baby brother tryin' to shoot Vida?" asked Tonio.

"Yeah," Samara said, still crying.

Tonio looked at his men and told them to go to the car. Looking back at Samara, he said, "Look, I need to meet this young dude, Tec. Tell him who I am and that we need to talk."

"Okay," Samara said, feeling a little worried that things were now about to get far more heated.

"I'll talk to you in a minute… I need to make a phone call." Tonio stepped off.

Samara went back upstairs with No Draws, Tia and Ms. Green, who were all sitting in the waiting area down the hall. They were crying and wiping their eyes; the scene was one of deep sorrow. Moments later, Tonio came upstairs and took a seat as well; he wasn't leaving until he heard something about Daddieo. He also had no intentions of leaving his brother unguarded.

"Where's Ice and Tec?" Samara whispered to Tia.

"They on the run, they can't be around all these police," Tia said.

"Lord, please have mercy on my baby," Ms. Green began to pray out loud.

Minutes later two loud gunshots went off down the hallway. Everybody jumped and looked toward Vida and Daddieo's rooms. Two police officers and a few security guards rushed down the hall with their guns drawn. A hysterical nurse ran down the hall scream-ing and pointing in the direction of the gunshots. "He went that way!" the nurse yelled as she ran by the police. The police ran down the back stairs. Samara gave Tonio a suspicious look.

In the midst of all the madness, the nurse went in the opposite direction of the police and hit the other stairway. She hurried down three flights of stairs and ran out the back door of the hospital into the cold night air in nothing but her little white uniform. Running across the parking lot, she jumped into a black Mitsubishi Eclipse RS.

The driver of the Eclipse pulled off as he cut his eyes at the nurse. "You take care of that?" he asked.

"Come on, young. You know I put that work in," Ice said. "Two to the head." She undressed and threw the uniform out the window. She'd shot Kareem in the head with a .44 magnum as he lay in his hospital bed. It was a bold move—cold-blooded too, but as Tec told her, she was white, so she could pull it off if she did it right.

"I knew you would take care of it," Tec said. He drove for a few minutes without another word as he headed for the beltway. Inside he was blaming himself for what happened to Vida, and it was killing him. Something kept telling him not to let her go see Daddieo by her-self while shit was still in the air. However, he didn't go with his gut feeling.

As Tec drove around the beltway, Ice knew what was eating at him; she knew him well. "It's not your fault, Tec. Don't blame your-self. Vee gon' be okay."

Tec had tears in his eyes.

"She's strong, she's a fighter." Ice tried to make him fell better, but the guilt was burning him up inside. His heart was heavy. If he would have never robbed Kareem none of this would have ever hap-pened. That's all he kept telling himself. "It's no way you could've stopped what was goin' to happen." Ice rubbed his arm.

Wiping tears away, he said, "I swear to God, Vida better make it. If she don't, I'ma make the Potomac run red wit' blood it's gon' be so much killin'; on everything."

Days later it came out that Green Eyes was driving the station wagon Kareem jumped out of. Her days were numbered.

Sitting in the car with Tia and Ice before going inside, Tec checked his .40 caliber and addressed the girls, "Keep your eyes open. If shit don't look right we gon' shut this muthafucka down." Tec didn't know what was up with the dude Tonio, but he decided to meet him out Rockville at the Cheesecake Factory in White Flint Mall. Tec picked the location. Tia and Ice had his back.

Tonio came with two of his young guns—dudes out of Southeast, D.C. that he dealt with. Tec was hoping Tonio didn't do anything stupid, but if he did shit was sure to get ugly.

The Cheesecake Factory was packed. Tec and Tonio sat at one table while Tia and Ice sat at another nearby; Tonio's young guns were nearby as well. The restaurant damn sure wasn't the place for a gunfight.

With no small talk, Tonio got straight to the point. "I'm glad you came to meet me," he said.

"I know your brother got caught up in this beef so it was only right, out of respect." Tec was wondering what would come of the meeting.

"I know how the streets work. The hospital shooting was some bold shit." Tonio looked Tec in the eyes as he sipped his water. "I ain't seen no shit like that in a while. He knew Tec was behind the shooting. "All I need to know from you is who else is involved with what happened to my brother."

"I feel you." Tec nodded his head; he understood where Tonio was coming from. "Everybody that played a role in what was goin' on ain't even around no more. It's a lil' bitch that was wit' it, but she on her last leg. You don't even have to worry about that."

"I see. Ay… uh, how old are you, shorty?"

"Sixteen. Why?"

"You seem older, son. You don't carry it like you sixteen," Tonio replied.

As Tec and Tonio talked, Tia and Ice had their eyes on everything moving. "What you think this joker wanna holla at Tec for?" Ice asked Tia.

"He just wanna know why his brother got shot. If he wanted to bring Tec a move he woulda did it."

"He woulda tried," Ice said.

Tia smiled. "You right, he woulda tried.

"So what we gon' do about Green Eyes?"

"I got her ass. I told Tec I would do it myself. I still can't believe she did some shit like that. I got her snake-ass though, don't even trip." Tia's mind was made up.

Tonio was feeling Tec after talking to him for a while. The young nigga was well before his time. "Well, I'm 'bout to slide to the hospital. If you need a favor or something like that just let me know. Feel free to holla at me."

"Bet," Tec said. It was never his style to burn bridges.

Sitting in Green Eye's hotel room out Maryland, Tia waited for her first cousin to return. Things had changed for the worse. Tia thought about killing Green Eyes and something kept telling her not to do it. Her mind drifted back to a dark corner of her childhood that she never spoke about.

When she was eight she was home alone and her uncle Moe, Green Eye's father, came home drunk and began touching her like he always did when he was drunk. However, on this day he went to the point of sticking his finger inside her vagina. After that day she stayed far away from him, praying that God would strike him dead.

Green Eyes walked into the hotel room and shut the door behind her, snapping Tia out of her hateful thoughts. Flicking on the light, Green Eyes screamed as fear paralyzed her. She saw Tia holding a TEC-9. "Please, Tee, I didn't know he was gon' hurt Vida." Green Eyes fell to her knees and began to cry, as if she was praying to Tia.

"I used to look up to you!" Tia stood up with the TEC-9 at her side. "You ain't shit, you a fuckin' snake!"

"I'm family!" Green Eyes sobbed. "I'm your blood! You can't kill me!" she screamed, grabbing at Tia's feet.

"Get off me, bitch!" Tia kicked her in the face and pulled a straight razor from her pocket. "You ain't shit." Tia sliced Green Eyes across the face.

Green Eyes grabbed her bloody face and screamed in pain.

"You don't know what family is!" Tia then sliced her throat in one quick slash and watched her squirm like a cut pig on the floor, holding her throat. "Snake-ass bitch." Tia stood over Green Eyes and watched her die, slowly.

As Tia left the hotel room she wiped tears from her eyes. It hurt her to the heart to kill Green Eyes. She'd thought it would be nothing considering what had gone down. But now that it was done Tia felt empty and soulless as she left her own flesh and blood dead on the hotel floor.

Chapter 12

The hospital stay was painful and scary for Vida. She didn't regain consciousness for almost two weeks and stayed in critical condition for another two weeks after that. Her memories of the shooting were clear. Ms. Green stayed by Vida's side every step of the way.

The police were all over her as soon as she was well enough to talk. They hounded her about murders and Tec's whereabouts. They even threatened to charge her with being an accessory to murder. Vida didn't break. Pissed off that she swore she didn't know a damn thing, the police charged Vida with possession of the gun she shot Kareem with. They also charged her with assault with intent to kill. However, both charges were juvenile charges. Plus, no one was alive to testify that Vida shot Kareem; considering the fact that Daddieo wouldn't take the stand, and he refused to answer any questions the detectives asked him.

Vida went home with her grandmother and rested and recovered for two months under Ms. Green's care. Daddieo had recovered as well; he spent a lot of time with Vida at her grandmother's. The whole situation had shaken him up pretty bad. All the girls and Tec stayed by Vida's side as well—when they weren't up to their old tricks. Daddieo was pressing Vida to leave the area with him once he finished school later on in the year. He wanted to take her to New York with him. Vida wasn't exactly excited about the idea; she told him she would think about it though. Although Vida was now sixteen, she felt thirty-six. Coming face-to-face with death had aged her. Life was short and serious; she'd had plenty of time to think about life while recovering.

"Vida," Ms. Green said, walking into Vida's bedroom, "I'm goin' to church. I'll see you when I get back, okay?"

"Okay."

Vida got up and got in the shower. She looked at her shapely body as she soaped up under the hot water. The bullet wounds had left painful memories. Looking at her scars, Vida frowned in disgust. *These scars are anything but sexy,* she thought. There was a long scar under her right breast where her lung had been removed. Five bullet wounds traced their way up her side and across the top of her breast. She thanked God for blessing her with another chance at life; she wanted more out of life. Something had to give.

Vida got dressed and called Daddieo over so they could go out to eat. It was their day to hang out all day, just the two of them. Daddieo scooped her and they were on their way.

"Where we goin'?" Vida sat in the passenger seat looking out the window as they headed west on the interstate.

"We goin' out to have some fun. I gotta get you away from D.C. more often." Daddieo popped in a Luther Vandross CD.

"Why is that?" She smiled.

"Come on now." He cut his eyes at her. "You too hood. I gotta show you some other things, boo."

"Is that right?"

"Yeah."

They drove for a few hours laughing and joking, just enjoying life. They ended up in West Virginia, where they had dinner and went horseback riding. Vida was scared to get on one of the big horses by herself so Daddieo put her on the back of his, and they took off into the woods. Vida screamed for him to slow down, but he paid her no attention. The woods opened up into a beautiful and green country-side. Even in the cool evening air of May it was still somewhat chilly as the sun began to set. Daddieo came to a stop overlooking a small waterfall and looked over his shoulder at Vida.

"It feels like we are out in the middle of nowhere, don't it?' he asked.

"We are." She laughed, holding on to him tightly. "You better get us back to the car before it gets dark."

Daddieo guided the horse slowly back into the woods. "It don't matter, we spendin' the night up here in the mountains."

"You must be crazy," Vida said as they headed up a hill and across a small creek. "I ain't stayin' up here in no damn mountains. They might got ax murders up here in these damn woods."

Daddieo laughed. "After all we been through together I know you ain't scared to spend a little time in the woods wit' me."

Vida could see wooden cabins ahead with smoke coming out of the chimneys and understood what Daddieo was up to. "Oh yeah... this how it's goin' down?"

Daddieo put the horse in the barn behind the cabin and took Vida inside. The cabin was old school, but had all the modern things that would be in a Marriott suite. Vida lay on the huge bed as Daddieo started a fire to warm the place up. He then went into the kitchen and came back with some Remy Martin VSOP and two glasses.

"This big boy shit right here." Vida was under the covers flicking the channels with the remote. *Coming to America* was just coming on Showtime. "We can get our laugh on, too."

"We can do whatever you want to do. The world is yours."

"How you get hip to this spot?"

"Tonio be comin' down here all the time to get away from New York."

Vida sipped her Remy. "I like it up here." They kicked back and watched the movie. As the fireplace warmed up they got comfortable. About an hour into the movie there was a knock at the door. Daddieo and Vida gave each other a puzzled look. No one knew where they were.

"Who is it?" Daddieo asked, as he went to see who was at the door.

"Tonio, nigga, open the door."

Daddieo let him in and gave him a hug. "What's up? I ain't know you was goin' to be out here."

"Yeah, I wanted to chill for minute," Tonio said looking at Vida. "What's up, Vee?" He liked her.

"Chillin', what's up wit' you?" Vida asked.

"Laid back," Tonio replied.

Tonio and Daddieo stepped out onto the porch and lit a blunt. "Who you got down here wit' you?" Daddieo asked.

Tonio smiled. "I got that lil' video broad wit' me." He had been fucking No Draws for almost a month—Samara had no idea what was going down.

Daddieo laughed. "Is she vicious as they say she is?"

"I ain't never met a bitch like her, son. She do anything."

"Damn." Daddieo's curiosity was getting to him.

"Don't even think about it. Vida fire that pistol," Tonio joked. They both laughed.

"I'll catch you later." Daddieo went back inside the cabin. Vida wasn't in the bed. The shower was running so he made his way in there. The bathroom was steamed up. Taking off his clothes while looking at Vida's sexy body under the water, Daddieo said, "I thought you ran off on me."

"I was waitin' for you." Vida's hair was soaked and her body was covered with soap.

"You don't have to wait no more." He got in the shower with her. Hugging and kissing her under the water, he said, "What did you have in mind?"

"A lot of things."

She rubbed and stroked his manhood, then turned around and let the water run in her face for a second while he rubbed her breast. She could feel him growing long and hard. Daddieo bent her over as the hot water came down on them. Vida grabbed the base of the tub as she felt him slide inside of her nice and deep, from the back.

"Aaaahhh," she moaned as he slow stroked her pussy just the way she loved it. With every stroke she got wetter. No matter how many times he filled her insides it always seemed to get better with every satisfying stroke. She began to moan and push herself back at him while he began to speed up and pull her to him, making their bodies slap together. "I'm cummin', aaaahhhh," she began to moan and shake as she bit her bottom lip.

Daddieo worked her nice and good for a while in the shower. They then made their way to the bed, soaking wet, where they started round two. Vida got on top and rode him; making love to him, taking him deep inside her while looking in his eyes.

"You like that?" she asked.

"Yeah, I love it, Vee. Ride this dick for me." He had his hands around her waist, digging up into her guts. She began to move around on him and ended up turning all the way around while he was still inside her. Her back was facing him while she was riding him.

When they had no more energy it was 5:47 A.M. They passed out in each other's arms.

"All Eyez on Me" was playing inside the white Toyota Solara that sat on the corner of G Street Southeast. Behind the dark tinted windows, Ice and Tia were scheming. Tec had started snatching niggaz and Ice and Tia were his partners in crime. Over the last few months they had snatched a number of money makers around the area. They quickly learned that some niggaz were all looks and no cake. Some of the dudes they snatched drove nice cars, wore expensive jewelry and clothes, but in the end they only had $40, 000 to $50,000 to trade for their lives. Tec, Tia and Ice only had to kill one dude in the process, and he wouldn't have taken a bullet if he didn't try to take Tia's gun.

"That's her gettin' in the car," Tia said.

"I got her." Ice began to follow the green BMW 740iL

Tec had them on a mission to snatch a nigga's baby's mother. The girls followed the BMW all the way out to Briggs Chaney, Maryland, where it pulled into a dark apartment complex.

Tia checked her Glock, slid on her ski mask and got out. Walking up on the female as she got out of the BMW, Tia grabbed her by the hair and put the Glock to her head. "If you scream I'ma put a bullet in your head," Tia hissed, as she forced the female into the trunk of the Toyota. "Let's go," Tia said, as she jumped back inside. Ice pulled off.

A little over two hours later, the kidnapped female found herself blindfolded in a dirty boiler room somewhere. She had no idea where she was, all she knew was that the ride from where she was snatched to where she was now was a long one. She had cried every step of the way and had never been so afraid in her twenty-three year of life. With a .45 automatic placed to her head, a phone was held to her ear.

"Tell 'em we want two hundred fifty Gs or you gon' be used for target practice," Ice said.

"Baby, are you okay?" Smitty asked with urgency.

"Smitty!" his baby's mother sobbed loudly. "They got a gun to my head. They say they gon' kill me if you don't give them $250,000. Please! Do what they say! Please!"

Ice snatched the phone away. "You understand what's at stake, right?"

"Who the hell is this?!" Smitty was enraged and afraid at the same time. He loved his baby's mother.

"Don't ask me no fuckin' questions! Just get that money together within the next hour, or Im'a blow this bitch's brains out!" Ice hung up.

An hour later Tec and Tia were in Tec's station wagon headed toward Rock Creek Park. Tec was on the cell phone with Smitty. "You got the money?"

"Yeah, but how do I know you won't kill her anyway?" asked Smitty.

"You don't. But if I wanted to kill her she'd be dead. Now check this out…" Tec gave Smitty detailed directions to Rock Creek Park in Northwest and told him to come alone to the big parking lot off of 16th Street, drop the money off and leave. "Got that?" Tec asked.

"Yeah, man. Just don't hurt my peoples, please."

"Don't trip. Just make sure you come alone or all bets are off and you'll be pickin' out a box for your baby's mother. Feel me?"

"When will I get her back?"

"When I get the money." Tec hung up.

Sitting across the street from Rock Creek Park on a dark side street lined with parked cars, trees and nice homes, Tec and Tia watched the parking lot. It was dark and empty. Any car that showed up had to have a good reason to be in the park at 11:00 P.M.

"If all goes well tonight we should be able to chill for a second," Tec said, rubbing the trigger of his .40 caliber.

He had big plans for the apartment complex that he and the girls lived in on Walker Mill Road, in Capitol Heights, Maryland. Ice and Tia had already thrown the pussy on a few dudes that sold coke a few buildings down from theirs. The girls knew who was who and how much weight they were buying. They also knew who was supplying the weight. Tec wasn't into hustling drugs anymore—he swore he would take what he wanted from now on—but he knew that the girls could hustle well so he planned to set up shop for them. He didn't care whose toes got stepped on in the process.

"You sure y'all can hold it down?" joked Tec, looking at the sexy killer beside him. He was now fucking her and Ice exclusively. What more could he ask for? In them he had good pussy and loyal comrades. He could care less about chasing any other bitches, unless it was Vida. But that was another story.

"Nigga, you trippin'." Tia smiled, looking down at the Glock in her hand. "Me and Ice got this covered. That spot is gon' be ours. You already know Vida a hustler by birth, it's in her blood. She gon' want in on it too."

"She family, it ain't in the talk, you know that. I just been lettin' her chill. I still feel fucked up about her gettin' shot." Tec was tapping his fingers on the wheel. His mind drifted to the Machiavelli book Ice had hipped him to. He had the whole crew reading it. "So when you front the coke to them niggaz and they takin' too long wit' that money, how you gon' carry shit?" he asked, watching the parking lot intently.

Tia knew he was testing her like he often did with Ice. She enjoyed when he tested her; loving the attention. "It's already understood. I done laid law wit' 'em, they know that the first fuck is on me, the second one is on them. But wit' all things, there's laws and force."

"That's right, baby girl." Tec rubbed her thick thigh; she was looking phat as shit in her tight Polo jeans. "So when fightin' wit' law or force what's natural?"

"Law is natural to men, but force is natural to beast. Like you always say, law don't be respected in these streets unless a nigga back it up wit' force and unleash the beast." Tia patted her Glock.

"That's right." Tec smiled just as he saw the headlights of a car enter the parking lot. "So when y'all set that work out I want y'all to make good use of the beast and the woman in you.

The allegory they were building on taught them to act according to the nature of beast and man, otherwise they would never survive in the streets, where at times one is forced to act a certain way. Nature gave many lessons in the fox and the lion. The lion is a feared killer, but is defenseless against certain tricks and traps. The fox is sagacious and shrewd, but defenseless against wolves. Therefore, one must learn to recognize tricks and traps like the fox, and kill off wolves like the lion.

Right now, we gotta keep our eyes open like the fox." Tec called Smitty on the cell phone and said, "Sit the money outside the car and pull off. Don't play no games." Tec hung up and watched Smitty do as he was told.

Driving into the thick woods of Rock Creek Park so no one could see what was going on, Tec parked and left Tia in the car as he jogged up a hill through the woods with his .40 in hand. He came out of the woods on the back side of the parking lot. Before stepping out into the open Tec carefully looked around, making sure everything was clear. He then snatched the heavy gym bag full of money. It felt like two hundred fifty million dollars instead of 250 G's. Quickly, Tec made his way back to the car.

Tec threw the money in the back seat and headed north through the dark and winding roads of Rock Creek Park. He and Tia went back to the apartment and counted the money. It was all there. Tec called Ice and told her what to do. Thirty minutes later he called Smitty and told him where to find his baby's mother. She was alive and well in the trunk of a stolen car at a gas station off Randolph Road, not far from where she'd been held captive.

Days later, Vida was sitting on the black leather sofa with Tec in the three bedroom apartment they all shared. The apartment was now laid out. Tec and the girls had put thousands of dollars into the spot; it was plush now. The $250,000 from the kidnapping had been broken down four ways. Even though Vida didn't do anything, she still got $62,000 to do with as she pleased. Now Tec was throwing the drug move her way. "Is you down?" Tec asked, smoking a blunt with his feet up on the coffee table while watching *GoodFellas* on the 60 inch TV. By the way he carried things one would never think he was still wanted for murder. "I got the shit all mapped out if you want in."

Vida really didn't want to mess with the coke move. Weed was far less stressful. "Check this out." She took the blunt. "Why don't we do this?" She suggested that they spread their wings. She could push weed, Tia could push the coke and Ice could push boat—since PCP was on the rise again. They had the muscle to set up shop out Maryland and around Montana Avenue. Since Kareem and his crew were gone, Tec and the girls could get things moving again around the way with no problems.

"I like that," Tec said. "I don't want y'all on front street though... I want y'all to get one of them young niggaz and make 'em your front man, cool?"

"Cool, I feel you on that. But what you gon' do about a connect? Who we gon' fuck wit'?" Vida asked just as Ice, Tia and Samara walked through the door with a bunch of shopping bags. Everybody spoke; it was all love.

Tia, Ice and Samara went in the back and put their clothes up. They could tell that Vida and Tec were talking business so they didn't want to interrupt them.

"Let me check a few traps," Tec said.

Over the next two weeks Tec stepped to a few dudes that were moving weight in the D.C. area, but they weren't trying to fuck with him. His reputation had dudes afraid to deal with him. The streets were talking. Tec was now seen as cruddy, even a snake that had killed his own homies. He didn't give a damn, his attitude was fuck it. It was more than one way to skin a cat.

In Ice's convertible Chrysler Sebring on I-95, Ice and Tec talked about finding a good connect so they could put their plan into effect. They had Tupac pumping through the system on their way back from buying some guns in North Carolina. Ice said, "Why don't you holla at the dude Tonio? He said he would fuck wit' you."

"Yeah, I'm hip. I was thinkin' the same thing." Tec was looking out the window. The day was clear and warm, without a cloud in the sky. Tec was still messed up about dudes not wanting to deal with him. His intentions were to take them all for bad. "I got a better idea, I'ma holla at Tonio, only because I told y'all we could chill out for a minute, but I'ma start takin' all these sucka-ass niggaz heavy. Since they think I'm cruddy, I'ma show 'em what cruddy is."

Days later, Tec was in New York riding shotgun in Tonio's silver Porsche 993 Cabriolet, smoking weed with him while they talked about doing business together. Nas' "If I Ruled the World" played as they cruised down Myrtle Avenue. Tonio said, "I done dealt with D.C. cats before. I know how y'all niggaz do things." He puffed on the blunt and continued. "I ain't got no problem fucking with you, but I don't want no shit behind fucking with you."

Who the fuck this nigga think he talking to? Tec thought. "You ain't got to worry about no shit like that. I ain't never crossed a nigga that looked out for me." After a little more thought Tec understood Tonio's concern. After all, D.C. niggaz weren't the easiest niggaz to deal with if they didn't really fuck with a nigga. "I'ma keep it up and up wit' you, all good money," Tec said.

A gold Rolex hung from Tonio's wrist as he pushed the car with one hand on the wheel. He wasn't scared to deal with Tec. As far as he was concerned, if Tec played games he was playing with his own life. Tonio smiled. "You know what? Tec, keep your money. I'ma give you two bricks, it's yours. I want to see what you do, since you never sold weight."

Tec laughed and leaned back in the passenger seat. "That's bird feedin' a nigga. I got sixty G's to spend."

"It's not bird feeding you. It's a gift, an offer of friendship. You can't have hang-ups. It's all about making money. We gon' stop talking business and just hang out for a while. When you get back home I'll have my man down there send you the coke up from B-more. Spread your wings; let me see what you made of."

"Bet." Tec gave Tonio five.

Tec returned to Capitol Heights and met up with Tonio's B-more man and got two bricks of powder. The plan was taking shape. Tia knew how to cook—Green Eyes had taught her—so Tec put her to work on the stove. After the coke was rocked up, Tec, Ice and Tia sat at the dining room table weighing and bagging up 8-balls, quarters, half-ounces and ounces.

"Time to get this money," Tec said. He then looked at Tia and said, "We gon' need another apartment to keep this shit in. Get wit' Vida and get another apartment."

"I got you." Tia stood up in her tight booty shorts and gray Polo T-shirt. "Let me holla at the dude Zoe first."

"Bet." Tec looked at his watch. "I'm 'bout to make a run real quick, I'll catch y'all when I get back." He slid his chrome .40 caliber Ruger in his waistband and hit the door.

Outside it was just getting dark but it was still real warm. Tia walked a few buildings down where there was a small crowd of dudes in their late teens and early twenties. They were hanging around a blue, 1996 Ford Explorer that had Tupac blasting out the speakers. The truck belonged to a dude by the name of Motor who was supposed to be "The Man" in the area. Motor was from D.C. but got his money out Maryland selling weight—bullshit weight—mostly out Capitol Heights and Landover. As Tia walked up switching, looking like a young Mariah Carey, all eyes were on her. All the niggaz in the complex were chasing her, but as Tec had instructed, she was only giving Zoe some play now.

"Zoe," Tia called out.

"What's up, Tee?" Zoe said as he walked over.

"Let me holla at you." They walked over to Zoe's Nissan 300ZX Turbo and got inside.

Zoe was eighteen years old with a real street look to him. He looked a lot like Prodigy of the rap duo Mobb Deep. Zoe was also moving up in the drug game. "What's up, Tee?" He rubbed her soft thigh, loving the way her smooth skin felt.

"Remember what I was tellin' you about last night?"

Zoe laughed. "Last night all I could think about was what you was doin' to me."

"For real, I'm serious. I got that coke. You gon' fuck wit' me or what?"

"You was serious?"

"You think I'm playin' games? I ain't bullshittin'," Tia said.

"As a matter of fact, Motor ain't on right now. I need a quarter key."

"I got that right now. You got the money?"

"Come on, boo, you know that."

"I'll be right back," said Tia.

Tia went back to the apartment and returned with a quarter key inside a Subway bag. Zoe gave her $4,500 and sealed the deal; they were in business. It was all a matter of time now. Tia would slowly cut Motor out the picture. After all, Motor sold quarter keys for $5,500; word would spread. Tia already had it understood that Zoe was to bring no one to her; if anything, he could bring her money only.

A little after 1:00 A.M., Tec walked in the apartment carrying a green duffel bag. Ice, Vida and Tia were on the sofa chilling, watching *The Usual Suspects* while sipping Remy.

"I thought you was comin' right back," Tia said.

"Me too," Tec said, as he dumped the contents of the duffel bag on the coffee table. Stacks and stacks of cash poured out along with five tightly wrapped bricks of powder coke. "It took me longer than I thought."

"Got damn, boy!" Ice began inspected the loot. "How much money is this?"

"I don't know. Why don't y'all count it for me?" Tec smiled and headed for the bathroom.

The girls gave each other puzzled looks and began counting the bank. It came up to $150,000.

In the shower enjoying the hot water, Tec wondered how and when his ways would catch up with him. *A nigga's ways always catch up with him,* he thought. *Fuck it.* If he was to die young he would die a paid muthafucker with his gun smoking. Tonight he'd killed two birds with one stone. One of the dudes that wouldn't sell him weight became his victim. Tec snatched the joker, duct taped him, robbed him for everything he had and left him murdered in his Fort Washington home. The victim was also the middleman between Motor and his coke connect; now Tia could make Motor come to her for his weight. Shit was falling into place.

Chapter 13

amara was more than thirty thousand feet in the air looking out the window down at the Grand Canyon. She really couldn't see anything, it was too dark. The plane had been in the air for hours. A dude she'd met from Roanoke, Virginia by the name of Black Top was taking her to Vegas with him for a few days. It was a first for her and she was excited.

Samara had met Black Top a few weeks ago at a Frankie Beverly show in D.C. They'd hooked up a few times since then and every time they hooked up she treated Black Top real good. He was the owner of a few Foot Locker stores in Roanoke, but his real money was from the drug trade.

A short while later their plane had safely touched down in Las Vegas. They mixed in with the crowd of people retrieving their luggage and grabbed their Louis Vuitton luggage. At the rental car company, Black Top snatched up a silver Jaguar. They hit the road and drove into Vegas, taking in the bright lights of the city of sin. Passing many high priced hotels, they checked into the MGM Grand. Their suite was plush, as if laid out for royalty. Samara was blown away, but played it cool. Black Top went to the fully stocked bar and grabbed an over priced bottle of Dom Perignon 1982. They sat back on the sofa and drank for a while.

"What's up for the night, Black?" Samara asked. She had her shoes off and was feeling real loose from the Dom P.

"I'ma take my ass to sleep tonight," Black Top said yawning.

"Come on, let's go out, Black." She kissed his face.

"You trippin'." He laughed.

"I know what will give you some energy."

Hell Razor Honeys

Samara unbuckled his black Versace jeans and pulled out his manhood. She began to lick it and kiss it. He put a hand on the back of her head and encouraged her to handle her business. Going to work, Samara looked up into his eyes from her position on her knees between his legs and got vicious. She was sucking the life out of him, deep-throating him and rubbing his dick all over her face. After he came all over her face they were just getting started. Samara knew how to heat things up. They came out of their clothes and moved to the bed.

"Roll me some smoke real quick," Black Top said, lying on his back.

Samara did as he asked. He watched her ass shake with every step she took. It made him hard again. Samara reminded him of Toni Braxton, with the short hairstyle and all. Samara returned with a lit Backwood and sat beside Black Top. She stroked his dick with her soft hand as they puffed. When they were done smoking and were high as a kite, Samara got on top of him and ripped open a condom with her mouth and rolled it down his dick with her mouth as well. With her hand she put him inside of her tight wetness and filled herself with satisfaction.

"Aaaaahhhh," she moaned, as she began to ride him slowly with her hands on his chest. "Ooooww… fuck me!" She was loving it and ready to fuck all night long. "Ssss… mmmmm." As they got into the mix and began to sweat and grab at each other Samara began to fuck wildly, making sounds like a porno star. "I'm cummin'! I'm cummin'!" She was slamming her pussy all the way down on him. They went on and on until they had no more energy. Samara made sure she always brought her A-game.

The next day Black Top met with a L.A. dude that he was doing business with and then took Samara up to Lake Tahoe for the day. It was hot and sunny and people were everywhere, tanning on the beach, swimming, boating and water-skiing. Black Top and Samara went water-skiing and then spent a few hours chilling, just laying out on the sand on thick beach towels. As the day turned to evening they headed back to Vegas.

People from all walks of life were on the crowded casino floor betting small and big. Samara got $2,000 from Black Top and went to the crap table while he tried his luck at the card table. In less than an hour Samara had lost all her chips and went back to Black Top for more money.

"Here you go." Black Top hit her off with $2,500 worth of chips. He was winning big at the poker table. "Holla back at me in a little while, you distractin' me, Sam."

Samara went back to the crap table and got a hot hand. As time went on she turned $2,500 into $10,000. People around the table were betting with her as she rolled the big dice.

"Damn, baby girl, you got a hot hand, huh?" a dude whispered in Samara's ear as she won another big pot of chips.

She looked over her shoulder and saw Black Top in his black Versace sweatsuit with his diamond encrusted Rolex dangling loosely on his wrist. "I'm up ten Gs and some. Trust me, nigga." Samara smiled.

"I see." Black Top started betting on her and together they raked in piles of chips.

When they'd had enough of the gambling they went back to their suite and fucked the night away on a pile of cash, for the hell of it.

Inside the same hotel, No Draws was in a suite with Tonio and two other New Yorkers that had met up with him in Vegas to meet the same L.A. dude Black Top was in town to see. Tonio brought No Draws along for the fun of it. There was an orgy going on in Tonio's suite. No Draws was taking on all three men with no problem at all. She was giving one head, while another hit her from the back Tonio had the video camera out while he waited his turn. No Draws was so vicious that she would wink at the camera from time to time.

The next day Samara was coming back from the Gucci shop with thousands of dollars worth of gear. She walked through the crowded lobby with a bellman in tow rolling the Gucci bags along on a cart. Samara stopped dead in her tracks. "I know this bitch ain't wit' Tonio!" she said out loud.

"Is there a problem, ma'am?" the bellman asked.

Samara paid him no attention; she stepped straight to No Draws and Tonio. "It's like that, huh? Y'all fuckin' behind my back, huh?"

Tonio and No Draws were busted.

"Sam—"

"Sam my ass," Samara hissed and punched No Draws in the face.

The two girls locked ass and went at it ghetto style right in the lobby of the MGM Grand. People stopped what they were doing to watch while Tonio and security tried to pull the two girls apart as they pulled each other's hair; swinging, kicking and cursing.

"Bitch, I'ma kill your dirty ass!" Samara shouted, as the police dragged her and No Draws off.

The girls weren't arrested, but they were put out of the hotel and drew a lot of unwanted attention to the dudes that had brought them to Vegas.

Back in D.C., a month passed with no one seeing No Draws. Samara told the girls how No Draws had crossed her with Tonio; the girls saw it as a snake move. Tia wanted to beat No Draws' ass. All the girls agreed that they weren't dealing with No Draws anymore.

Speaking of No Draws, a Nas video came on BET while Vida and Tia sat in the apartment counting money. "Look at that freak-ass bitch," Tia said. "She bet' not let me catch her ass."

Vida laughed as she put a rubber band around a stack of money and sat it in a Nike shoe box on the floor. "You fired up about that

Tonio shit, huh?"

Before Tia could say anything the front door was kicked in with a loud bang. Two masked gunmen rushed inside. The girls had no time to react, they were slammed facedown on the carpet, fearing for their lives and shaking nervously.

"Watch these bitches," one of the gunmen said to his partner, as he grabbed the money filled shoebox. "If they move blast they ass." He then went into the bedroom and grabbed two pillowcases. Returning, he put the cash inside a pillowcase. "I'ma check the place."

Laying on the floor at gunpoint made every second seem like an hour for Vida and Tia. They knew the robbers were going to kill them after they got what they came for. All Vida could think about was her grandmother and how Daddieo wanted to take her away from the world in which she lived. Tia had her eyes closed, bracing herself for the gunfire that was to come. She secretly prayed for God to save her and Vida. She swore she would change her life if she made it through the night with her life. Vida began to wonder how the robbers knew where the stash house was. The apartment was a nice ways away from D.C.—it was in Mitchellville, Maryland. Someone had to have followed one of the girls or Tec to the spot.

The gunman that was standing over the girls, looking at their phat asses and thick thighs in their tight blue jeans, began to have other thoughts. "You got somethin' on you?" He began to search the girls, feeling on their body parts. The girls assured him that they had nothing on them, but he still made them strip down to their bra and panties.

"What the fuck your dumb ass doin'?" The other gunman returned with ten bricks in a pillowcase. "We ain't come here for that shit!" He snatched Vida off the floor by her hair and jammed his pistol into her stomach with a sharp stab. "Open the safe, bitch!" he hissed as he threw his partner the pillowcase. He then dragged Vida to the back room and ordered her to open the safe. "Hurry the fuck up!" He was growing impatient; he had been in the apartment for more than ten minutes now.

With tears in her eyes, down on her knees inside the walk-in closet, Vida nervously tried to open the big safe. Her hands were shaking so bad that she messed up on the combination twice.

"I'm not playin' wit' you, bitch!" The gunman smacked Vida in the back of the head with the pistol.

"Oww... I'm trying, muthafucka!" she yelled. A few seconds later she finally got the safe open.

"Lay on the floor, bitch!" the gunman barked. He grabbed another pillowcase and emptied the safe of close to $450,000. He then called his partner and told him to bring Tia into the bedroom, which his partner did. "Tie these bitches up."

While tying the girls up the other gunman said, "Let's fuck these lil' bitches before we kill 'em."

"Shut the fuck up! Dumb-ass nigga, we got what we came for."

After the girls were tied up with telephone cords the gunman that was calling the shots said, "Let's roll." The gunmen left, leaving the girls unharmed, but scared to death.

Thirty minutes after the gunmen had gotten away with everything the crew had hustled up over the last few months, Vida and Tia untied themselves.

"You okay, Tee?" Vida hugged Tia like it was the last time she would ever see her.

"Yeah, I'm okay."

They were both still visibly shaken up and looked like they had seen a ghost as they stood in the ransacked bedroom in their underclothes. After they calmed down they beeped Tec, who was out shopping with Ice at Tysons Corner Center.

Tec and Ice rushed to the stash house, balling on the highway. When they got to the apartment Vida and Tia put them on point. Tec was in a murderous rage, even though he kept calm. He was relieved that Vida and Tia were still alive; they meant the world to him. The crew sat around trying to figure out who had hit them for everything. Whoever hit them had done their homework.

Looking at the girls, Tec said, "Get your most important shit. We through wit' this spot. I'll come back tomorrow and get everything else."

The next day Vida was hanging out with Daddieo, who was now finished with school and ready to go back to New York once he wrapped up his business plans in the area. He was still pressing Vida to go with him to New York, but she was playing hardball. She didn't want to leave her crew behind, they were her family. She also had to look after her grandmother.

Daddieo and Vida went to lunch at Crisfield and then hit the movies at City Place Mall and caught *Set It Off*. Daddieo noticed that Vida was perplexed the entire time. Even though she tried to enjoy spending time with him, she was still messed up about the robbery. After the movie they walked out into the cold winter night and found that it was snowing. They jumped inside Daddieo's car and headed for Ms. Green's apartment. On the beltway with the radio on WPGC, Daddieo asked Vida what was on her mind.

"I'm okay, why you ask me that?" Vida wondered if Daddieo somehow knew what she had been through yesterday. She didn't want to tell him about the robbery.

"I know you. I know when somethin' is wrong wit' you. What's up?" Daddieo had to press her for a while, but Vida ended up telling him what was up. "See what I'm sayin'? That's why I want you to go up top wit' me. You gon' get yourself killed down here."

"I can get killed in New York."

"Not where I want to take you."

"Daddieo..." She looked him in the eyes. "I love you, but this is home for me. This is where my heart is. I can't leave it all behind. I'm sorry."

They discussed the situation all the way to Ms. Green's, but Vida had her mind made up. Daddieo was messed up about it, but respected it.

A week passed and there were still no leads on who robbed the stash house. Tec was fucked up and had no one to blame for the loss. He owed Tonio $180,000 and had no way to pay him. In any other situation Tec would have said fuck a nigga, but Tonio had played fair with him.

Tec decided to take a trip up I-95 to holla at Tonio in person. The girls went along as well. They all checked into the Marriott. While Tec when to meet Tonio at the Shark Bar, the girls put their old credit card move into effect and attacked Gucci, Bloomingdale's and Macy's. They were broke, but they damn sure would go home with enough top-of-the-line gear to make a few dollars.

At the Shark Bar, Tonio and Tec were talking business. Although Tonio heard Tec out, he thought that Tec was starting the typical D.C. bullshit. On top of that, a notorious D.C. hustler that was doing life in the Feds had just started snitching. Tonio's L.A. connect had been arrested; it was a three hundred kilo connect down the drain. Even if Tonio wanted to front Tec ten more bricks, now wasn't the time.

"Look here," Tonio said. "Shit fucked up on my end right now. I couldn't extend my hand if I wanted to. I understand your situation so I'ma give you some time to pay me back. Whenever I get my shit back in order I'll holla at you. Cool?"

Tec felt as though Tonio was cutting him off and just wasn't man enough to tell him so. "I feel you. I'll be in touch as soon as I can." Tec gave Tonio a pound and left. *If this nigga think he gettin' paid he a damn fool,* Tec thought as he left the Shark Bar.

Back at the hotel with the girls, Tec told them that Tonio wasn't fucking with him and why. He also told them what he thought about the whole situation. "I know the nigga think I'm playin' games wit' his money."

"So what we gon' do about the money we owe the nigga?" Tia asked, trying on new clothes.

"We ain't payin' that nigga shit. I done played fair wit' his punk-ass and he gon' cut a nigga off when a nigga take a fall. Fuck that nigga!" Tec was looking out the window of the 41st floor, taking in the view of the New York City skyline.

"He might be fucked up for real." Vida didn't want Tec and Tonio to fall out over money. Although she could care less about Tonio, he was still Daddieo's brother.

Tec looked over his shoulder with a frown on his face. "What? You takin' sides because of that soft ass nigga Daddieo… the same nigga that was the reason you got shot."

"I ain't takin' no muthafuckin' sides, nigga," Vida snapped. Tec's statement didn't sit well with her. "I was just lookin' at both sides of the coin. You can talk that crazy shit to somebody else. You know muthafuckin' well what side I'm on; win, lose or draw."

"She right, Tec. You dead wrong questioning her. You know where Vida stand," Ice said. She was closer to Vida than anyone else in the crew. Vida had shown her the most love from jump street. Ice had to earn her keep with everyone else. It was no secret.

Tec studied every face in the room. He was surrounded by the only family he'd ever known. Nothing was supposed to come between them. He was so fucked up about the loss they'd taken that he was snapping out of anger.

"Come on, y'all. This ain't for us." Tia stood in the middle of the room with a look of disgust on her face. "We all we got."

"You right," Tec said. He then looked at Vida and said, "My bad, Vee, I ain't mean that; we family."

"Don't trip. I know you fucked up about the money and shit, but we can always get that back. I'm just sayin' the bamma Tonio might be fucked up for real. Yeah, he Daddieo's brother and I don't want us to get into no shit wit' 'em, but right or wrong I'm wit' the home team. You know that, slim."

Tec smiled. "That's why I fucks wit' y'all bitches so tough, y'all real niggaz."

"If you just don't want to pay the nigga fuck 'em, but he might be tellin' the truth," Vida said.

"What you think we should do?" Tec asked Vida.

"That bullshit ain't nothin', let's pay the nigga what we owe him. If he true to his word and he really fucked up when he get back on he'll look out for us," Vida said.

"How we supposed to get the $180,000 we own him?" Tec asked, already knowing what had to be done.

"We get money the fast way,' Tia rapped, "the ski mask way, wit' the ransom note." The whole crew burst out laughing. It was lock and load time.

Hell Razor Honeys

Chapter 14

Tupac's "No More Pain" was playing inside the green Chevy Impala with light tints as it cruised along the beltway in light traffic just after 8:30 P.M. About four car lengths ahead was a milk-white Isuzu Rodeo. Ice was in the passenger seat, looking good as always. A dude by the name of Ralph was behind the wheel. Ralph looked like Usher with a few extra pounds and a little hair on his face. Ice had met him at a club called the East Side. Tec had done his homework on the dude and put Ice on him.

Weed smoke filled the Rodeo as Ice took Ralph's attention off the road behind him. He seemed to watch his back like a wanted man. Ice didn't want him to pay attention to the green Impala that was trailing them so she undid his pants and pulled out his manhood while looking up into his eyes. "Let me get a taste of this big dick. I can't wait 'til we get to the hotel."

"Do your thing." Ralph looked down at the vicious white girl that seemed eager to suck him off.

Trailing the Rodeo in the Impala, Tec and Vida were stalking their prey. "When Ice get finished wit' 'em he gon' be high and tired as shit," Vida said, holding a chrome Ruger 9mm.

"No bullshit." Tec nodded.

A short while later Tec and Vida were parked in the back of a dark parking lot behind a Days Inn in Temple Hills, Maryland. Ice had been in the hotel with Ralph for almost an hour. While watching the hotel room carefully, Tec cut his eyes at Vida and said, "What would Daddieo say if he knew you was out on a caper wit' me?"

Vida laughed. "He messed up at me right now. I don't know what he would say."

"He still fucked up that you ain't go up New York wit' him?"

"Yeah… New York ain't home for me. I love slim, but home is where the heart is," Vida said.

Tec was pleased but kept his game face on. "I feel you on that."

Meanwhile, Tia was chilling with Zoe at his apartment. She was feeling him, and the sex was a plus as well. Tonight they were just sitting around watching HBO wile eating pizza and drinking ice-cold Pepsi; nothing much. Out of the blue, Tia said, "Where Motor been? I ain't seen big boy in a minute."

"I just seen 'em the other day around Brightseat Road. Why you ask me about him?"

"Just wondering." Tia bit into another slice of hot pizza with melting cheese dripping from it.

Tec and Vida waited for close to three hours for Ice and Ralph to leave the hotel and then followed them to an apartment in Capitol Heights that Ralph believed was where Ice lived. After that, Tec and Vida followed him to Hillcrest Heights where Tec got fed up. "Let's just snatch this nigga," he hissed.

"Come on," Vida said. "Let's get 'em."

They followed Ralph to a nice house on a dark street lined with cars and trees. Ralph pulled up and parked in a tight space in front of the house. Tec swiftly pulled up beside his truck, trapping Ralph in the parking space. High and drunk, it took Ralph too long to understand what was going down. In a flash, Tec was yanking Ralph out of the truck with a Beretta to his head. Ralph tried to struggle with Tec, who was wearing a ski mask with the hood of his Eddie Bauer over his head, but Vida hit him in the side twice with a small high-voltage stun-gun. It knocked Ralph out.

Vida and Tec got Ralph in the Impala and drove around back to the alley. They parked behind the house and dragged Ralph through the dark backyard. Tec got the keys to the house off of Ralph and opened the back door. Inside the plush house, Tec searched every room while Vida watched a handcuffed Ralph at gunpoint as he laid face-down on the living room floor.

"Ain't nobody else in here," Tec said as he came back downstairs. "Let's wake this nigga up." Tec went to the kitchen and returned with a jug of ice water that he poured down Ralph's pants, he then smacked the taste out of his mouth. Ralph slowly came around. "Where that money at, nigga?" Tec had his pistol to Ralph's temple.

It took Ralph a minute to understand what was going on. Then a painful fear set in. "Please don't kill me!"

"Where the fuckin' money at, nigga!" Tec hissed, cocking the hammer of his pistol with a loud click.

Vida was peeking out the front window. "A car just pulled up out front."

Panic set in when Ralph heard those words. His girl was supposed to be coming over.

"Some broad comin' up to the house." Vida was a little nervous; she didn't want murder to be involved. However, she knew that if anything went wrong Tec would kill everything moving.

"Man, look, I got money upstairs. You can have it all. Just don't hurt my girl, man," Ralph begged.

"Take care of that," Tec said to Vida.

Ralph's girl, Meeka, put her key in the door in a rush to get out of the cold. She opened the door and stepped into the dark house. Vida grabbed her by the coat and slung her to the floor. Meeka screamed out in fear. "What the hell is goin' on?" she screamed as Vida slammed the front door. Meeka's eyes adjusted to the darkness and she saw the masked gunmen.

"Just do what they say, Meeka," Ralph called out.

Tec tied Meeka up with the laces of her boots and told Vida to watch her while he took Ralph upstairs to the safe. Ralph opened the safe at gunpoint. Tec didn't see what he expected in the safe; it couldn't have been more than $50,000 inside. "What the fuck is that?" Tec smacked Ralph in the back of the head with his pistol.

"That's all I got. I swear to God." Ralph was on his knees looking over his shoulder at the masked gunman that held his life in his hands.

"Don't play wit' me. I know you got more than this small shit." Tec smacked him with the pistol again. Ralph cried and swore over and over again that he had nothing else. Tec dragged him back downstairs and threw him to the floor. Ralph was still crying and begging for his life.

Vida had a bad feeling in her gut. She knew shit was about to get ugly.

"Watch this!" Tec grabbed Meeka, who was crying hysterically. He put his pistol to her head. Looking at Ralph, he said, "I'ma ask you one more time and them I'ma blow this bitch brains out."

"Okay... okay... you got it, man," Ralph sobbed. He had to think of something. "That's all I got, for real. I swear to God. But my man got at least two hundred strong." He went on to explain. Tec was interested.

Tec and Vida marched Ralph and Meeka out to the Impala and stuffed them into the trunk. With the money from Ralph's safe, they headed for the next spot. On the beltway headed for Suitland, Maryland, Vida looked at Tec and said, "You know this wasn't the plan."

"Yeah, I know, but fuck it." Tec was checking the rearview. He knew he was pressing his luck with two kidnapping victims in the trunk.

"What we gon' do wit' them?" asked Vida.

Tec said nothing, just gave Vida a sideways glace as he tapped his fingers on the wheel.

They pulled up in front of an apartment building on Suitland Road. Tec really didn't have a plan, he was shooting from the hip but he didn't care. All he could think about was the cash. "Stay in the car and keep your eyes open. If anything don't look right blow the horn. If you have to, bail out," Tec said.

Tec got out and looked around the parking lot. Empty. He popped the trunk wearing no mask and snatched Ralph out. Taking off the handcuffs, he said, "If anything go wrong it's your ass." Tec walked Ralph to the building with his pistol jammed in his back. "Knock on the door," Tec ordered as they stood in the hallway. Ralph did as he was told.

Hell Razor Honeys

Boo, Ralph's man, looked through the peephole and opened the door without a second thought. "What's up—"

Tec shoved Ralph inside and pointed his pistol at Boo's head as he slammed the door. Tec took control in seconds. "Get the fuck on the floor!" he barked. Both Ralph and Boo fell to the floor, facedown. BOOM! BOOM! Tec shot Ralph in the back of the head twice—point-blank.

"Oh shit!" Boo screamed. "Oh shit! Man, what the fuck I do?!" Blood and brain matter was all over Boo's face. He felt warm piss all around his midsection.

Tec grabbed Boo by the collar and made him take him to the safe. "Open it up!" Tec hissed. As soon as Tec saw the money stacks he shot Boo in the head twice and watched his body slump to the floor. Tec emptied the safe into a brown trash bag and hurried back to the Impala. As he drove back to Capitol Heights with Meeka in the trunk he stared aimlessly at the road feeling cold and empty inside. Vida didn't have to ask what went down inside the apartment; she knew Tec. Tec pulled up in front of their building and they took the money inside. Tec still had to get rid of Meeka and the stolen Impala. He left Vida and Ice counting the money and went to take care of the girl.

As Tec drove toward Walker Mill Road he just shook his head. He knew that if there was really a God that he would burn in hell for the life he lived. *What the fuck,* he thought. For him, murder was just another day at the office. His time would come one day and he knew it. In fact, he was cool with it. As he cruised down the street with only a few cars out at the late hour, he lit a cigarette to calm his nerves. Stopping at a light, he could hear Meeka crying in the trunk. For a second he thought about letting her go, but she'd seen his face—she had to go.

As Tec turned onto Walker Mill Road a Prince George's County police car got behind the Impala. For the hell of it, the officer ran the plates. As the Impala made a left turn into an apartment complex the cop did the same. Before the read on the plates came back Tec stomped on the gas and sped through the back of the complex. He saw the flashing lights and heard the blaring sirens as he took the Impala up to ninety miles per hour, swerving dangerously around other cars. Sliding into a flying fishtail as he shot around a corner and down an empty street, Tec kept his eyes darting back and forth from

136 EYONE WILLIAMS

the road to the rearview mirror. There were now four police cars on his back.

"Shit!" Tec snapped. His heart pounded out of control. At top speed, all he could think about was the broad in the trunk. "I ain't going to jail," he declared to himself. He knew the broad would connect him to the double murder, plus he was wanted in connection with the Metro Club murders. He wasn't going out like that. Putting it down like the Dukes of Hazzard, Tec knew the stakes were high. He continued to hit corner after corner with P.G. police on his back like heat-seeking missiles. Tec always tried to duck P.G. police; they were known to shoot a nigga dead.

Tec felt a hard bump to his rear left side. The police were trying to force him off the road at close to one hundred miles per hour. Fed up, Tec rolled down his window and fired three shots at the police car. There was no turning back now. The police car that he fired at swerved dangerously and fell to the back of the pack. Struggling to keep control of the speeding Impala, Tec felt another strong bump to his right rear side. The Impala spun wildly out of control and flipped over three times before sliding off the road and into the woods. The sound of the crash was just as deadly as the results. Moments later the whole car exploded into flames as the police looked on. Tec and poor Meeka didn't stand a chance.

Chapter 15

The girls were crushed by Tec's death. It shook their whole foundation. Vida was hurt the most, by far. She and Tec came out the sandbox together. He was like blood. Once she'd seen the scenes of the burning Impala on the news the following day she knew why Tec had never returned to the apartment that night. Ice was crushed as well, she hadn't cried so hard since Tupac was murdered. Tia had lost many people that were close to her growing up in Barry Farms, but she still took Tec's death hard. Her pain was all inside— she didn't shed not one tear.

Ms. Green put together all the funeral arrangements. From the wake to the funeral, the only people to show up to pay their respects to Tec was Ms. Green, all the girls, Tec's pipehead mother and two homicide detectives. The homicide detectives asked a few questions, but didn't really sweat the girls.

Standing over Tec's gravesite a week after he was buried, Vida fought off the cold in the deserted cemetery. Her eyes had tears in them. She didn't know why she'd driven out to the cemetery; she'd just got behind the wheel of her car and ended up there. "I can't believe you gone, young." Vida wiped her eyes as she looked down at Tec's headstone. "No bullshit, I'm still fucked up about this shit."

Vida stood over the grave talking to Tec for thirty minutes. She'd lost a part of her soul when he died. When she was done she walked back to her car crying. It was time to move on and she knew it. "I'll never forget him," she told herself. She knew that Tec would want her to be strong and move on. He always told her that when he died he didn't want anyone to mourn him. "No more pain," Vida said out loud as she got in her car.

It was sunny and clear outside in the middle of January, 1997, as No Draws walked into the production company of Mario Miles III on Beverly Boulevard in Hollywood. Mario was up and coming in the film business. He had directed two box office killers and he had just turned thirty-two. His upcoming film was called *Around the Corner*. Jasmine Guy was starring as a successful New York defense attorney who becomes so caught up in her career that she loses her husband to a young gold-digger that lived around the corner from her and looked up to her as a child. Mario was banking on the film earning him the Hollywood respect that he felt he deserved as the force behind two box office hits within the last two years. He and No Draws met three weeks prior at Nora's Café; they had a few martinis and clicked well, but never got together again until now.

No Draws was escorted into Mario's office; he was expecting her. As she walked in Mario motioned for her to have a seat while he wrapped up a phone call. Mario was a smooth brown-skinned dude that looked somewhat like Mekhi Phifer. Mario sat behind his desk in a cream Ferragamo suit; black shirt, tie and pocket square by Ralph Lauren; and cream Ferragamo loafers. His black and gold Movado watch was cool, but his wedding ring was like something out of a Pharaoh's tomb with diamonds everywhere.

No Draws took it all in while she sat on the cream colored leather sofa in a black and silver Scaasi dress that showcased her sexy, light brown legs that were crossed. She had on a pair of black Prada open-toed heels that exposed her freshly pedicured toe nails. Her hair was done in a way that made it look flowing and lustrous as it fell down her shoulders.

"I understand all that, John, but I pulled in more than fifty million on the last project." Mario spun around in his high back office chair and faced the window, taking in the beautiful day. "I should be good for at least seventy million to do this film. I want you on board."

No Draws was where she wanted to be. She'd been in L.A. for close to a month now. She came to L.A. for a video shoot and now she was in the office of a man that was having a conversation about millions of dollars. *L.A. is the place to be, I'ma get mine,* she thought.

"Shelly," Mario walked over to No Draws and shook her hand. "Glad to finally get to talk business with you." He sat beside her.

"I feel the same. I really didn't think you'd call." No Draws smiled, turning on the charm.

"Let's talk about acting. I know what you can do in a video, but can you act a part?"

"I took actin' lessons in high school. I can do anything I put my mind to."

"My people tell me that you are good people. I'll take their word on that. I'm looking for a new face, so we can try a few things. I know you're from D.C., how long do you plan on staying out here?" Mario walked to the bar for some water.

"If I can find work I plan to stay out here for a while."

"Well, I can help you with that." Mario sipped his water. "Have you had lunch yet?"

"No, I was in a hurry to get here."

"Let's talk more over lunch."

Mario and No Draws rode in the back of Mario's Benz limo as they headed to P.F. Changs at the Beverly Center Mall. There, Mario introduced her to Ice Cube and Mack 10, who were leaving as they were being seated. No Draws felt like a star. This was the life she had always wanted to live. She didn't care whose bed it would lead her to. She was willing.

After the food arrived and they began to eat, Mario said, "I have a friend doing a small straight to video movie. I'm going to plug you in and see how you do. We'll take it from there. How's that sound?"

"Great." No Draws couldn't believe that Mario was all business and hadn't brought sex up. 'When do I meet your friend?"

"I'll give her your number. Expect a call from her within a week or two. In the meantime, feel free to call me if you need anything." Mario smiled and winked.

"Thank you so much. Is there any way I can repay you?"

"Don't worry about it."

No Draws had Mario drop her off at a condo in Santa Clarita, about thirty miles north of Beverly Hills. With no more than a handshake, No Draws thanked Mario again and stepped out of the limo. Once she got inside she took a hot shower and then had a glass of Dom Perignon as she lay in bed in a pink Victoria's Secret chemise that was damn near see-through. She couldn't wait for Nigel to return from the set of his new video shoot. He told her that he would take her places, and all he wanted in return was her loyalty. He couldn't get enough of her. At eighteen, No Draws had him sprung. All No Draws wanted was a shot at wealth and fame. She could sure get it in L.A.

Nigel arrived about an hour later in a black and gray Coogi sweater, blue Versace jeans, black Timberlands and the jewelry of a rap star. "I guess you heard me come in." Nigel was always turned on by her.

"I met your friend Mario today." No Draws spoke in a sultry tone as she fingered herself with her legs wide open, inviting Nigel. Every time she laid eyes on him he reminded her of Puff Daddy, who she thought was the sexiest man she'd ever met. "Mario said he gon' look out for me."

"I told you that." Nigel threw his keys on the nightstand and took a sip of the Dom Perignon from the bottle. "I guess you in a good mood, huh?"

"Yeah, I want you to fuck the shit out me." No Draws got on her hands and knees on the bed. "I want you to cum all over me." She licked her long tongue at him.

"Work ain't hard." Nigel got undressed. "I can do more than just that."

"What you waitin' for then?"

Smoothly, Nigel climbed in the bed and pushed up her chemise. He took a good look at her round ass. He then did what a nigga had to do to be respected by No Draws in the bed; he took control like a beast master. He roughly flipped her onto her back.

"Yeah, just like that! Show me who's the man, fuck me!"

Nigel raised her legs high in the air and dug in like a shovel into soft soil. She let out a deep moan as he slid deep inside her wetness.

The bed began to bang and slam against the wall as he gave her what she wanted. She began moaning in different cords as if she was a grand piano that he was playing with royal expertise. The more she fucked him back, the more he put his back into it. She loved the satisfying pounding she was getting. Her moans became screams of lust and passion the farther he bent her legs back.

"Fuck me in the ass," she hissed.

Nigel flipped her onto her stomach and slid inside her tight ass like it was her pussy. It was that wet.

"Oooooowwwww… mmmmmmhhhhmmmm. Don't stop." She felt him plowing in and out of her asshole with barbaric energy and vigor. "Awww, it's stinging…." It made her come in seconds. Orgasms came back to back like a one-two punch. "Oh yeah!" she screamed, using her hands to help push her ass up to meet his plowing. It was pleasure and pain—the best of both worlds in one session of erotic exhibitionism. "I'm cummin'! Don't stop! Damn, don't stop! Sssss…"

Nigel knew what she wanted. He fucked her hard and deep in her asshole and pulled out just as he was about to cum and shot it in thick globs all over her lower back and ass cheeks. He then jerked the last of his warm load out with his hand and kept cumming on her.

"I love it when you cum on me." No Draws lay on her stomach while he finished coating her with his cum like lotion. "Uuummmm."

Two weeks after Tec was buried Ms. Green asked all of the girls over for dinner. They all spoke freely as they sat in the dining room eating baked red snapper, Cajun rice and steamed broccoli covered with cheddar cheese. Vida, Tia, Ice and Samara all wondered why Ms. Green wanted them all to have dinner together. She was loving to them all, and they respected her as if she was their very own grandmother.

Wiping her mouth and taking a sip of water, Ms. Green looked around at the young girls and said, "I'm worried about you girls." She paused to see if the girls were paying attention. They were. "Since Little Timmy died I've been having bad feelings about you all. I don't know what the world is coming to, but I know the Lord don't like ugly. Times have changed so much." She let out a small sigh. There was a lot on her mind. "Life is short… I want you girls to make the most of the time you are blessed with here. Don't let Timmy's death be for nothing, learn from it. Pay attention to the signs of the Lord and see that you can be here one minute and gone the next. I didn't ask you girls over here to preach to you, I just wanted to say a few things to you all that might make you think. Have any of you even thought about where you want to be in the next five years?"

"I plan on goin' to Tulane University in September," Samara said. The other girls had heard her talk about college but thought she was faking. They all cut their eyes at her as if to say, *Yeah, right!*

"New Orleans, huh?" Ms. Green was born in New Orleans and had lived there for years before her father moved to Southeast D.C.

"Yes, ma'am," Samara said.

"I have family there," Ms. Green continued.

"I've been lookin' at a few schools down there." Samara and Ms. Green exchanged a few words about going to school and how it is a good thing.

"So what about the rest of you?" Ms. Green asked. The other girls had nothing to say. "I want you all to think about life for a second. Ask yourselves are you ready for the next life. Have you done enough in this life?" Ms. Green stood up to leave the table. "If it so happens to be your time to go tonight have you even done all the things you want to do in this life?" She stepped off on that note.

Later on Vida lay in the bed in her room at her grandmother's apartment. She was thrown into deep thought by the piece her grandmother had dropped on her and the girls. Vida was going on seventeen and had dropped out of school, was deeply involved in crime and had an open case in court. She wasn't living right and she knew it. Her soul was uneasy about her lifestyle. It was time for a change.

Not a day went by that she didn't think about where she would be if she was in the car with Tec when the police got on his back that night. She had deep regrets that haunted her conscience like assaulting demons every time she thought about the three lives that had been taken for the $156,000 she and Tec had taken that fateful night. The girls had split the money up three ways. Vida was sitting on $52,000. They didn't owe Tonio shit, Tia established that. As far as the girls were concerned, Tec was the one that had business dealings with Tonio. As Vida lay in the darkness thinking about everything she once again told herself that it was time to get her shit together. Daddieo came to mind; he was supposed to come down and spend the weekend with her. She looked forward to that, knowing that she could talk to him about her dilemma, and he would have some good advice for her.

Vida grabbed the remote and cut the TV on. Before she could focus on the show the phone rang. "Hello."

"Vee!" Tia was excited and spoke with urgency. "We need you to come get us!" She was talking fast.

"Slow down, what's wrong?" Vida sat up.

"We got into it wit' some uptown bitches in the go-go and sliced they ass up. They went and got some niggaz and got us trapped inside the joint. They fucked my car up and everything."

"I'm on my way. Stay inside. You'll know when it's safe outside." Vida hung up the phone with a sigh. It was on again. The madness was never ending. She shot over to their Capitol Heights apartment to get one of the many guns Tec kept in the closet. Grabbing a smoke gray MAC-11, she checked the clip. It was packed with thirty-six 9mm bullets. Vida headed uptown.

Nativity was a Catholic school on Georgia Avenue, Northwest that sat across the street from the 4th District police station. It was packed with youth who came to see Backyard Band. There was light traffic as Vida cruised by the front with the MAC-11 on her lap. She saw small crowds in front of the entrance and down the sidewalk. She made a right turn on Peabody Street, drove through the McDonald's parking lot, where other small crowds were clicked up, and circled the block. Vida spotted Tia's car parked with the windows busted out. A group of rowdy girls and a few dudes had it surrounded. Vida nodded her head, she figured they were the opposition but she wasn't sure. She played it smart and went inside the go-go, leaving the MAC-11 in the car.

The go-go music was blasting. The place was dark and hot. An old auditorium was being used for the go-go. Crews of thugs played the wall in the back looking like they came to start shit instead of party. Honeys of all flavors filled the dance floor looking like they were straight out of a rap video. It was *Go-Go Live* for real. Dudes that came to party were freaking with the honeys.

Vida made her way through the thick crowd in search of her crew. She had to fend off dudes that were trying to holla at her, she was used to it. Vida found the girls with a small crowd of honorary Hell Razor Honeys. Samara had been carrying the Hell Razor torch with pride and conviction while Vida, Tia and Ice were playing the streets with Tec. Tia told Vida what went down. Somehow a bitch mistook Ice for a white wannabe and got her face sliced in a quick "X" motion, simple as that.

"Meet me at the door in five minutes," Vida said. She went and got the MAC-11 out the car and returned to the front door to give her crew a safe passage. As she and the other girls strolled down Georgia Avenue Vida led the way.

"That's them bitches right there!" a girl yelled from the McDonald's parking lot. She and her crew began to mob toward the Hell Razor Honeys.

Vida smiled and without warning pulled the MAC-11 and opened fire with a deadly rapid fire burst from the submachine gun. Crowds began to scatter in quick dashes like gazelles in fear with a cheetah on the scene. Vida kept bussin'. The police came from all directions. Vida and the girls took off running and mixed in with the masses that were all trying to get the fuck out of dodge. As Vida ran she threw the MAC and dashed down a dark alley and across 13th Street.

Just as Vida crossed the street, two police cars with flashing lights and blaring sirens pulled up on the sidewalk. Four officers jumped out with Glocks in their hands yelling, "Freeze! Put your hands in the fucking air!" Putting her hands in the air slowly, Vida knew she was caught. Not knowing uptown streets well, she had nowhere to run. She was arrested.

Chapter 16

Vida was charged with assault with a deadly weapon; she shot one of the dudes that were with the bitches that were beefing with the Hell Razor Honeys. The bamma pointed Vida out when he was shown a picture of her at the hospital. Bitch nigga! Ice was also arrested and charged with assault for slicing the girl's face that night. Tia, Samara and the other girls got away. Vida's open case kept her in custody; she was still a juvenile so she was sent to the D.C. Jail for an eight day hold. Ice's juvenile charge for the Black Hole shooting was dropped and she made bond on the adult assault beef. Tia paid the $2,000 to get her out.

On lock down Vida had more than enough time to think things over. She didn't know what she was thinking when she fired twenty some shots at a crowd of people across the street from a police station. It was good that she didn't kill a muthafucka. She would surely be facing an adult murder beef if that was the case. However, she would soon learn that the assault with a deadly weapon beef was the least of her worries.

Tia was in the bed sleeping good when Ice woke her up. "What the hell is wrong wit' you, Ice?!" Tia didn't get in the house until after four in the morning.

"I'm pregnant!" Ice had just tested herself—twice.

"What? By who? How the fuck that happen?" Tia asked. The girls had a pact that they would always use rubbers. "I know you ain't let no nigga go up in you raw!" Tia jive snapped.

"Come on, bitch. You know better. You not gon' believe this shit." Ice stood beside the bed in a white bra and panty set with her blond hair in a ponytail. "Tec was the only nigga I let hit it raw, right before he died. We was high as shit and he ain't have no rubber." Ice sighed. "I couldn't tell slim no. That's my nigga. You know that."

"Damn," Tia said. Neither girl wanted a child at the time. They were living on the edge. "What you gon' do?"

Ice sighed again. "I can't get rid of it. It's Tec's baby. I'm sure of it."

"You sure?" Tia sat up and rubbed her eyes.

"Come on, Tee... I ain't gon' let nobody else hit it raw. I would get rid of it in a heartbeat if that was the case."

"I feel you. You gotta keep it if it's Tec's baby. It's a part of him; a part of us."

"You right." Ice knew she had to have the baby. It was nothing to talk about.

A week later Ms. Green went to see Vida—her pride and joy. Dressed in institution clothes with her hair in a ponytail Vida looked like a tomboy. She had a small scratch on her forehead from a fight she'd been in a few days ago with some bitches that said Vida thought she was cute. Vida's words to the bitches were, "I am cute, bitch!" She then tore into the leader of the pack like a wild dog. After crushing her it was understood, Vida wasn't going for shit. She was a Hell Razor Honey.

Sitting across from her grandmother, Vida told her that she was just fine. Like any loving grandmother, Ms. Green was still worried and concerned. After a while, Ms. Green took a deep breath and said, "Every time I look into your beautiful eyes I still see the same sweet little girl that used to make me "I love you" cards every day as a child."

Vida smiled, remembering those days.

"You are just like your mother, Lord rest her soul, loving, sweet and so strong-minded." Ms. Green paused for a moment, reflecting. "Vida, you are all I have in this world. The Lord called my baby girl home but eased my soul's pain with you. You have always been a blessing to me." A tear rolled down Ms. Green's face. "I want you to listen to me real good... and promise me one thing."

"What, grandma? Anything" Something about the vibe her grand-mother was giving off was making Vida nervous, even fearful. "Is somethin' wrong wit' you?" Vida grabbed her grandmother's hand, feeling the urge to cry.

"I'm sick, baby... I've been sick for a while. I didn't want to say anything to you about it."

"Sick?" Vida's heart pounded like a death row inmate being led to execution. "Sick like what?"

Ms. Green explained that she'd been living with lung cancer for the past few years, but it was getting worse. She didn't know how much time she had left. Vida began to cry. She felt like God was pun-ishing her for her wrongs by taking her grandmother away from her.

"Don't cry, baby." Ms. Green wiped Vida's tears away. "Death is not a bad thing. This world is only a stopover. We all will move on. This is not our true home. I'm not telling you this to make you cry. I need peace. I need to be able to rest in peace, and the only way I can do that is if I know that you are okay once my time is up." She squeezed Vida's hand. "I need you to promise me that you will get your act together. Promise me that, Vida."

"I promise, grandma. I promise you that."

"That's my baby." Ms. Green gave Vida a big hug. Vida held her tight, thinking of how much she loved her. Life was too short.

On the West Coast, months later, the summer sun was bright and glowing in the picture-perfect sky over Venice Beach. Countless peo-ple covered the beach, flooded the walk and filled the water of the Pacific Ocean. Laid out in the hot sand on a thick red Polo beach towel, wearing a $750 Gucci bikini and a pair of $325 Christian Dior shades, No Draws was high on life. Almost over night she'd met a number of important people and made crucial connections in L.A.

She now had her own condo in the Brentwood section of West Los Angeles. She and Nigel were still cool. After all, he had plugged her in and made her new lifestyle possible. However, he spent most of his time in New York; all of her dreams were in L.A. The sky was the limit as far as No Draws was concerned.

Mario's friend, Liz Whitaker, and No Draws hit it off well. Liz was in her mid to late thirties and resembled Phylicia Rashad. She was respected and had a nice standing among Hollywood blacks. No Draws was just what Liz wanted in her life, someone young, sexy and a little hood. No Draws and Liz met when Liz sent a limo to pick No Draws up and take her to Liz's house in Hollywood Hills—a residential section of Hollywood that's one of its most glamorous districts. Liz's house was beyond No Draws' wildest dreams; it sat far up in the green slopes of the Santa Monica Mountains. Inside Liz's house, No Draws was escorted through the plush home to Liz's home theater. It was a smaller version of a real cinema environment—the screen was ten feet wide. There they got to know one another.

Now, months later, the film *Under the Hollywood Sky* was done and was going straight to HBO. In the film No Draws did well in her supporting role as a high-priced Hollywood call girl. She couldn't wait for HBO to air the film. On top of that, within the next two weeks she was about to begin shooting for Mario's film. Excited was an understatement. Being on the big screen with the likes of Jasmine Guy was intoxicating for No Draws.

Spending a little over an hour tanning on the beach, it was time to hit the road for No Draws. She got in her triple black 1997 convertible Lexus ES300—a gift from Liz—and cruised along Sunset Boulevard as she often did when she just wanted to soak up the West Coast. It made her feel like a star. With her hair dyed blond and blowing in the wind, looking like Faith Evans, No Draws cruised through the Strip, passing all the expensive restaurants, cafes and nightclubs. Her cell phone rang. "Hello."

"Shelly, how are you?" Liz was in the back of her limo cruising down Wilshire Boulevard, coming from her office.

"Just lovin' life," No Draws said with a smile.

"Good, sweetie, life is short. I have good news. HBO loves the movie so much they're moving up the airing date, and their numbers are perfect."

"Oh my God!" No Draws was so excited that she wanted to jump out of her skin.

"They'll be airing this fall. You'll start getting royalty checks in the mail soon. It won't be much, a few thousand dollars or so. Nevertheless, your foot's in the door. That's what really counts."

"Things are lookin' up"

"Let's have a drink," Liz said.

"Where?" No Draws asked as Tommy Hilfiger cruised by in a fire engine red Ferrari 360 Spider F1.

"Let's make it the Sky Bar."

"I'm on Sunset Strip right now."

"I'll be there in a few minutes. Just tell Marcus you are meeting me. He'll seat you."

Minutes later No Draws was inside the Sky Bar seated at a table reserved for Liz. Dennis Rodman was a few tables away to the right. A few seats behind No Draws sat X-rated queen Vanessa Del Rio, who was enjoying a drink alone. In her mid-forties, the fiend queen still had the curves of a young Pam Grier. As she looked around, No Draws saw a lot of stars.

Liz arrived shortly. She and No Draws had vodka and cranberry as they spoke about the Hollywood lifestyle. Liz took it upon herself to school No Draws to how things went. "Out here…" Liz paused to sip her drink; the diamonds in her bracelet sparkled. "You have to do whatever it takes to succeed. I like you. You understand how the game is played. I can tell you have what it takes to succeed. It took me almost ten years to grasp a concept that you've grasped in months. You've got a bright future, kid."

"We learn that comin' where I'm from," No Draws said.

"It's no different back in Chicago, but I came out here with a degree in Performing Arts, I'd been acting since 9th grade. I thought I was going to be the next big thing." Liz laughed at herself with a dismissive shake of her head. "Boy was I dreaming. Anyway, I had to apply the old saying, when in Rome, do as the Romans do." She winked at No Draws. "Always keep your eyes open for your next come-up. Opportunity is always out there, one just has to be able to capitalize on it."

"That's what I'm all about. If it don't make dollars, it don't make sense. I came out here to come up, by all means."

"I love the way you think. You're going to go far out here. I'll give you all you need to know. Think of our friendship as an apprenticeship of sorts. I got you," Liz said. She went on to school No Draws for a while

After they'd had a few drinks they left and went to Liz's house. Liz's dining room was graced by wood walls, modern furnishings of French taste and a beautiful handmade carpet—a true luxurious Hollywood setting. "What do you have a taste for?" Liz asked as she and No Draws sat at the dining room table.

"Lobster and shrimp." No Draws was feeling the Vodka and cranberry.

Liz had her maid prepare some lobster and shrimp. When the food was done she and No Draws drank champagne and ate the food. They also discussed other business plans.

When they were finished eating Liz said, "Let's go down to the theater and check out the final cut of the film." They went down to the home theatre. Liz dimmed the lights and cut the film on. It was at a part where No Draws was on a date with a rich oil tycoon. She was giving him a passionate kiss. "You are a natural," Liz said, putting her arm around No Draws. "Sexy, too." She lean over and kissed No Draws in the mouth. They tongue kissed like old lovers.

No Draws had never been with a woman before she came to L.A. Liz had begun to test the water with her from the first day they met. It took some time, but money, power and influence had a way of getting people to conform and compromise their principles. It started out with soft touches of the hand, next a kiss and so on, until Liz had her face between No Draws' legs licking her clit. Before long No Draws began to enjoy the things she and Liz did together. Liz was a vicious freak that was down to do anything at least once. However, as far as No Draws was concerned, Liz really took the cake the day she gave No Draws the Lexus. That same night she put on a strap-on and fucked No Draws better than any man had ever fucked her before. It was no turning back after that.

On the theatre floor, No Draws and Liz came out of their clothes and were moaning and breathing hard as they went to work in the sixty-nine position with Liz on top. As No Draws ate Liz's pussy she felt Liz slide a finger insider her asshole. It made her cum instantly. No Draws did the same, sliding her finger deep inside Liz's ass she heard Liz grunt with satisfaction. They went at it on the floor as if they were shooting a porno flick. They traded positions and kept going hard as if in a race to make one another cum. The orgasms came quick and hard for them both.

"Let's go up to my room," Liz panted after cumming for the second time; her face was glistening with No Draws' cream. "I'm feeling naughty." Liz was into the bondage shit also. She liked being handcuffed and whipped while being talked dirty to. No Draws had gotten used to giving Liz what she wanted and had even grown fond of whipping the freak.

In Liz's plush bedroom No Draws lay on the huge bed watching Liz bend over and pull some things from her dresser. Liz's body was in great shape from hours of swimming in her pool. She could easily get a spread in Playboy. Her ass was wide and plump. Her thick, brown thighs and small waist, along with her nice breast and shoulder-length hair turned No Draws on.

"Here, put this on." Liz handed No Draws her strap-on contraption fully equipped with a black, ten inch dildo. "Cuff my hands behind my back and fuck me from the back. Be rough, too."

No Draws didn't ask any questions. She strapped up and went to work.

The D.F. Jenkins Academy was a residential placement program for troubled youth. It sat on a huge estate deep in Georgia. It looked like a university. There were no fences around its huge, green compound. The youth—males and females between the ages of fifteen and twenty-one—moved freely from one class or activity to the next. It wasn't a bad place at all, and if a young person wanted to change the program would help them.

Vida had been in the program for four months now. The courts ordered her to be committed to the academy for two years. However, if she did well she could go home by her eighteenth birthday. So far she had already gotten her G.E.D. and was now taking college classes as well as real estate courses.

Vida shared a room with an eighteen year old female from St. Louis that was a diehard Blood. Her name was Mary Hawkins, but she went by Bloody Mary or Bloody. Bloody and Vida got along real well.

Vida and Daddieo were still cool but weren't together. He was always busy; he stayed back and forth out of town on business. He was doing well for himself. Daddieo had come to visit Vida twice; both times he brought Ms. Green along. He also sent Vida packages and money.

Tia and Ice, who was seven month pregnant, came to see Vida twice a month. They did everything for her and took care of Ms. Green. They respected the fact that Vida was trying to do something with herself. At first they tried to get Vida to run away from the program, but she shot the idea down. Vida was shocked when she found out that Ice was carrying Tec's baby. In a way Vida wished she was carrying the baby. Nevertheless, they had a piece of Tec to hold on to.

Samara went to see Vida once. She'd stopped through on her way to Miami for a South Beach party. Samara told Vida how excited she was to be going away to college. It was time for her to get away from D.C. for a while. In the last six months two dudes she was dealing with had been murdered, both were shot multiple times after a go-go.

Sitting in her room on the bed listening to a Rare Essence go-go tape, Vida missed the Murder Capital. Bloody walked in the room wearing a red Jordan short set with black and red Air Jordans. She was a thick girl, one with style, and she was cute also. She had the look of a young Lady of Rage—the female Death Row rapper.

"Who is that? Essence?" Bloody asked. Vida had turned her out on go-go music.

"Yeah." Vida smiled. "I'ma have to take you to a go-go wit' me one day."

Bloody sat on her bed and grabbed a Source magazine. "I'm serious, I'ma come up there and hang out wit' you when we go home."

"You can come hang out wit' me anytime. You'll love it in D.C. It's live, just the way you like it."

"I know I gotta bring my heat," Bloody said.

Vida laughed. "Yeah, you might need that when you come through."

Bloody had been at the academy for eighteen months and would be going home shortly. Gang banging was her way of life. Her mother was an L.A. Blood that had been murdered in a drive-by slaying in Compton. Bloody—then five years old—and her two brothers, who were already Bloods, were sent to live with their aunt in St. Louis. By the time Bloody was ten she was already claiming Blood and holding guns and drugs for her brothers and homies. By fifteen she had stood firm, represented and survived a number of shoot-outs. At sixteen she shot up a club where Crips were clubbing and was later arrested and sent to the academy.

Through all the madness Bloody had never seen a lot of money. Armed robbery was her thing; she lived from caper to caper. When Bloody and Vida talked about the streets Bloody was amazed that Vida had touched so much money at such a young age. Bloody had her mind set on getting real money once she was back on the streets; she was also pressing Vida to put her down with Tia and Ice. Vida knew how Tia was when it came to strangers so she didn't really want to hook Bloody up. However, the closer Vida and Bloody got, Vida's feelings began to change. She told herself that she would put Bloody down with the crew.

"You ready to hit the gym?" Bloody asked. On Fridays after 4:00 P.M. there was music and food in the gym. Most of the time it was like a big party, everybody hit the spot.

"Yeah, let's see what's goin' on down there." Vida popped a stick of gum in her mouth.

Vida and Bloody stepped inside the crowded gym and were greeted by the sounds of Notorious B.I.G.'s "Hypnotize" blaring hypnotically through the system. It was like stepping into a popular nightclub. Everything was live and full swing. Most of the people in the gym were black, but there were a few other races in the spot as well. Bloody saw some of her Blood homies and told Vida that she would be right back; she had to check on a little situation from earlier.

Walking around the gym Vida spoke to the handful of people that she knew from back home and the few she'd become cool with from other places. Vida had the around-the-way-girl look down to a science and was drawing more than enough attention. Her hair was done in little braids that she had pulled back into a ponytail. She was wearing a gray and black striped Polo shirt, tight blue Guess jean shorts, no socks and a pair of black Reeboks. She was one of the baddest honeys in the spot, for sure.

Navigating his way through the thick crowd with his eyes on Vida, a dude by the name of Moe-Moe slid up behind her and hugged her, pressing up against her ass with his midsection. Vida spun around to see who was behind her; she smiled. "You act like you was about to put some work in or somethin'." Moe-Moe laughed.

"I was gon' fuck a muthafucka up, I ain't know who was all up on me like that." Vida playfully caught an attitude. She was really feeling Moe-Moe on the real. She knew him from back home. He was the cousin of the dude Chris that Ice used to fuck with for a minute. Moe-Moe used to try to holla at Vida, but she was fucking with Daddieo tough at the time.

"Not even me? I can't be all up on you like this?" Moe-Moe wrapped his arms around her waist, resting his hands on her phat ass.

"Nah, you cool, baby boy." Vida grinded against him to the sound of J.M.'s "Get Money Remix." "I fucks wit' you."

Moe-Moe was nineteen years old. He was from Condon Terrace, Southeast D.C. He'd been at the academy for over a year for armed robbery and two gun charges. They were charges that he'd racked up when he was seventeen. Moe-Moe was smooth and had a top-flight rap game. If a honey would just listen to him he would get somewhere with her. He looked like a young Mike Tyson and was built just like a boxer. He had a chipped front tooth, but it didn't make him look fucked up. In fact, Vida thought it was cute. Moe-Moe radiated confidence to such a point that he made himself appear to be the flyest and best looking dude in the world. He and Vida were on some homie-lover-friend shit, which was cool for them both. No feelings were a good thing, plus it was safe.

"I'll be gone on Monday," Moe-Moe said. He had a tight grip on Vida's ass as they grinded on the dance floor.

Vida was loving his grip on her ass. "You know I'ma miss you. So what you gon' do wit' yourself?" she asked.

"I'ma find a way to get me some money. I really don't want to hustle no more. My next charge is an adult beef. I ain't wit' bein' locked in no cage. I hate that shit." Moe-Moe paused for a second, checking out the crowd. It seemed like something was going on. "I'ma take it slow, one day at a time."

"That's all you can do. You know how to hustle for real. You a real hustla', you ain't gotta limit yourself to sellin' drugs. It's a million and one other ways to get money." Vida knew that Moe-Moe had completed a number of vocational courses.

"Yeah, I feel you on that. I'ma try my hand."

A cute dark-skinned girl walked up and cut into their conversation. She told Vida that she needed to go get Bloody before she got herself in trouble. Bloody was about to get into a fight. Vida, Moe-Moe and the girl slid to the bathroom where Bloody and a tall, linky dude were already going toe to toe, as if they were in a back alley somewhere. A small crowd encircled them. Bloody was landing loud, powerful punches with violent force. She was getting down like she was a dude. With authority, Vida forced her way through the small crowd and broke the fight up. Bloody had busted the dude's nose and he was making it clear that he wasn't done fighting. Bloody still wanted to rec as well, but Vida held her back.

Looking at the dude with the bloody nose Vida said, "You done had more than enough for one day."

"You better get out my way, Vida," the dude said.

"Or what, chump?" Moe-Moe stepped up. "You gon' do somethin'?"

"That nigga fakin', let's roll," Vida said, pulling Bloody along by the arm. She didn't want her to get caught up when she was on her way home. Vida was like a big sister to Bloody and was always keeping her out of trouble, even though Vida was the younger of the two.

Back in their dorm room, after Bloody had calmed down, she told Vida what the drama was all about. It was behind some stolen shoes—a Blood in another dorm had gotten her shoes stolen. Bloody took it upon herself to straighten out the situation. Vida loved her loyalty.

"I'm glad you pulled me off that crab-ass nigga. I was in a zone." Bloody knew her temper was out of control.

"I fucks wit' you. That shit was small shit. You put the work in and y'all got the shoes back."

"You right, Vee. You good peoples, you like the sister I never had. I got big love for you."

"It's all love. Bein' real is in my blood."

"That's right, Blood." Bloody laughed. Vida had shown her nothing but love from day one. Bloody gave Vida five. "We peoples for life."

Chapter 17

L ying in her hospital bed hooked up to all kinds of life support
machines, Ms. Green held Vida's hand as tight as she could, as
if life depended on it. She was very weak and frail and she
looked like she was living in her last days. Vida had been given a pass
to leave the academy to be by her grandmother's side since doctors
said that Ms. Green didn't have long to live. With tears in her eyes
Vida listened to the struggling whispers of her grandmother.

"Baby..." Ms. Green took long pauses between her words.
Breathing was a painful challenge. All her hair was now gone due to
the painful chemotherapy she'd been undergoing. "Always remember... remember that I love you... and I did the best I could do, baby.
I didn't have much... but I gave you all I had."

"I know, grandma. I know." Vida wiped tears from her eyes.

"You told me that you—" Ms. Green was overcome by a painful
coughing fit.

"You need to rest, grandma."

"The Lord is calling, baby... I'll get all the rest I need." The old
lady forced a smile. "I just want you to always remember... remember that my soul will always be at ease as long as I know that you're
doing right. Do something with yourself, Vida." After those words
Ms. Green drifted off to sleep.

Vida thought about what her grandmother had said and what she
asked of her. It was now December of 1997, and Vida had been doing

great in the academy for months. Even now, she was still focused on bettering herself. The pain of losing her grandmother was tearing her apart. However, her grandmother had prepared her for the reality of death. Everyone was sure to taste it.

For the next four days Vida spent almost every minute with her grandmother. On December sixteenth of 1997 Ms. Green passed away. Tia and Ice were there to help Vida deal with the painful loss and help her with the funeral arrangements. Family members Vida didn't even know popped up. Some even had money. She wondered where they were when she and her grandmother were doing badly.

Out in the cold, flanked by Tia, Ice and Samara, Vida cried as her grandmother was lowered into the ground. Family and friends all looked on as the sweet woman was laid to rest.

"It's gon' be okay, Vee." Ice put her arm around Vida. "She's wit' her Lord now."

"I know." Vida replayed all the final words of her grandmother in her head. Vida knew she had to stay strong, focused and do the right thing with her life.

A few family members offered to help Vida out. She didn't feel any connection to them at all, but she tried her best to be nice. Nevertheless, the only family she really had left was Tia, Ice, Samara and Ice's twins—Timmy and Tony.

Later on at Tia's apartment, Vida sat on the soft leather sofa holding Ice's first born, Timmy. Ice sat next to Vida, breast feeding Tony. Tia sat across from them in the love seat.

"You gon' be okay goin' back to that program?" Tia asked.

"Yeah, I'ma be okay. I'ma be missin' my grandmother, but she wants me to go on wit' my life and do positive things. I gave her my word that's what I'd do." Vida saw the brown-skinned baby in her arms smile.

"I respect that, Vee," Ice said.

"It comes a time when enough is enough," Vida said. "It's time for us all to get something on our minds. Life is short."

"I agree wit' you, Vee, but I ain't got time for school and shit. The cost of livin' is high as a muthafucka. I gotta do what I gotta do. You know how that go baby," Tia said. She was now buying two bricks a week from her homie Lil' Ed.

"I know how it goes." Vida looked at Ice and continued. "But what about you? You got two kids now."

"Yeah, I know. You right," Ice said. "I been thinkin' the same thing."

"We done done a lotta dirt. That shit comes back around, every time," Vida said. "We gotta start slowin' down."

"This the only lifestyle I know, Vee. Plus, it works for a bitch like me," Tia said.

"I feel where you comin' from, I'm just throwin' it out there. It's just somethin' to think about," Vida said. "Ice, you ain't gotta carry it like you do. Your mother will make sure you straight."

"You already know how I feel about that," Ice said. "I don't ask her for nothin'. I can take care of myself. Plus, she fucked up I got two black babies."

The girls sat around talking for a good while. Vida's mind was on getting her life together. Tia had other plans; her mind was on getting money. Ice was forced to think about what Vida was saying. After all, she did have two kids to think about.

A month later, Tia was pushing Zoe's white 1997 Acura Integra along Suitland Parkway. "Ain't No Nigga" by Jay-Z and Foxy Brown was pumping through the system. She was on her way to meet Lil' Ed around Hunter Pines on Stanton Road, Southeast. Lil' Ed told her he had some serious shit to holla at her about.

Tia pulled up in front of the Hunter Pines apartments. A group of dudes were standing on the sidewalk beside a smoke grey Mercedes Benz 500SL. Scarface's "Smile" was blasting out of the car. Tia knew most of the dudes that were dressed in thick black skull caps, huge Eddie Bauers and Timberland boots. She got out into the cold morning air and stepped to Lil' Ed, who was off to the side talking to Lil'

Rick. Tia, Lil' Ed and Lil' Rick went inside the building and up to Lil' Rick's apartment. Sitting on the sofa in the living room, Tia gave Lil' Ed a look that said, *what's up?*

Lil' Ed looked at Lil' Rick and said, "Put her on point for me."

"You hip to the nigga Motor, right?" Lil' Rick asked Tia while he rolled a Backwood.

"Yeah, why?" Tia knew that Motor had been locked up for a few months on a gun charge; he'd just hit the streets a week ago.

Lil' Rick lit the Backwood and said, "The nigga was running his mouth over the jail, talkin' 'bout he was behind the move when y'all got hit for like $400,000 and some bricks. Anyway, the nigga he was talkin' to is my man, he put me on Motor. When I told Lil' Ed about it he said that you was his peoples, so here we are."

Tia squinted her eyes with an evil look and said, "Is that right?"

"No bullshit." Lil' Rick passed her the Backwood that he'd stuffed with weed. I do my homework."

Tia looked from Lil' Ed back to Lil' Rick and said, "What's in it for you bringing me this information?"

Lil' Rick smiled and said, "I could say I brought it to you because we peoples, which is true on the strength of Lil' Ed. But on the real, I want to rob the nigga, and I know you want to get back for what he did, right?"

"Oh, he gon' get dealt wit'. That ain't even in the talk," Tia said. "Check this out, I'll locate the nigga and we can go on the move together, on the strength that you put me on point. Cool?"

Lil' Ed laughed and looked at Lil' Rick, saying, "I told you she was gangsta."

"I see," Lil' Rick said. He then looked at Tia and said, "That's a bet."

For the next two days Tia stalked Motor's girl. Like clockwork, she got the drop on the bitch-nigga. Motor was staying out Germantown, Maryland. She called Lil' Rick. "I got it all mapped out. We can take care of that situation tonight, feel me?"

"Cool," Lil' Rick said. "Meet me around Atlantic Street at six this evenin'."

Tia hung up the phone and walked into the living room. Ice was sitting on the sofa watching the movie that No Draws was in. HBO was airing it. Tia sat beside Ice and said, "The bitch done fucked her way into a movie, huh?"

"Yeah, she made it happen. I give it to her," Ice said and then changed the subject. "What's up, you and Lil' Rick gon' handle that nigga Motor tonight for sure?"

"Yeah, we got that bitch-nigga," Tia said.

"I can't believe that nigga got us like that."

"We shoulda guessed he had somethin' to do wit' the shit when he stopped comin' around."

"It was a lot of shit goin' on at the time though, Tec died right after that, we had our hands full." Ice's cell phone vibrated on the table, she checked the number and saw it was the dude Chris. He'd just got out of prison and was trying to holla back at her. He could wait. "You think Zoe had somethin' to do wit' that shit?"

"I asked myself the same question. I don't think so, but I don't put shit past neir nigga. If I find out he had somethin' to do wit' it or even knew somethin' 'bout the shit he gon' get it, too."

"I hear that."

Just after 6:00 P.M. Tia pulled up and parked on Atlantic Street, Southeast. She was pushing a huge, dark blue 1976 Caprice Classic with dark tinted windows. The car was one of those joints that would make niggaz pull their hammers if it bent the wrong corner late at night. Tia got out the car and acknowledged the dudes she knew that were on the block. Baby J, T.R. and Lil' Twon had grown up with Tia.

After kicking it with them for a second, Tia and Lil' Rick jumped in the Caprice and hit the beltway. Tia had the plan mapped out in her head; it was jive sweet too." Ice had a Montgomery County police that she was working. Tia got Ice to get a police uniform from the bamma so she could use it for the move. Tia handed the uniform to Lil' Rick.

"Fuck I'm supposed to do wit' that shit?" Lil' Rick laughed.

"You gotta put it on." Tia smiled. "Come on now. You gon' get us inside."

"You a wild muthafucka," Lil' Rick said, as he started taking off his clothes to change into the uniform.

A short while later there was a knock at Alexis' apartment door. She looked through the peephole and saw a police officer in full uniform, cap and all.

"Who is it?" Motor asked his girl as they sat on the floor watching BET.

"The police."

"What?" He jumped up to see for himself. "Damn!" he hissed, pointing at the bedroom and signaling for Alexis to go put up his pistol; it was sitting on the bed. He opened the door and said, "Is there somethin' wrong, officer?"

Lil' Rick kicked the door all the way open and slammed Motor to the floor. Tia rushed in behind Lil' Rick and checked the apartment; she dragged a crying and screaming Alexis back into the living room and made her lay facedown on the floor.

"You thought you could get away wit' robbin' us, bitch-nigga?!" Tia kicked Motor in the face with her Timberlands. He screamed out in pain.

"Where the money at?" Lil' Rick smacked Motor in the back of the head with a .45 revolver.

'It's in the safe. Just don't kill me, please, man," Motor begged.

Lil' Rick dragged him to the bedroom by his collar. Moments later Tia heard two loud pops come from the bedroom. Alexis knew what had happened; she screamed and pissed on herself right before Tia shot her in the head at point-blank range, without as much as a blink of an eye. Lil' Rick came back into the living room with a duffle bag thrown over his shoulder. "Let's get the fuck outta here," he said to Tia.

Just like that they were gone, with $160,000.

Vida was dealing with the death of her grandmother as best as she could. She missed her so much; not a day went by that she didn't think of her. However, she had to stay focused on her classes if she wanted to make things work.

A knock at her door grabbed Vida's attention. She opened the door and saw the girl that slept next door; she looked like something was wrong. "What's up?" Vida asked the girl.

"Vee, Bloody on the phone. She said she needs to talk to you. She said it's important… I think somethin' is wrong."

Vida rushed to the pay phone in the back hall. She was filled with anxiety, knowing how much trouble Bloody stayed in. For the few months that Bloody had been home she'd been staying in touch with Vida and sending her money. Vida got on the phone. "Hello."

"Vida, I need you," Bloody said. She was in a South Carolina hotel. The police in St. Louis were looking for her in connection with a murder.

"What's wrong? Are you all right?"

"I really can't talk about it on the phone, but I need for you to holla at your peoples in D.C. I need somewhere to lay low for a while. I'll tell you all about it when I get a chance."

Vida sighed and shook her head. "I got you, Bloody."

Chapter 18

Vida finished her time at the academy and returned home just after her eighteenth birthday, in May of 1998. Tia bought her a red 1998 BMW 318i to come home to. Vida enrolled in Maryland University to study business management. She also got a job working at Bloomingdale's in Tyson's Corner Mall in Virginia. Vida had a good understanding of the real estate business and had $50,000 to try her hand with. Not to mention the fact that Tia was getting money and would slide Vida whatever she needed.

With a million things on her mind, Vida walked through the busy mall on her lunch break headed for Taco Bell. She heard a voice call her name from behind. As she turned around she saw a dude walking her way.

"What's up, Vee?" Moe-Moe hugged her. He was looking good, rocking a black and gold Iceberg short set.

"Damn, you lookin' good, playboy." Vida smiled. She hadn't seen Moe-Moe in months, although he had kept in touch through the mail.

"Where you on your way to?" Moe-Moe asked, checking Vida out, she was looking better than he remembered; phat as shit.

"I'm on my way to get some lunch."

"Can I hang out wit' you for a minute?" Moe-Moe asked.

Vida smiled. "Sure."

They hit Taco Bell and ordered something to eat. Over lunch they spoke about what was going on in their lives. Moe-Moe as working as a mover while doing odd jobs in between; he was holding on and doing well for himself though. He had his own apartment and a used Acura Legend. He wasn't selling any drugs nor was he involved in any crime. Moe-Moe's game plan was to walk a straight line until some doors opened for him. Vida respected the fact that he was standing firm on his plan to stay out of the game.

"You look like you still pumpin'," Vida said, checking out Moe-Moe's outfit and the light jewelry he was pushing. He looked like he was doing a little something on the side. "Let me find out you tellin' me all this positive shit so I'll think you got your shit in order."

Chewing a mouthful of food, Moe-Moe shot Vida a stern look and said, "You know me better than that, Vee. I'ma always be real wit' you. If I was still fuckin' around I'd tell you... you know that."

Vida gave him a sly look, as if she was trying to figure out if he was telling the truth. "I'm proud of you, boy. You stickin' to ya guns."

"I got to, too many niggaz I know doin' time. The Feds got a spot for a nigga, that's for sure. Shit gon' work out for me, money gon' come."

"You got that right."

Vida and Moe-Moe spent a good forty minutes together enjoying each other. They agreed to hook up again, real soon.

Vida and Moe-Moe began to see more and more of one another over the next few weeks. They had nice chemistry. Sometimes they would go out to eat and then go back to Vida's and just chill. They hit the movies and other spots together as well. The sex was top-of-the-line. Vida began to really feel Moe-Moe, but kept her feelings on the low. That was always her style.

During this time Daddieo would pop up from time to time to check on Vida, but her feelings for him had changed. They'd grown apart. In addition, Vida felt that the success that Daddieo was gaining was going to his head. He was changing. Therefore, Moe-Moe was really in the running.

Vida was sitting in Tia's living room on the sofa reading the Washington Post. She was watching the twins for Ice while she went

to see her probation officer. The twins were a year old now; they reminded Vida more and more of Tec each day.

Bloody came out of the bedroom talking on her cell phone. She was family now. Tia and Ice had accepted her as one of their own on the strength of Vida. Bloody and one of her homeboys back in St. Louis had caught a Crip that was the gunman in the murder of one of their homeboys, and they gunned him down in broad daylight. As soon as she heard that the police were looking for her she left town and had been in the D.C. area ever since. She loved it too. She fit right in with the crew and was just what Tia needed, a partner in crime.

"I'll be back, Vee," Bloody said as she ended the call. "Tia want me to meet her up in M.L.K."

"Don't get in no trouble," Vida said, as she continued to look through the paper at houses for sale in the ghetto. She was ready to put a few things in motion.

On the West Coast, down in Malibu, at a beach bar called Full Moon, the party was in full swing. Jay-Z was promoting his *Hard Knock Life* album out west. Stars of all kinds were in the spot. The music was a serious blend of East Coast and West Coast hip-hop, with some R & B hip-hop slid in. Jay-Z had free drinks flowing, free food and CDs. Afterward, he had an exclusive after party for a select few on a private yacht.

On the back patio taking in the cool evening breeze mixed with the fresh scent of the Pacific Ocean, Daddieo was drinking Belvedere with a dude by the name of Jalil Wilson. Jalil was a young aspiring entrepreneur from the South Bronx that Daddieo had met through Tonio. Tonio put them together after seeing that they shared some of the same business goals.

Daddieo and Jalil had a plan to produce documentary films about real-life street legends such as New York's Rich Porter, D.C.'s late, great, Michael "Fray" Salters and others. Tonio was backing the project. Jalil estimated that they would need at least $20,000 for their first film, which was to be about Daddieo's dead brother, Ricardo, who was one of the first young blacks to go to war with the mob in New York's crack-era. Ricardo ended up making more than five million dollars before the mob paid the N.Y.P.D. to gun him down.

"Niggaz gonna wanna see real shit like this, son," Jalil said as he watched a bad ass honey sitting across from him, they'd been sending each other eye signals all night. "All we gotta do is get a few rap niggaz to promote the shit for us, that'll get the word out. Tonio will put the word on the streets for us."

"Yeah, but what about this nigga Nigel? I wonder if he gon' act right." Daddieo sipped his drink.

"Don't worry, son. He gon' get wit' the program."

While Daddieo and Jalil were talking, Nigel walked up with Jay-Z and introduced Jay to them. Nigel was directing Jay-Z's next video.

"So what's the deal?" Nigel joined the conversation after Jay-Z stepped off. Business was discussed for a while. Nigel was on board.

By 3:00 A.M. the party had moved to the private yacht. Daddieo was pissy drunk; he went out on the deck for some fresh air. The first thing that caught his eye was a phat ass and a pair of sexy legs. "Ay, ma," he said.

"Daddieo?" No Draws asked with a smile. She was on the scene hunting for Jay-Z; he would be a mean catch for her. She was having a hard time getting close to him. "Is that you, Daddieo?"

Daddieo was shocked when he recognized No Draws. *Damn, this bitch lookin' good as shit,* he thought. "I didn't know you were here." He looked her up and down in her stripper outfit. All the freak shit his brother had told him about No Draws came to mind. "I hear you makin' moves out here. I seen your movie."

"I'm workin' my shit as best as I can. What's up wit' you? I hear you and Vida ain't like that no more." No Draws slid beside him as they both looked out at the dark ocean.

"We cool, we just goin' in two different directions right now. What made you ask about her?"

"Just askin'," she said in a sexy tone.

"Check this out, it's an after party so let's party. What you think about that?"

"We can have a private party if that's what you want." No Draws winked.

"Cool."

Daddieo and No Draws slid upstairs and found an empty room. "Take your clothes off." No Draws wasted no time; she undressed while watching him do the same. She got a good, long look at Daddieo's manhood and quickly understood why Vida was on him so hard. He was hung like an elephant! She wanted to taste him. Getting down on her knees, she grabbed his huge dick with one hand while rubbing his balls with the other. Looking into his eyes while rubbing his dick all over her face, she made it grow to its full length. "It's so big. I don't know if I can put the whole thing in my mouth." She began licking the tip of his dick in circles with the tip of her tongue.

Placing a hand behind her head, Daddieo said, "Let me see what you can do."

"Okay." She kissed the head and slowly slid every inch of him in her mouth and began working her head back and forth while looking him in the eyes. She played with her pussy while she sucked him off, taking him deep in her throat with no problem. Taking him out of her mouth, she licked all over his dick and then put his balls in her mouth and sucked on them. Putting his dick back in her mouth, she did every trick in the book, driving him crazy. Knowing that he was about to cum she hungrily deep-throated him, almost gagging.

Daddieo exploded in her mouth with force, grabbing the back of her head with both hands. She swallowed some of his explosion, but then pulled his dick out and jerked nut all over her face and in her hair. When he had nothing left, she wiped the dick all over her face.

"I can show you a lot more, daddy." No Draws licked her lips. "I love it in the ass."

Daddieo was in a daze, but he still wanted more. "Show me more. Give me the works."

No Draws worked her magic and got him hard again. She took it in the ass and loved it. "Ohhhh, Daddieo, I can't take it no more!"

Vida put her book knowledge to the test and put her real estate move into effect. Samara's mother worked at Bank of America so Vida went to holla at her and laid her real estate plan down. With the

$50,000 she had in the bank—Vida already had good credit and no debt—the bank granted her a loan for the property, and in days she had a check for $150,000 to begin her mission.

The house Vida was focused on was in a nice middle-class section of Northwest, D.C. It had once been a crack house that was now boarded up. It was a nasty eyesore among the houses on the block with it. Vida purchased the house for $95,000.

Sitting in front of the boarded up house in her BMW, Vida went over her game plan with Moe-Moe. After months of messing with each other they were now in an official relationship and trusted one another. "Other houses on the block are appraised at prices as high as $400,000. I'm sure I can get at least half of that once I get the joint fixed up," Vida said. "That will be double what I paid for it."

Moe-Moe looked at the house with its boarded up windows; high, uncut grass; and fading paint. The joint looked like something out of a horror flick. "I'm gon' need a lotta help, but I can help you fix it up. All we need is a little bit of time."

"We got a deal then," Vida said as she pulled off and drove down Jefferson Street. "Tia said she gon' help me cover the cost of the renovations. All you gotta do is put a small team together."

All the way to Moe-Moe's apartment they discussed the game plan. Once they got there they ate Chinese food and enjoyed spending time together while watching *Friday* and smoking a little weed.

Rubbing Vida's thigh, Moe-Moe said, "I got claims on you now, right? You all mine?"

Vida smiled and said, "I should be askin' you that. I know you still got bitches chasin' you."

"Cut the jokes out. When I'm not wit' you I'm at work. You know that." He brushed her hair out of her face. "Besides, I got all the woman I want and need right here." He popped her on the ass. "Ain't that right?"

Giving him a quick kiss on the lips, Vida said, "I guess so." She then smiled and playfully rolled her eyes. "I'm all yours as long as you act right."

EYONE WILLIAMS

Just after 11:30 P.M., the parking lot of Tia's Capitol Heights apartment complex was jumping like a '64 Impala. Music was pumping out of cars. A crap game was in full swing. Dudes were serving coke at one end of the court in front of the buildings. Tia and Zoe were sitting in her BMW drinking Remy. Bloody was leaning in a car serving sacks of Boat (PCP) to some young dudes.

Sitting on the hood of her BMW wagon, Ice had her arms around a guy named Walt's neck. He was standing face-to-face with her, trying to get her to hit the hotel with him. Walt slid his finger inside Ice's pussy and felt her gush. He knew she was ready to fuck. Her Polo jacket hid Walt's hands so no one knew what they were doing.

As she got wetter between the legs, Ice whispered in Walt's ear, "Can you work your tongue like that?" She then licked his ear.

'Let's hit the hotel and find out." Walt was rock hard, so much so that it was painful.

"Let me see if you worth the time." Ice slid her hand inside his pants. "Mmmmmm, I'm impressed."

Walt laughed. "It gets greater later." Still working her with his fingers, his whole hand was covered with her cream.

"That's how you feel?" Ice sighed in a sexy way.

"No question." Walt felt Ice cum and saw her eyes roll back in her head as she humped his fingers.

Bloody was making a killing with the Boat. Cars kept pulling into the parking lot looking for the Boat that she was pumping. Word on the streets was that the Boat she and Ice had was like the shit from the 1980s that had muthafuckas jumping off of apartment buildings and running down Georgia Avenue ass-naked, lunching good. A brown Monte Carlo with three dudes in it pulled into the parking lot. Bloody stepped to the passenger side window and said, "What y'all want?"

"Let me get four of them sacks," the passenger said, sipping a cup of Remy. Master P was pumping through the system. Bloody had the sacks in her hand; she handed them to the dude and the car pulled off on her with its occupants laughing.

Bitch-ass niggaz, Bloody thought. She whipped out her Ruger and opened fire on the car. The Monte Carlo had no way out of the parking lot unless it made a U-turn and came back toward Bloody. That wasn't going to happen. Holding her pistol with both hands,

Hell Razor *Honeys*

Bloody ran after the car firing repeatedly. POW! POW! POW! POW! POW! POW! POW!

"What the fuck?!" Ice pushed Walt off of her, whipped out her 10mm and ran after the Monte Carlo firing shots as well. Gunfire filled the air.

Taking heavy fire, the Monte Carlo skidded to a halt at the end of the parking lot. Two dudes jumped out firing TEC-9s. The third dude was dead in the back seat, hit in the head by Ice's 10mm. Bullets were flying in every direction. People caught in the crossfire were running, screaming and taking cover wherever they could.

Bloody had one of the dudes pent behind a parked car. She fired through the window, making him duck as she ran around the car. He popped up and spit five shots, making her duck behind another car. The dude then tried to make a run for the woods, but Bloody was right on him, firing round after round until she ran out of bullets.

Ice was running after the other dude, trying to take his head off. She chased him between the buildings. The dude fired the TEC-9 over his shoulder as he ran for his life. Ice stumbled and fell, sliding face first into the grass. Two slugs had caught her in the throat.

Tia was right behind Ice, also firing shots at the dude. When she saw Ice fall she thought Ice had just slipped. Gun in hand, Tia stopped to help Ice. The dude continued to head for the woods. "Come on, Ice, get up." Tia turned Ice over and felt her heart drop. Ice's throat looked like she'd been bit by a pit bull. "Ice! Ice!" Tia yelled frantically. Ice tried to smile as she blacked out in Tia's arms.

I notice repetition creeping in; let me stop and finalize.

EYONE WILLIAMS

CARTEL PUBLICATIONS PRESENTS

Chapter 19

The funeral home was decorated with countless flowers. Ice's mother and father held hands standing over her casket crying, each claiming the blame of her demise. Her life was cut short and they could not understand why. *Our child wasn't supposed to die the death of an average inner-city youth,* they thought. *What is the world coming to?*

Bloody and Tia were no-shows at the wake. They were being sought by the police in connection with the shooting that left three dead that night. Vida, Samara and a number of other mourners came to pay their respects. They all took their last look at Ice. There would never be another Ice; she was one of a kind.

Moe-Moe held Vida close to him as they walked up to view the body. Vida began to feel faint as she looked down at her girl. "You gon' always be my girl." Vida said out loud, as she rubbed Ice's face. Tears rolled down Vida's face non-stop. Enough was enough. The madness needed to stop. Thoughts of her grandmother's dying words came to mind as Vida looked down at Ice's lifeless body.

Ice was only nineteen; she left two twin boys behind. Her death was sure to be felt far and wide.

Vida got a chance to talk to Ice's mother before the wake was over. She knew how much Ice loved her mother. Vida only spoke to her for a second; she let her know how sorry she was for her loss. Ice's mother vowed to take care of the twins and give them the best life possible. Vida was pleased.

"I know how my daughter felt about you, she loved you like a sister," Ice's mother said as she wiped away tears of pain and hurt. She hugged Vida tightly, full of love. "If you ever need anything feel free

173

to call me. Now that I have the boys I'm sure we will see a lot more of each other."

"Yes, we will." Vida nodded, still crying. To be such a young woman she had seen and felt more than her fair share of pain and loss. She'd lost too many people close to her, people she really loved and considered family. "We will see a lot of each other."

Weeks passed quickly after Ice's funeral. The pain of Ice's death stacked on top of the pain of the death of Tec and Ms. Green weighed heavy on Vida's heart. With Samara away at school and Tia and Bloody down south laying low because they were wanted for murder, Vida grew even closer to Moe-Moe. She was in love with him. He always knew exactly what to do to make her feel better when she was down. He helped keep her focused. By the end of the year Vida and Moe-Moe had moved into a condo together in Lanham, Maryland. By March of 1999 Vida's real estate game plan had come to fruition. The old crack house she'd bought was now on the market for $250,000.

On the West Coast, No Draws was into everything but a casket. She'd now been in her first major motion picture and had been given a $150,000 check up front for her supporting role as a home wrecker. Checks were still coming in the mail for the movie she did with Liz. No Draws had also made guest appearances on WB's "Steve Harvey Show"; that put her face out there on another level. Daddieo wanted her to assist with his upcoming film. Among other things No Draws had her mind made up that she was going to start her own production company. Liz was teaching her everything she needed to know. No Draw's connections were growing stronger with every move she made.

In her spanking new silver Mercedes Benz 500SL, No Draws headed to Mario's office in Hollywood; her mind was on Liz's words of Hollywood wisdom. Liz kept her ever mindful of the fact that she had to work her shit to get ahead in her line of business.

"How are you?" Mario hugged No Draws as she came through the door.

'Just tryin' to get things movin'… you know how it is." No Draws took a seat on the sofa. She was feeling a little nervous.

Mario took a seat beside her. "So tell me about this plan you need my help with."

No Draws laid out the first part of her plan. Her name was respected in some Hollywood circles, but if she were to star in a movie it would raise her stock tenfold and then some. Mario had a box office killer in the making that was to be directed by John Singleton. No Draws wanted the lead female role.

Mario laughed. "I'm already working with Vivica Fox."

"Come on now, Mario." No Draws smiled.

"I'm sorry, I can't do that."

"I don't think you understand. I'm not asking." No Draws got up and walked over to the VCR and popped in a tape while Mario looked on, dumbfounded. No Draws let the tape play. Mario's eyes got big as shotgun barrels. He was the star of the movie on the screen; he was bent over with ten inches of dick in his ass in a hotel room somewhere.

"Where the hell did you get that?!" He jumped to his feet in a homicidal rage.

No Draws felt her hands begin to shake, but she kept her game face on and did just as Liz told her to. "That's not important." She folded her arms. "What's important is that no one has to know what I know if you act right."

Mario walked up and got in her face. She felt the heat of anger coming from his body. "You don't know who you're fucking with." He pointed his finger in her face; it took everything in him not to knock her funky ass out cold. "Liz put you up to this, didn't she? You're playing a dangerous game. You could wake up one morning with your brakes cut, you know. It would be just another car crash," Mario hissed.

"I doubt it." No Draws rolled her eyes. "I want the lead role and you're going to give it to me, plus a million dollars to help me start my company."

"I treated you good you trifling bitch!" Mario sighed and walked to his desk. "I'll give you what you want, but that tape must disappear, forever."

Got 'em, No Draws thought. "Don't worry... I don't intend to ruin you; I just need to make sure I'm set. It's not personal."

Later on, sitting on her living room sofa, No Draws told Liz how things went with Mario while they drank wine and laughed.

"You learn fast." Liz rubbed No Draw's thigh. "We're going to be great business partners."

"I agree. You have taught me so much. I know we're gonna do big things together." No Draws smiled.

"You've done a lot for me as well. You make me feel twenty years old again." Liz stood up. "I see bright things in our future. We're going to make a great team."

"Let me ask you somethin', Liz."

"Anything, darling," Liz replied.

"You and Mario are friends, so why'd you let me work him wit' that tape?"

Liz smiled. "Its business, you know that."

"Yeah, I know."

No Draws understood the game. She also understood that Liz was a snake who would do anything to succeed. No Draws had made up her mind to use Liz for what she was worth and then to move on. At the same time, No Draws knew that she had to make Liz feel as though she was in control.

"Do you always keep tabs on your friends?" No Draws asked in a joking way.

Liz winked at her student. She knew what No Draws was getting at. "You can trust me," Liz said, sipping her wine. "On another note, you're a millionaire now. Let's celebrate."

"What does such an accomplishment call for?" asked No Draws.

"Have you ever been to Barbados? It's beautiful all year round."

"No, but I'd love to go."

"Pack some clothes, I'll have Frank get the jet ready," Liz said.

Like true stars, Liz and No Draws flew to the island country in the West Indies. Liz checked them into the Fairmont Plaza in Bridgetown—the capital. Bridgetown was also the largest city, chief port of the city and the tourist center. No Draws loved everything, the pleasant climate, sandy beaches and the black people that spoke English. Some of them even knew who she was. That was a hell of a high. Liz took her to eat at all the top spots. They drove along the coast on the left side of the street taking in the beautiful sights. They went shopping in the business district and spent tens of thousands. After three days of ballin' they decided to rent a yacht and enjoy some time on the beautiful Caribbean Sea.

No Draws stood under the hot water taking a shower on the yacht. She had soap all over her body with her eyes closed, enjoying the heat. Her mind was focused on the moves she wanted to put in motion once she got back to L.A. Things were coming together well. She'd only need Liz for a little while longer.

"You didn't invite me?" Liz stepped in the shower with a playfully sad face. She slid up behind No Draws and hugged her, pressing breast against her back as she cupped No Draws' full breast. Liz sucked on No Draws' neck while playing with her nipples. "You know I need to be close to you."

"You know I always got time for you, Liz." No Draws began to grow warm inside. Liz always had such an effect on her. "I was just thinkin' 'bout you," No Draws said. As Liz slid one hand down No Draws' wet body and slid a finger inside her pussy, No Draws put her hands behind her and began rubbing Liz's wet ass. They both began to breathe hard.

"You make me so wet, Shelly," Liz panted as she licked No Draws' ear, sticking her tongue inside. She continued to finger fuck her while grinding on her ass at the same time. No Draws squeezed Liz's ass hard. "You know how to bring the freak out of me."

No Draws began to shake and cum as she closed her eyes. Liz was working her clit so good that No Draws began to moan. "You make me cum so hard. Sssss… mmmmmhhhmmm… you make me feel so good."

"I want you to do the same for me, Shelly."

"Yes… yes… yes, I'll do whatever you say, Liz, just don't stop."

Liz smiled and used her other hand to work No Draws over. She slipped her thumb in her asshole. "You like that, Shelly?" she whispered into her ear.

"Oh yes, yes… yes… I love it." No Draws was cumming again, harder. With fingers working her pussy and her asshole at the same time, No Draws felt like a sports car being pushed to its limits at top speed. "Aaahh…."

"Good girl… cum for momma, Shelly… cum for momma."

No Draws bit her bottom lip as her eyes rolled back in her head. She began to feel faint, close to passing out from an overload of her pleasure senses. "I'm cummin' again, Liz! Don't stop!" No Draws sank to the floor after she came; her legs could no longer hold her.

Zoe sat at his dining room table talking to two homicide detectives. He had given them Tia and Bloody's whereabouts down south. However, when FBI agents raided the spot Tia and Bloody were no longer there. Now the detectives were threatening to charge Zoe in connection with the triple homicide.

"I swear to God, I don't know where they at. I ain't heard from them since the last time I told you." Zoe had the look of deep dread on his face.

"You need to start thinkin' real quick, buddy," the tall detective said.

"Look, man, let me see if I can find out where they are. You need to check with the girl Vida I was tellin' you about. I'm sure she knows somethin'. Let me check around and I'll call you in a day or two—"

"You don't have a day or two!" the other detective hissed.

"Hold on, Jim," the tall detective said. "Let's see what he can give us."

"Okay," his partner said. The detectives stood to leave.

The tall detective said, "We'll be waiting."

After the detectives left his apartment Zoe paced back and forth in the living room. He was in a frantic state of mind, like a man trapped inside a tank that was quickly filling with water. Zoe wasn't going to prison for nobody. *Fuck that,* he thought. He had to do something, fast. He knew Tia and Bloody were running low on cash; he'd just wired them $2,500 a few days before the detectives put the press on him.

Zoe grabbed the phone and called Vida. Moe-Moe's cousin, Chris, answered the phone and put Vida on. "Vee, what's up? What you doin'?"

"Studyin' for school," Vida said.

"I ain't heard from Tee, I'm startin' to worry about her. I ain't heard from her since the last time I sent her some money."

"I ain't heard from her or seen her since she hit the road," Vida lied. She didn't feel comfortable talking about Tia on the phone. Alarms went off in her head as soon as Zoe asked her about Tia on the phone. He'd never done so before. Vida knew damn well where Tia and Bloody were, she was sending them money through Samara twice a month. "Is somethin' wrong?"

"Nah, I'm just a little worried, that's all," Zoe said.

"Well, I gotta finish studyin'. Let me know if you hear from Tee," said Vida.

After getting off the phone with Vida, Zoe needed to clear his mind. He jumped in his car and hit the beltway blasting Ja Rules's "Holla Holla." He felt like shit for working with the police. Lighting a blunt, he took the weed to the head and thought about how he could locate Tia and Bloody so he could get the bodeans off his back.

A few days later, Zoe still didn't have anything new for the detectives, and he could feel the pressure. He was trying to duck them, but how long could that last? Coming home from the go-go, Zoe was thinking about pussy. He thought about calling one of his hoes on the side. As he stuck his key in the door two sharp coughing sounds from a silenced pistol came from behind him. His whole world faded to black as slugs crashed into the back of his head. His limp body slumped to the ground with a strong thud. The killer disappeared into the night.

The next morning Vida was greeted by two homicide detectives as she left for work. "What the fuck do they want?" she asked herself as she stepped outside. Her nerves became jumpy.

"We'd like to ask you a few questions," one of the detectives said.

"About what?" Vida sucked her teeth and rolled her eyes.

"About the murders your friends are wanted for?"

"Look here, I don't know shit about no got-damn murders, and I wish you muhfuckas would leave me the fuck alone. I ain't heard from Tia and Bloody in I don't know how long. Okay?!" she snapped.

"What about the murder of Mr. Zoe Smithers?" the detective spit with a smug look on his pale face. "We know you spoke to him a few days before he was murdered. Do you mind telling us what that conversation was about?"

Frustrated, Vida looked at her watch and said, "Look, I'm late for work. I don't have time for this shit!" Vida tried to walk past the detectives.

Stepping in front of her, the tall detective said, "We'll be seeing you again, soon."

"Kiss my ass. I ain't broke no damn laws, so you won't be talkin' to me, you'll be talkin' to my lawyer." Vida jumped in her BMW and headed to work.

Although she carried shit like a soldier, she was still a little shook that the detectives were sweating her. She didn't need the heat that Zoe's murder was sure to bring. When the murder made the news Vida knew the police would be paying her a visit. She tried to clear her mind when she got to work, but when her shift was up she found the detectives following her. Even when she got home she noticed that they just sat across the street from her spot.

Zoe's murder had his man Walt trippin'. Walt couldn't put it together. It had him puzzled. He hit the streets trying to find out who had smashed his man. Sitting in a car on Pomeroy Road, Southeast, Walt was waiting for Zoe's cousin to come out of his apartment. Walt kept his eyes on everything moving. It was just after 10:00 P.M. A few dudes were at the top of the block pumpin', but other than that shit was cool.

Walt turned his attention to the blunt he was rolling. Suddenly, bullets from a silenced pistol came crashing through the driver side window. The whole side of Walt's head opened up like a cracked coconut. Lifelessly, he slumped onto the wheel, causing the horn to blare nonstop. His killer dashed down the street and around the corner where a black Mazda RX7 awaited.

Walking down Elvans Road, Southeast after dark with a pipehead, a young man in an over-sized winter coat handed the pipehead two $20 rocks and took the $35 from him. The two went their separate ways. The young man's beeper vibrated in his pocket as he crossed the street. He fumbled with the beeper to check the number. A black Mazda RX7 came down the street. The driver side window was already down. A .32 automatic with a long silencer on it appeared and fired five rounds, dropping the young man. His beeper fell to the ground. A gunman jumped out of the passenger side, ran over to the dying young man and pumped four more slugs into the back of his head.

Chapter 20

Tia turned herself in to Prince George's County police two weeks after the murders of Zoe, Walt and the dude on Elvans Road. She and Bloody had put that work in, off the no bullshit. After their hotel was raided they began to second guess Zoe. But after Vida told them how he had called her acting all funny and shit they knew they had to take his ass out. Tia and Bloody put their plan into effect and headed back to the D.C. area where they smashed Zoe, Walt and the dude on Elvans Road—he was the dude that killed Ice. Poor Walt really got a bad one; Tia and Bloody decided to smash him on the strength that he was the only person alive that could connect them to the murders.

With no witnesses that could testify against her, Tia only spent two weeks in jail before the murder charges were dismissed and she was free to go.

"You gotta chill, Tee," Vida said, pushing her BMW up I-95 headed to New York. "You goin' too hard. It's time to slow down, baby girl."

"I'm hip, I'ma chill. I just couldn't take no chances wit' that murder shit over my head. I can't go out like that. When Bloody said we should just wipe shit out, I was like, yeah, no bullshit. Dead niggaz tell no tales."

"I know that's right." Vida shook her head." So what's up wit' Bloody?"

"She called me this mornin'. She said they should drop her shit in St. Louis some time this week and send her to Maryland. We already know what's gon' happen when she get to Maryland." Tia dropped her seat back and rested her arm behind her head. "Shit gon' work out just fine."

Vida smiled and shook her head. "You too many things, girl."

Once in New York City, they checked into the Four Seasons Hotel where they unpacked. They were only spending the weekend in the Big Apple; a little shopping, a club or two and then back home.

Coming out of the bathroom, Tia said, "When Moe-Moe comin' over?"

"Why you worried about my man, bitch?" Vida joked.

Tia smiled and rolled her eyes playfully. "I'm just tryin' to get out the way for a minute. I know y'all need some space. Plus, Chris keep tryin' to holla at me, is he wit' Moe-Moe?"

"Nah, he ain't come here wit' him," Vida said.

"Yeah, I wish that nigga would stop tryin' to holla at me. I told him I don't fuck wit' niggaz my girls used to mess wit'. Even though I know Ice ain't have no feelings for him." Tia began rolling a Backwood. "Now that nigga Styles that Moe-Moe be wit', I'm feelin' him, a little bit." She laughed.

"Yeah, right." Vida looked at her watch "Moe-Moe should be here in a little while." She stood up and threw on her leather jacket. "Let's go get somethin' to eat."

"Cool, I'm tryin' to get out and about anyway." Tia followed Vida out the door.

They hit Junior's restaurant in Brooklyn. Vida loved cheesecake. They both ordered shrimp scampi and had fun just hanging out with no drama.

"Tee, main man keeps checkin' you out." Vida cut her eyes at a dude that was sitting behind them.

Tia took a quick look and the dude winked at her. She smiled and gave him a quick wave before turning back to face Vida. "He jive cute too."

"He got that whole Allen Iverson thing goin' on," said Vida.

Tia smiled. "He do look like A.I. a little bit." She took another look and saw that the dude was walking their way.

"How you doing?" the dude spoke.

"I'm good, what's up wit' you?" Tia checked out his gear. He wore a black leather jacket, blue jeans and Timberlands. He was Tia's type; he was smooth, with street swagger.

"Y'all alone?" The dude didn't sound like he was from New York.

"Not really, we just eatin' alone right now," Tia said.

"Can I join you two for a second?"

"Yeah, why not?" Tia patted the spot next to her in the wrap-around booth.

The dude had style. He made Vida feel at ease and comfortable while he laid his thang down with Tia. He had them both smiling and laughing the whole time. His name was Wendell. Wendell was from Northwest, D.C., but lived in New York where he and his cousin sold car rims.

"I don't mean to run after such a short time, but I gotta meet my cousin." Wendell looked at Tia as he stood. "I'll call you. I'd like to take you out before you go back home, if that's cool wit' you."

"We can do that." Tia smiled, she was feeling Wendell.

Wendell shook their hands and said, "Your meals are on me." He dropped four hundred dollar bills on the table. "I'll catch y'all later." Wendell strolled out the door.

Vida and Tia talked about Wendell for a second. "I think slim feelin' you. You gon' give—" Vida cut her sentence short and zoned out. "Look at this shit here!" She got dead serious.

Tia looked over her shoulder to see what was wrong. Looking back at Vida she said, "What you wanna do, Vee?"

Daddieo and No Draws walked through the door holding hands like two lovers. The shit made Vida's stomach turn.

"Fuck that shit; he ain't my man no way." Vida stood up. "Let's go."

Tia took it upon herself to step to Daddieo and No Draws. Looking No Draws in the eyes, Tia said, "You just fuck every nigga that a bitch been wit', huh, ho'?"

"Bitch, you better get the fuck out my face," No Draws snapped.

Tia couldn't understand where the bitch got so much heart from. Before Vida could grab her, Tia smacked the shit out of No Draws and threw a glass of water in her face. Vida grabbed Tia and Daddieo grabbed No Draws.

Vida looked at Daddieo and said, "I guess you like trash. You got the right to sleep wit' dogs."

"Fuck that! Let me go!" No Draws screamed, trying to snatch away from Daddieo.

"Bitch, stop fakin', I'll mop the floor wit' your ho-ass!" Tia hissed, ready to work. "You hip to me. You better be lucky I ain't slice your muhfuckin' face open, bitch!"

Vida began pulling Tia out the door before shit got too far out of hand.

On the way back to the hotel Vida tried to calm Tia down. "Fuck that shit, Tee. I ain't even trippin'. I been through so much in the last few years that I don't even got time for the bullshit no more. I ain't got time for the drama. Feel me?"

"I feel you, but that snake ass bitch needs her ass kicked." Tia rolled her eyes. "You shoulda let me fuck that bitch up."

"Don't trip. She'll get what she got comin'. She ain't even worth the time." Vida was trying to distance herself from the bullshit by all means.

Chapter 21

Vida walked across the stage to receive her degree; the smile on her face was full of pride and accomplishment. She looked into the crowd and saw Moe-Moe, his man Styles, his cousin Chris, Samara, Bloody, Tia, Ice's mother and the twins. It was the best day of her life. Her grandmother would have been proud. Vida did what she had to do. She'd gotten her life together and settled down. A huge load was lifted off her shoulders. At twenty-four years old she had seen and done more than most people twice her age.

Hours later, Vida was celebrating her graduation at the home she and Moe-Moe had bought in Alexandria, Virginia. It was a huge Southern Colonial Victorian with a long wrap-around porch, two car garage, and a deep green lawn. The price tag was $649,000. Down in the basement, Jay-Z played in the background as Vida and Tia were shooting pool. Samara sat on the deep leather sofa talking to Styles. Bloody and Moe-Moe were beefing on the PlayStation playing John Madden Football.

Vida sank the eight ball. "That's you, baby girl. I told you… you can't get in my business." She laughed.

"Bet back." Tia threw a hundred dollar bill on the green surface.

"Make it light on yourself."

Tia and Vida played two more games—Tia punished her. Tia's cell phone vibrated in her pocket. It was Wendell. She told Vida to hold on and answered the call. "What's up, sexy?"

"What's up wit' you?" Wendell asked.

"Chillin'."

"I'm uptown. I'm tryin' to see you."

"I'll meet you in thirty minutes, cool?" Tia asked.

"Bet."

Tia said her goodbyes to everybody and hit the road.

Bloody went up to the kitchen to get something to drink and ran into Samara and Styles all hugged up in the living room. Bloody smiled and went on about her business. *It's good to be back around family,* Bloody thought. She'd just gotten out of prison for a drug beef she'd caught in Silver Spring, Maryland; she only did eighteen months on the beef. Now she and Tia were back at it, moving weight together.

Vida walked out the back door into the cool spring air and took a deep breath. She felt good about herself. Looking around the dark back yard, she saw Moe-Moe smoking a Backwood as he leaned against the side of the house in a gray Rocawear T-shirt, black Mann's World jeans and a pair of white S. Carter tennis shoes.

"I'm proud of you, baby," Moe-Moe said as Vida walked over. He blew smoke into the air and continued. "I know you feel good about that."

"Yeah, I do," Vida said as their black pit bull Jaws ran up to her wanting to play. She rubbed his head. "I feel like I made it. You know? I'm thankful that I had you by my side." She gave Moe-Moe a kiss. "You kept me focused. I love you so much for that."

With his arms around Vida, Moe-Moe said, "You had your mind made up, and you didn't let anything get in your way. I love that about you. When you put your mind to something you get the job done."

"I really wish my grandmother was here to see how far I've come," Vida said.

"Believe me... she knows that you put your work in." Moe-Moe took one more pull on the Backwood and plucked it in the grass. Jaws ate the roach. Vida and Moe-Moe laughed. "I guess I need to stop smoking wit' slim so much," Moe-Moe said.

"It's too late for that." Vida laughed.

"Check this out... I'm glad you slid out here. I got somethin' to holla at you about."

"What?" Vida's eyebrows went up. "Don't tell me you in love wit' another bitch or some crazy shit like that," she joked.

"On the real, check this out." Moe-Moe dug in his pocket and pulled out a small black box. Vida's eyes grew big with excitement. "I told you that I want to spend the rest of my life wit' you. Now that you are done wit' school and we are doin' our thing wit' the real estate thing, I think we need to make this thing official, baby." Moe-Moe opened the box and exposed a huge, sparkling diamond ring.

"That's the smoothest way you can ask me to marry you? You ain't gon' get down on your knees and all that romantic shit?"

Moe-Moe laughed. "Come on, baby. It's all or nothin' wit us anyway, you know that."

"I know, I'm just messin' wit' you, boy." Vida stuck her hand out and Moe-Moe slid the ring on her finger. She hugged him and kissed him on his lips.

"I take that as a yes."

"Yes, you know it's a yes, nigga." She playfully punched him in the arm.

Leaving the L.A. court house, No Draws spoke with her lawyer for a few minutes and then jumped in her Benz and headed home as the sun set. Pissed off was an understatement, she was fucked up! No Draws felt like a fool; she had called herself being on top of her game and had decided that she no longer needed Liz, so she tried to cut Liz off. However, Liz was on top of her game for real. In the paper work that they'd signed when they started their production company, there were complex clauses that stated if No Draws ever broke their contract that Liz was to take over the company. Trying to be slick, No Draws tried to back door Liz, but Liz was waiting for such underhanded shit from No Draws. Now Liz had her by the balls and was taking everything.

No Draws and Liz had made a lot of money together during the past few years. With three movies under their belt and millions of dollars in profits, they were taking care of business. Greed drove No Draws to try to cut Liz out of a big movie deal with Warner Brothers.

Liz let No Draws hang herself.

Later on, at the Sky Bar on Sunset Strip, No Draws sat alone drinking a martini. It seemed like all of her dreams were coming to an end. *I can't believe this shit,* she thought. *At times things seemed too good to be true anyway.* Hate began to boil inside her heart, hate and anger.

Daddieo showed up a few minutes later and took a seat beside No Draws. He now lived out west also; they were still fucking around in spots as well. "How'd things go in court?" Daddieo asked.

"I'm gon' lose all I've worked so fuckin' hard for. That bitch is goin' to laugh in my face and walk away wit' it all."

"I don't mean to sound cold," Daddieo rubbed her hand, "but you can do it all over again. You got what it takes. Don't forget that."

No Draws smiled. "Thank you. I really needed to hear that, but it still breaks my heart to know that she's gonna take away my fuckin' company. How could I be so stupid?"

Daddieo had his hands involved in a lot of things; he was trying to open up the doors of network TV. In a way it was good that No Draws was taking a fall, as far as he was concerned. She would be more hungry, just like she was when she first hit L.A. Daddieo could use that hunger. "You know we could go at this TV move together… you'd be perfect for it. Your name is still hot. This would keep your face out there until you get back where you want to be. It'll put you back in the pocket. What you think about that?"

On the real, No Draws didn't like the TV idea; it was going backwards in her book. Nevertheless, it was the only move on the horizon at the time. "Let me think things over and finish wit' this legal shit and I'll let you know somethin', okay?"

"Sounds good," replied Daddieo.

Days later No Draws had pulled herself together after licking her wounds. She gave Liz a call and asked her to meet her at the Garden of Eden—a nightclub that Liz loved because it allowed her to meet young men.

"So you submit… is that what you're telling me, Shelly? You give up?" Liz smiled, loving the thought of still being in control of No Draws in some kind of way. The thought alone made Liz wet between the thighs. Sipping her Watermelon Pucker, Liz waited for an answer.

"You win, Liz." No Draws was defeated. She was way out of her league.

Liz leaned forward as if she were about to tell a secret and said, "I always win. You should know that." Liz killed her drink. "Now, I'm still gonna take everything, just to teach your young ass a lesson. But, I'll give you a chance to get back on my good side now that you know who the top bitch is on this end." Liz patted No Draws' hand. "Now you be good, you hear." She got up and walked away without another word. No Draws was burning with anger.

Liz's blue Mercedes Benz pulled up in the driveway of her Hollywood Hills home. Her driver got out and opened the door. "Oh my God!" he gasped. Liz was sprawled across the back seat covered in her own vomit. The driver tried to wake her, but she would not come around. Shaking her, the driver thought she'd had too much to drink. Nothing he did got her to come around. He began to panic and quickly got the paramedics on the scene. Liz was rushed to the hospital.

"I do," Vida sealed the deal. The pastor told Moe-Moe he could kiss the bride. He did. They were now husband and wife.

It was a cool September afternoon. A few clouds filled the sky. The backyard of their house was filled with only close family and friends. In a row of white chairs sat Ice's mother, Ice's twins, Tia, Samara, Bloody, Moe-Moe's mother and his two aunts. There were a few others on the scene to witness the event that joined Vida and Moe-Moe in marriage. It was a great day. Vida and Moe-Moe had spent top dollar to make everything about their wedding a royal event.

Later on, everyone mixed and had a good time, eating and drinking while music filled the backyard. Vida still had on her beautiful white Versace gown and was glowing with happiness as she played the role of the best hostess.

"You look beautiful, Vida." Ice's mother hugged Vida, they'd grown very close.

"Thank you, you look great as well."

"You have really done something with your life. School... real estate... now you're married. All you have to do now is start a family."

"Let's not move too fast." Vida laughed. "I still have a few things I want to do first."

"You're still young. You have your whole life ahead of you."

While Vida was talking to Ice's mother, Moe-Moe and his man Styles were down by the small man-made pond talking. At this point in his life Moe-Moe had been crime free for years. Real estate was his hustle; he and Vida were partners in crime on that. However, as of lately, Styles was on some other shit, trying to get Moe-Moe to finance a drug move he was trying to put together. Moe-Moe wanted no parts of the move.

"Styles, you my nigga, but I don't want my hands in none of that shit you talkin' 'bout. For real, slim. I told you what I'm tryin' to do. You act like you can't respect that. I ain't even tryin' to have this conversation. This my weddin' day... I'm tryin' to chill, slim. You blowin' me wit' this bullshit." Moe-Moe was fed up. If he and Styles weren't so close he would have really snapped on him.

"That's fucked up you ain't tryin' to see me get no money," Styles said.

"Look, man, I'm through wit' this shit here," Moe-Moe replied.

"Whatever, nigga. You wanna get all brand new on a nigga." Styles stepped off. Moe-Moe looked at him like he was tripping.

Drinking Remy at the table with Samara, Tia and Bloody, Vida got her laugh on as the girls cracked on her about how Moe-Moe was going to start pumping babies up in her. "I want kids, just not right now. I got some moves I want to make first." Vida sipped her drink as Jay-Z played in the background.

"Moe-Moe ain't goin' for that," Bloody said. "You might as well accept it; you got that ring so you done signed over all rights." All the girls laughed.

"That's why I'm still havin' fun until I finish law school." Samara was going to Georgetown Law; she had plans on being a heavy weight defense attorney. "Once I'm done wit' school and I've made a name for myself then I might settle down."

"Bitch, please!" Vida laughed. "You on dick too hard to settle down… cut the jokes out."

"No bullshit," Tia cut in. "You still got niggaz payin' all your bills, car note, rent, tuition and everything else." All the girls burst out laughing.

"I ain't forgot how to work good pussy." Samara snapped her fingers with pride.

"I know that's right," Bloody said.

"Look how far good pussy got No Draws." Samara sipped her Remy.

"Yeah, you see what that got her slut ass." Tia rolled her eyes.

No Draws had been arrested and charged with Liz's murder a month after her death. Traces of arsenic and nitroglycerin were found in Liz's bloodstream. The police immediately began to look at No Draws as a suspect, but couldn't make an arrest until an informant came forward with details about No Draws buying arsenic capsules. No Draws was awaiting trial on the murder beef.

While the girls were talking Styles came over and told Samara that he was ready to leave; they were on their way to the Poconos for the weekend. Samara had a few more laughs with the girls before she rolled out.

Just after 11:00 P.M. Vida and Moe-Moe were alone in their bed with Frankie Beverly playing in the background. They had just finished making good love and were soaking wet, breathing like they'd just sprinted two miles.

Out of breath, Moe-Moe said, "You jive tried to get out on me."

Vida laughed. She was lying on her side, rubbing his chest and admiring his body. Moe-Moe had the look of a dude that had spent years in prison doing all kinds of different work outs. "I gotta throw this pussy on you, make sure you don't stray. If I do my job I ain't gotta worry about you fuckin' none of these other bitches out here."

"You already know that you do your job just fine." He smiled then kissed her for what seemed like minutes. He began rubbing her hair. "You ain't gotta worry about me. I got all the pussy I want and need right here in the bed wit' me. That's why I married you, Vee, I love you." He kissed her again. "Don't you ever forget that."

Vida kissed his lips. "Don't you ever forget it, nigga." She smiled. "Not to change the subject, but I meant to ask you somethin'. What was up wit' Styles? He acted like he had an attitude about somethin' when he left."

"That nigga trippin'." Moe-Moe told Vida about the conversation he and Styles had. Moe-Moe was messed up about the whole thing but was trying not to think about it. "I'm 'bout to pull back up off slim and all the rest of my homies that got one-track minds. I'm on some different shit now."

"Don't let that shit get to you, boo." Vida seductively straddled him and placed both of her hands on his chest while grinding against him with her wetness. She felt him grow hard again between her legs. "We got other things to worry about." She slid down on his thick manhood and began to ride him.

Hell Razor Honeys

Chapter 22

For their honeymoon Moe-Moe and Vida flew down to Miami where they rented a luxury yacht with a small three-man crew, and cruised to the Virgin Islands. Their first stop was St. Thomas, the harbor city of Charlotte Amalie, which was also the capital. It was surrounded by high tree-covered hills. Huge ocean liners docked in the harbor. The tropical climate, attractive beaches, lovely scenery and tropical flowers and trees gave Vida a euphoric sensation.

Sitting on the top deck of the yacht in the afternoon sun wearing a Prada T-shirt and Polo jean shorts, Vida ate lunch with Moe-Moe, feeling like royalty. Off to her left, rising above the skyline, was Crown Mountain. It towered 1,556 feet above the sea, surrounded by a range of beautiful trees that were in clear view of the ocean.

"This is life here," Vida said.

"It gets better in time." Moe-Moe rubbed her hand softly. "As long as we remain a team we can do whatever we set our minds to, you know that?"

"Once we get them other houses fixed up we gon' really come up like the mob."

"Everything gon' work out, baby. I'm gon' make it all work for us."

Vida smiled, she was deeply in love with Moe-Moe. He made her feel like a queen. He always made her feel loved and special. "I know you'll make it work, boo. You always do."

After lunch they went to the market district to shop. They hit the beach after that and enjoyed the water.

In Moe-Moe's arms as they floated in the clear blue water, Vida

194 EYONE WILLIAMS

looked in his eyes and said, "I'm ready for a family."

Moe-Moe gave her a puzzled look. "Where did that come from, baby?"

"I been thinkin'; life is short. I just want us to have kids—"

"Kids?" He smiled

"Yeah." Vida smiled

"You sure you ready for that?"

"Yeah, I'm sure." She kissed him deep and passionately.

"Let's get started then, we got work to do." He dunked her in the water. They began to play fight, enjoying the rest of the day.

Two weeks later, Tia pulled up in front of Vida's old building on Montana Avenue. It was dark outside but the action was still in full swing, just like old times. A group of young dudes stood in front of the building selling coke hand-to-hand. Most of them were working for Tia, the others were buying weight from her and Bloody. Recognizing Tia's black Corvette, Lil' Rose walked over to holla at her. He bent down to lean in the driver's side window and began discussing business with her.

Rose was a smooth eighteen year old that was buying a brick a week from Tia. He was also trying his best to fuck her, which she found amusing. Lil' Rose looked like he was Spanish due to his light skin and slick, curly, black hair. He was also known to fire his pistol.

"You ain't stepped to me in almost a week, what's the deal? You ain't fuckin' wit' a bitch no more?" Tia joked, watching the action in front of the building with a sharp eye.

"Hell nah, you know it ain't like that, Tee. I told you it's some Panamanian dudes around here that just opened shop up the street. A few niggaz done started fuckin' wit' them," Lil' Rose said.

"The Panamanians fuckin' up the cash flow, huh?" Tia asked.

"Kill my mutha, mo, that's on everything." Lil' Rose swore his strongest oath.

"We can't go for no shit like that." Tia had been hearing about the dude Lito for the past few weeks. He had snatched a few of her weight customers. "I jive checked the dude out wit' the Panamanian dude I be dealin' wit' over Southeast, my man say the nigga got ran from up New York for steppin' on toes. I guess he think he gon' come down here wit' that bullshit." Tia's cell phone vibrated. It was Vida. "Hold on real quick, Rose," Tia said and then answered the phone. "What's up, Vee?"

"Tee, I need to see you, right now, it's important!" Vida sounded frantic.

"You okay, Vee? You sound like somethin' wrong." Tia's alarms went off.

"I don't want to talk about it over the phone, just get over here as fast as you can, okay?" Vida said in a rush.

Tia felt a sudden sense of anxiety rush through her body. "I'm on my way, Vee." She snapped her cell phone shut. Looking at Lil' Rose, Tia said, "I gotta go take care of somethin' real quick. We gon' bake a cake for that Panamanian nigga."

"Bet," Lil' Rose said, giving Tia five.

On the highway Tia was pushing the Corvette at high speeds with BG playing. The way Vida sounded had Tia worried; Vida hadn't sounded like that since Tec died. Tia called Bloody on her cell phone.

"What's up?" Bloody was also on the highway racing to Vida's house.

"Where you at?" Tia asked.

"I'm on my way to Vida's house. She called and said she needed to see me," said Bloody.

Bloody and Tia had no idea what was wrong.

"I'll meet you there," Tia replied.

A short while later Tia pulled up and parked behind Bloody's BMW. Tia jogged up the walkway and let herself into the house. She was almost holding her breath in dreadful anticipation. She found Vida sitting on the sofa with Bloody trying to comfort her. Vida's face was covered with anger and despair. "What's wrong, Vee?" Tia demanded, standing in the middle of the living room.

"Somebody kidnapped Moe-Moe!" Vida blurted out, holding

back tears.

Moe-Moe had gone to check on his mother and never came back. Vida got a phone call a few hours later demanding $500,000.

"I think I know who's behind this shit," Vida said.

"Who?" Bloody put a hand on Vida's shoulder. "We gon' get Moe-Moe back."

Vida told them how Styles had been acting. "I'm almost certain that nigga got somethin' to do wit' this shit." Standing up, she said, "I swear to God, muhfuckas gon' pay for this shit!"

The phone rang. Vida answered it.

"You get that money together yet?" a deep voice asked.

"I'm workin' on it now. Please don't hurt him. I'll have the money in an hour." Vida felt her old fire beginning to burn again. "Where do I take the money?"

"I'll call back in thirty minutes." The caller hung up.

Vida looked at Tia and Bloody when she got off the phone. For a moment no one spoke a word. Tia and Bloody waited for Vida to speak. They knew what time it was. "I need $500,000 in cash," Vida finally said.

"We can get that," Tia spoke up.

"I want to find this nigga Styles in the meantime." Vida looked at Bloody.

Bloody gave a nod. "I got that." She headed for the door, on a mission.

Tia left to round up the cash, leaving Vida with a .45 automatic. Holding the pistol, Vida thought about her future. She thought about all she'd worked for. She thought about her grandmother and back to Moe-Moe. Shaking her head she said out loud, "Somebody's gon' pay." She cocked the hammer of the pistol.

Bloody knocked on Styles' apartment door, her Desert Eagle .357 was in her hand, behind her back.

Styles opened the door in nothing but his boxers. "What you doin' knockin' on my door like you crazy?'

In a flash, Bloody had the huge pistol in his face. "We need to talk, muhfucka." She put the pistol to his forehead and pushed him backward as she walked in slowly and shut the door.

"What the fuck is goin' on?" Samara came out of the bedroom in her bra and panties.

"Vida wanna talk to Styles." Bloody cut her eyes at Samara, keeping the pistol to Styles' head.

"For what?" Styles asked, shaking like a leaf in the wind.

"I'll let her tell you." With her free hand Bloody pulled her cell phone from her pocket and called Vida. "I got the nigga right here," Bloody said to Vida. She passed the phone to Styles at Vida's request.

Samara was scared to death and wanted to leave. She had no idea what she was caught up in. "I'm leavin'," Samara said.

"Don't move. Sit your ass down!" Bloody ordered. She was cool with Samara, but at the moment no chances would be taken.

Samara did as she was told. "You're not goin' to kill me, are you?"

"You did somethin' I should kill you for?" Bloody asked calmly, watching Styles like a hawk, paying close attention to his conversation with Vida. He was trying his best to convince Vida that he had nothing to do with what was going on with Moe-Moe.

"We all family," Samara said to Bloody, she was about to cry.

"I hope that's true." Bloody was ready to kill everything in the apartment if Vida said so.

Styles gave Bloody the phone back. "What you want me to do?" she asked Vida.

"Stay there and watch them. Answer the phone, check his beeper and everything. I'll call when I hear somethin' else," Vida said.

"What about Sam?"

"Let me speak to her."

Samara got on the phone. "Vee, tell Bloody not to hurt me, please," she blurted out.

"She not gon' hurt you. You family, I trust you. I know you wouldn't cross me, but some serious shit is goin' down right now. I need you to stay there until shit is cool. I'll explain it all. Bloody won't hurt you. I promise you that." Vida left it at that.

Trying his best to untie himself, Moe-Moe squirmed about on a dirty floor. Darkness covered him and the smell of piss and cigarette smoke filled his nose. He could also hear and smell a dog in the back room. His captors had left him blindfolded, gagged and tied up at the wrist and ankles. Facedown, as he struggled to free himself, he thought of the two men that had kidnapped him. They were rookies, they didn't even search him. He still had his cell phone clipped on his belt. However, what hurt him the most was the thought of who was behind the kidnapping—his cousin Chris.

Chris had also been pressing Moe-Moe to put him on with some cash so he could get back on his feet in the drug game. On the D.L., Chris believed that Moe-Moe still had his hands in the drug game. Chris wasn't buying it that Moe-Moe was doing so well with just real estate.

Moe-Moe freed himself and cracked the door to the back room. The pit bull began barking and growling menacingly. Moe-Moe quickly shut the door. His heart was pounding, fear set in as the dog kept barking. Moe-Moe knew someone upstairs would be rushing down the stairs to investigate. Just as the thought crossed his mind he heard the door at the top of the stairs open. The basement lights came on and someone rushed down the stairs.

Moe-Moe had to think fast; his life was on the line. Swiftly, he slid up against the wall alongside the stairs. A slim, brown-skinned dude bent the corner. Moe-Moe fired a crushing left hook that staggered the dude. The dude tried to reach for his pistol, but Moe-Moe rushed him and slammed him to the floor on his back. The pistol went off with a loud boom. Moe-Moe emerged from the scuffle with the pistol—a 9mm Glock. Wasting no time, Moe-Moe fired five shots into the dude's head.

Hearing someone coming down the stairs, Moe-Moe fired shots up the stairs. A quick burst of gunfire came back down the stairs. Moe-Moe sidestepped the gunfire and fired up the stairs again, out of sight this time. Dashing to the back room, Moe-Moe kicked the door open and shot the pit bull in the head twice. He then ran pass the dead dog and kicked the back door open. Stepping out into the darkness he ran up some concrete steps and down a narrow alley. Cutting through two apartment buildings, Moe-Moe ran across a busy section of Southern Avenue, Southeast. Crossing over into Maryland, still running top speed with the Glock in hand, Moe-Moe headed for a friends apartment in Oxon Hill.

Inside his man Frank's apartment Moe-Moe calmed himself down and told Frank what had just gone down.

"Damn, you sure it was Chris?" Frank asked in disbelief. "That's your blood."

"That's what I thought," Moe-Moe said, as he dialed Vida's number. "He may be blood, but he sure ain't family."

"Hello?!" Vida answered the phone. "Are you okay, baby? Where are you?" she fired countless questions.

"Hold fast, Vee. I'm okay. I'll tell you everything, just come get me." Moe-Moe told her where he was.

"I'm on my way right now, baby." Vida hung up.

"So what you gon' do?" Frank asked.

"I'ma take care of it," Moe-Moe said. He wanted to strike fast. Cousin or not, Chris was going to answer for what he'd done.

Moe-Moe jumped in the passenger seat of Bloody's BMW wagon and saw a MAC-10 lying across Vida's lap. Tia and Bloody were in the back with Beretta CX4 Storm Carbines that were loaded with fifty shot, .40 caliber clips. They had beams on top of the carbines. "Damn!" Moe-Moe said. "Y'all strapped for real."

"We got your back." Vida pulled into traffic. "Now tell me what the fuck is goin' on." Moe-Moe explained everything to the girls. Vida couldn't believe Chris would pull some shit like that. He'd sat at her table and ate her food, even slept at her house when he was on the run. "What's our next move?" Vida asked.

"Let's check his baby's mother's house," Moe-Moe said.

Vida headed for Congress Park. "I thought Styles was behind this bullshit," she said. She told Moe-Moe how she'd sent Bloody over to Styles' apartment. After she'd heard from Moe-Moe, Vida told Bloody to let Styles and Samara go.

Moe-Moe smirked. "That might be a problem." He knew how

Styles was going to react to that situation.

"It ain't like he can't get dealt wit'," Bloody said as the car pulled up at a stop light behind a gold Benz.

Vida's cell phone rang. "This the nigga Styles right here," she said.

Moe-Moe answered the phone. "What's up?"

"What's up?!" snapped Styles. "What's up wit' your bitch?!"

"Bitch?!"

"You heard what the fuck I said," Styles confirmed. "When I catch that bitch and her slut-ass crew I'ma blast they ass... you can get it too!"

"Fuck you, nigga!" Moe-Moe snapped the phone shut. He didn't say anything for a second, just glared out the window. *More money, more problems,* he thought. "We gon' have to deal wit' Styles, too."

I was gon' do that anyway, Bloody thought.

"As pissed as I am right now, anybody can get it," Vida said.

A speeding Cutlass Supreme flew by going in the other direction. The car caught Tia's eye; her head turned all the way around, damn near. "Bus' a U! That's that nigga right there! That's Chris in that Cutlass!" Tia yelled.

Vida stomped the gas and shot into a u-turn. Pushing the BMW pass sixty miles per hour, she began running the Cutlass down.

"You sure that's slim?" Moe-Moe didn't recognize the car.

"I'm positive!" Tia saw Chris and his man Johnny."

Vida followed the Cutlass up South Capitol Street. "I'ma pull up beside the joint."

"I got they ass," Bloody said, letting her window down, ready to let loose.

"Ease up slow," Moe-Moe said, taking the MAC-10 off Vida's lap.

Just as the Cutlass turned onto Atlantic Street, Vida pulled up next to it. Johnny was behind the wheel. Before he knew what was going down Moe-Moe and Bloody were spraying into the car. Two flames of fully automatic fire roared out of the BMW. It looked like a scene out of the movie *Dead Presidents.* Chris jumped out of the passenger seat and ran toward the apartment buildings as bullets flew by his head. He fired blindly behind his back as he ran for his life. People outside began to run for any cover they could find as gunfire tore through the night.

"You ain't goin' no muhfuckin' where, nigga!" Bloody hissed, as she jumped out of the car and gave chase.

Moe-Moe went after his cousin as well. Firing countless rounds at Chris, Moe-Moe and Bloody chased him between two buildings into a dark alley. Chris ran down the back steps of an apartment and dashed into the building. He could taste death. Running up the stairwell with his empty .45 in hand, Chris made it to the ground floor and stopped in his tracks. Tia stood in the doorway holding the Beretta Carbine like Tony Montana at the end of Scarface.

"Lights out bitch-nigga!" she hissed and then open fired, spraying Chris with one wave of fully automatic gunfire. Countless .40 caliber shells spit all over the place as bullets tore through Chris' body. Moe-Moe and Bloody came running up the stairs just in time to see Tia stand over the body and spray it with one last flaming barrage of heavy fire. "Let's get the fuck outta here," Tia said as she led the way back to the car. Police sirens were thick in the air and closing in with every passing second.

"Come on, y'all," Vida yelled. "The police comin'!" She sat behind the wheel looking over her shoulder.

A police car was flying around the corner at the end of the block. Bloody sprayed at the police car as she jumped in the back of the BMW. Once everyone was in the car Vida took off flying with screeching tires, passing two police cars at the top of the block. An officer opened fired on the BMW. Tia fired back as Vida bent the corner and shot down 4th Street. It was off to the races. Bending corner after corner, Vida hit Southern Avenue and stepped down, taking the BMW wagon up to eighty miles per hour. Bloody and Tia were in the back seat slapping fresh clips into the Beretta carbines. One police car seemed to be keeping up.

"Get that car off my back!" Vida ordered as she concentrated on getting away, running lights and all.

With no hesitation, Tia and Bloody turned around and shot through the glass of the back window. On their knees in the back seat they unloaded on the police car, turning its windshield into swiss cheese. They destroyed the police car in seconds, causing it to slam into a tree and flip over onto the sidewalk. Vida got them to Suitland

Parkway and never looked back.

TO BE CONTINUED...

HELL RAZOR HONEYS II:
TIL DEATH DO US PART

Books From Our Friends In The Publishing Industry

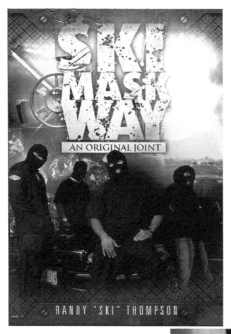

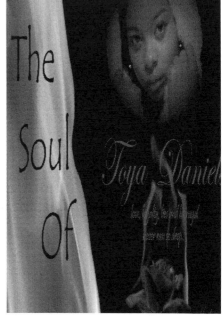

THE CARTEL COLLECTION

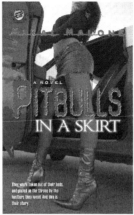

Cartel Publications Order Form
www.thecartelpublications.com

Titles	_Select The Novels You Want Below_	_Fee_
Shyt List	_____	$15.00
Pitbulls In A Skirt	_____	$15.00
Victoria's Secret	_____	$15.00
Poison	_____	$15.00
Hell Razor Honeys	_____	$15.00
A Hustler's Son 2	_____	$15.00
Black And Ugly As Ever	_____	$15.00

Please add $2.00 per book for shipping and handling.
Total: $_____

Mailing Address
*The Cartel Publications * P.O. Box 486 * Owings Mills * MD * 21117*

Name: _____

Address: _____

City/State: _____

Contact #: _____

Email: _____

Special Note:
Please allow 5-7 business days for delivery. The Cartel is not responsible for prison orders rejected. **We accept stamps**.

Made in the USA
Columbia, SC
24 September 2024

42891243R00129